Tangled Vines

BOOK TWO IN THE
Tales of the Scavenger's Daughters

Also by Kay Bratt

Silent Tears: A Journey of Hope in a Chinese Orphanage
Chasing China: A Daughter's Quest for Truth
The Bridge
A Thread Unbroken
Train to Nowhere
Mei Li and the Wise Laoshi

TALES OF THE SCAVENGER'S DAUGHTERS
The Scavenger's Daughters
Tangled Vines
Bitter Winds (coming in April, 2014)

Tangled Vines

BOOK TWO IN THE

Tales of the Scavenger's Daughters

A Novel

KAY BRATT

lake union publishing

Printed in the United States of America.

No part of this book may be reproduced, or stored in a retrieval system, or transmitted in any form or by any means, electronic, mechanical, photocopying, recording, or otherwise, without express written permission of the publisher.

Published by Lake Union Publishing, Seattle

www.apub.com

ISBN-13: 9781477808818
ISBN-10: 1477808817
Library of Congress Control Number: 2013912318

To my dad, Tony.
I'll never forget that you once helped me out of my
own desperate situation.

"Our sorrows and wounds are healed only when we touch them with compassion."

—*Buddha*

Chapter One

Suzhou, China, 2011

Li Jin ducked to the left as the familiar but dreaded fist flew toward her face and hit the concrete wall behind her. It was getting easier to predict his actions and sometimes her quick moves helped her avoid the pain. But not always.

"You'll do what you're told and if you don't, Jojo will pay the price." He cradled his fist as he spat the words at her.

Li Jin was glad Jojo was at school and not there to witness her shame. The man she'd once considered her rescuer cradled his bleeding knuckles against his chest and glared at her as if his pain was her fault. She huddled in the corner of the room, transfixed by the dots of spittle on his upper lip. Erik knew how to get her to do what he wanted. Her son meant the world to her, and she'd do anything to protect him, even if it meant jeopardizing her freedom.

"Okay. I'll do it," she answered, careful to keep her eyes downcast. If she looked straight at him when he was angry, he'd take it as a challenge.

Erik snorted in disgust and pushed the piece of paper into her face, crushing it against her nose. She took it and slapped his hand away. He turned to leave, throwing out one last warning.

"Be there by noon. Don't make me come find you, Li Jin. You're an old woman now. You can't hide from me."

The bitter sound of her name rolling off his foreign tongue made her glad once again that she hadn't shared her secret with him. *Dahlia*—just a name but it was the only clue about her birth that she'd been able to flush out from the director at the orphanage. The nontraditional name had been given to her by parents who didn't want her, but it at least made her wonder if they may have loved her even a little. She'd almost told Erik about it when he'd asked about the tattoo on her foot, but now she never would. He didn't deserve to know and she didn't want to share something so special with such a vindictive person.

Surprisingly, Erik spoke good Chinese and his South African accent made it sound almost poetic. When he had swept her off her feet a year ago, he'd told her she was lovely and didn't look all of her thirty years. Now that he'd been in China long enough to understand much of the culture, he knew being an unmarried mother at her age was a social stigma. In the eyes of her people, she was a disappointment to society.

He'd used that weakness and longing for respectability against her. He was younger than her, though not a lot, but his muscular body had immediately attracted her attention. He'd approached her as she sat watching Jojo play in the park. She hadn't encountered too many foreigners and his golden-boy looks, blond hair, and blue eyes had startled her. At first she was wary, but he won her over with his smooth way of talking. After some flirting, he'd told her he was an investor. They'd hit it off and she couldn't believe such a worldly man would choose her. He had smothered her with attention and for the first time in her life, she had felt what it meant to be romanced. They'd moved fast—too fast. Within weeks she had helped him secure an apartment for a great local price, and he'd begged her to move in with him. At the time, she and Jojo had been staying in a hostel and barely making it. With the new living arrangements, she'd felt like fate had finally sent her a reprieve.

Unfortunately, Erik's behavior changed quickly once she was securely ensnared in his web. Those blue eyes that had captivated her now turned icy when he was having one of his fits. And these days he was constantly reminding her that he could easily get a younger, more beautiful girl to do his bidding.

Now that she knew who—or what—he really was, Li Jin wished he *would* find someone else. But then who would pay for Jojo to go to school? Without an education he'd be just another boy on the street, forced to hustle to make a living like the migrant workers' children. The financial support from Erik had allowed her to put Jojo in school for the first time and he had flourished ever since. To Jojo, an inquisitive ten-year-old, school was a constant adventure and source of entertainment. And she loved her son more than life itself. He was her only spot of light in what before him had been a world of darkness. This was her chance to provide for his future. She'd suffer the abuse as long as it didn't touch her son. There was no limit to what a mother would do for her child and she was determined Jojo would never have a childhood like hers. He would have a family and feel protected. And wanted.

When she heard the front door slam she stood and released a ragged sigh of relief. He'd be gone for the rest of the morning. She rubbed her hands down her clothes to wipe away the invisible feeling of filth from Erik's latest demand. She didn't approve of what she had to do, even if she'd done it several times already. The truth was that it never got easier. She resolved to just get it over with and not think about it. She'd focus on the face of her son and pretend she was just a normal mother out to finish her daily errands. She'd done it before and she could do it again. But only for Jojo. And just maybe before the next round she'd find a way to stop the madness.

Chapter Two

Old Town Wuxi, China

Linnea exhaled a big breath to move the sweaty strands of hair off her forehead while she rummaged in the deep recesses of her bag to find her keys. Too many commuters and the lack of space had made her morning bus ride hot and miserable. Now she could relax because she was here. At her store. She still couldn't get used to the words! Feeling a burst of impatience, she dug beneath the old packs of chewing gum, a few folded love notes from Jet, and a half-empty bottle of water until she finally touched metal.

She pulled the key ring out and took a step back to look up at the sign over the door. VINTAGE MUSE. Jet had hung it the day before and Linnea had stepped outside at least a dozen times to look at it. She'd painted it herself and loved the elaborate characters and the buds of pink Linnea flowers, the symbol of her own name, etched around the border. It was a little piece of her up there, and she couldn't be more proud.

It was hard to believe, but she was finally getting her chance to rise above the low expectations that society had set for her as an orphan. More importantly, if she succeeded, she would make her Nai Nai and Ye Ye proud—the only parents she'd ever known—and show them the years of love and care they'd given her after finding her abandoned on the street were all worth it. She felt a lump rise in her throat as she realized she'd no longer have to bow down to obnoxious boss men, or work in the streets in the freezing winter or the scorching summers. She'd done it! Or at least she'd almost done it—time would tell whether she'd be a success or have to go back to slinging tires or hawking wares from the sidewalk.

She quickly looked around at the other shops and could see by their still-dark store windows that she was the first one on the block to arrive. It had been hard to get up so early, but today was the most important day of her life thus far. If she didn't get going, her *grand opening* wasn't going to be so *grand*.

She looked through her large, empty picture window and sighed. Yet another huge project to throw together this morning. Now she wished she'd asked some of her sisters for help but in her usual stubborn way, she hadn't wanted to burden anyone else. Now she had a long list of tasks befitting at least a dozen workers to accomplish on her own, all in only a few hours. Overwhelming, but it would be a while before she could actually afford to hire employees, so she'd just have to make do with her own two hands.

Ready to tackle the day, she unlocked the door and walked through.

She stood in the middle of the room and put her hands on her hips. There was so much to do! She approached a box, opened the flaps, and began to pull out shirts and stack them on the shelves next to it, trying to sort by size. The shirts were her signature item—and the money earned from their sales had helped pay back the original business loan to Jet.

She held up one of her favorite shirts. Printed across the front was a graphic she had sketched of what used to be called a tiger kitchen range. In the old days, the Wuxi people would line up at local shops to buy hot water to shower with. On the shirt, the huge pipe—what they called the fuel mouth—that brought in the water looked like the head of a tiger; the two big pots it poured into resembled the body, and the chimney mimicked a swishing tail. From afar it was simply a tiger but close up the detail on the shirt was amazing. Now there were only eight such kitchens remaining in all of Wuxi. Linnea didn't want those pieces of history to disappear—and given the sudden success of her shirts, obviously neither did the Wuxi residents who had bought from her.

Other shirts sported graphics of old street signs, subway tickets, and other Old China memorabilia. Her shirts had been categorized as urban vintage—and Linnea was still astounded at their popularity of them. Somehow, without any real advertising, she had sold out repeatedly until she'd finally found a supplier to help her keep up.

But now that she had a real store with walls and a door, and no longer relied on selling from a small cart on the street, she could sell other vintage pieces in addition to her signature shirts. Many of the things she'd already collected were strategically scattered around the room, waiting to be displayed to entice buyers. Linnea wiped the sweat from her brow and picked up the pace. She had left too much undone the day before. She'd never finish in time.

An hour later Linnea looked up when the bell hanging over her door jangled. Backup had arrived; leading her sisters in the charge was her feisty Nai Nai, pushing a wheelchair through the narrow entrance with such energy that the gray bun on top of her head jiggled back and forth. Over her plump middle she wore her blue gingham going-out apron, but Linnea noticed by the bulges that she'd still packed her pockets full of odds and ends.

"We've got to talk to the city about the buses being inadequate to get wheelchairs in and out. You should have seen what we just went through." She fussed as she pushed the chair farther into the store, then broke into a wide smile crinkling her face into a thousand tiny lines.

Linnea's sister Maggi waved from her wheelchair as Nai Nai pushed it over the doorjamb. On Maggi's lap, Poppy, their youngest addition, sat wide-eyed and curious, just happy to be out for a ride.

"Linnea! Nai Nai brought us to help you. What can I do?" Maggi asked, her pigtails swinging back and forth as she looked around the store, taking it all in. At nine years old, she acted like she was big enough to tackle any task.

Linnea laughed. "You mean you're going to stop knitting long enough to do something else with those talented little hands?"

She was relieved that despite her stubbornness in not asking for help, they'd come anyway. She should've known they would. And her army of sisters was just what she needed to help her out of the time crunch she had created. She was speechless with gratitude.

"Linnea," her Nai Nai began, her face set in determination, "we'll whip this place into shape in no time. You just give the orders. Where's Jet?"

"Oh, he was going to be here but this is the day he already promised to help his father with some special project. He'll be here tomorrow. He was so upset to miss this." At least, that was what he'd said when he broke the news to her last night. Sometimes Linnea got so frustrated with his busy schedule but then he'd flash those twinkling eyes at her and make her forget why she was even irritated. And he always went out of his way to make it up to her—she felt her cheeks warm as she thought of some of the ways he went about it.

Linnea dropped the T-shirt she was folding and jumped up. She ran to the old woman and, skirting around the chair, hugged her tightly. "Nai Nai. Thanks for coming. I thought I was going to have to do this alone!"

Nai Nai shooed her away and pulled a wrapped steamed roll from her apron pocket. "*Bah.* Of course I was coming. Do you think I'd miss your grand opening? This is a big moment for the Zheng family. You're going to be a business owner—and at only nineteen. *Aiya!* We're so proud of you, Linnea. And here, eat your breakfast and don't be sneaking out on an empty stomach again. Ivy, hand me that playpen for Poppy."

Behind her, Ivy deposited the playpen against the wall as she and the other girls bickered about who would get to do what. Lily, Ivy's twin, kept her hand on Ivy's arm as the girl guided her around the unfamiliar territory. Lily swung her new walking cane to find her way, but she wasn't quite used to it yet and still depended on her sister to help her around unfamiliar areas.

Linnea still recalled when the girls had been brought to them at only five years old. Officers had brought them by after their mother had been taken away by the police. The girls were meant to be transferred to the orphanage in the next city over but knowing their Ye Ye like they did, the officers asked if he'd take them in. The girls had huddled behind the officer, bedraggled and reeking of smoke. Nai Nai had shuffled them through their door and tried to comfort them. Even then Ivy had protected Lily and refused to allow anyone else to touch her. She'd helped her sister eat, bathe, dress—everything until she'd finally felt like they were in a safe place.

Now they were fifteen and Ivy was the loudest. Her voice carried over everyone else as she walked to the front window display box.

"I wanna work in the window!"

Lily followed along. She never complained about being blind, probably because she'd always had Ivy to depend on. The two were so connected that many times Lily didn't even need to hold on; she could just feel where her sister was leading.

"But what about their lessons?" Linnea asked Nai Nai.

Nai Nai shook her head. "The only lesson they'll learn today is how to follow their hearts and keep at their dreams until they come true. And Peony is thrilled to skip school. You can probably get her to do anything you want."

Linnea scanned the room and saw Peony busy on the other side of the store, already scoping out the new items and probably trying to figure out how she could swipe some things for herself. Of all her sisters, Linnea thought ten-year-old Peony the most beautiful with her mixed blood that gave her golden eyes and fair coloring. Even the natural auburn highlights in her hair added to her exotic look, and Linnea knew that when Peony grew older, she would be even prettier. But the most amazing thing was that her little sister didn't have a clue of her own beauty. She was tomboyish and into everything. She usually went to the local elementary school, but she didn't like it and wanted to stay home and be tutored.

It was unfair, but whether they'd get school registration or not usually depended on how they were abandoned or where they were found. It'd be much easier if they all were allowed public education—or at least easier for Nai Nai to set rules about it then.

Linnea stopped looking at her so intently before Peony noticed.

"Where's Ye Ye?" she asked Nai Nai.

"He's coming. Jasmine pulled him over to watch those old buzzards on the lane playing mahjong. Now that he's feeling better I can't get him to stop all his *socializing*." She waved her hand dismissively in the air. "You'd think he was a celebrity or something the way everyone wants to have time with him."

Linnea smiled at her Nai Nai's words, which she knew hid a deep affection for Ye Ye. She had never seen two people more in love. Even after all their years together they were still totally devoted to each other. And she should have guessed her little sister, Jasmine, would have gotten Ye Ye sidetracked. Even though she'd never spoken a single word, the six-year-old had Ye Ye wrapped around her little finger. And her grandfather *was* a celebrity of sorts—but then so was her Nai Nai. They'd both been recognized a year ago for their contribution to the community for taking in abandoned girls and raising them as their own over the last few decades. Linnea was one of those orphaned girls—but she couldn't love the two old folks more if they were blood related. In her mind, she wasn't an orphan because she had Nai Nai and Ye Ye, as well as her sisters, and they were a family.

She left those thoughts behind and put her hands on her hips. "Okay, we have two hours before the doors open. Peony, you and Ivy are in charge of that display window. I want you to find a way to display my T-shirts but also add some of the antique items sitting over there next to the wall. Make it look like an old Chinese living room with a flash of urban."

The two girls came back to get the box of T-shirts, racing against each other to be first to look through the styles. Linnea figured she'd let them work for a little while before she intervened to explain the definition of urban.

"Maggi," Linnea began again, "it'll be a huge help if you just entertain Poppy while Nai Nai helps me clean up." Her sister was doing great after her recent surgery by the Shanghai doctor to remove the sac of membranes from her spine, and Linnea was surprised that the operation had given Maggi such a different outlook on her future. Spina bifida could be cruel and her sister might not ever be able to walk, but at least now she had control over her bladder and no longer had to wear the embarrassing diapers. And since the surgery had done so much to minimize her pain, Maggi was gaining more strength in her lower body and had even learned to lift herself up and could get in and out of her chair by herself. And Linnea couldn't believe how talented she was with the knitting needles! She was even learning how to embroider and crochet. In her eyes, Maggi was nothing short of amazing.

"Nai Nai, the broom's back in the storeroom. You can sweep, or I'll sweep while you polish the glass countertop. As soon as the girls get the display going, I'll help them get it perfect."

Nai Nai answered her by immediately going to the storeroom for the broom.

Linnea looked at her other sister, Lily. What could she have her do to feel helpful?

"Lily, I have a box of porcelain teapots and cups over there in the corner. There's a shelf right in front of the box. Please unwrap everything and set them up. I'll put them in the right places after you get them all out."

Lily would probably be even more careful than her sighted sisters, Linnea thought to herself as she watched Ivy lead Lily to the corner where the box of porcelain sat. The empty wall behind the girl caught her attention and she sighed. She'd forgotten she needed to hang one example of all her vintage shirts across the wall for a display. Luckily her Ye Ye would be there shortly. He could help her attach the lines and then clip the shirts up. He could also open the register and get her starter money organized. *He'll feel important to be handling my money,* she mused.

With her hand on her chin, she stared up at the wall, imagining the best way to hang the shirts to get the most attention from shoppers.

Behind her she felt a poke of something prickly on her backside and turned around.

"What are you standing around gawking at, girl? You've got work to do!" Nai Nai prodded her again with the broom and smiled, showing the adorable gap between her two front teeth.

Linnea jumped into action. She felt a shiver of excitement traveling up her spine and tingling through her fingertips. Thanks to her family it was all going to be okay—everything was coming together and in a few hours she would embark on the next stage in her life. Vintage Muse was going to be a smashing success—she'd settle for nothing less.

Chapter Three

Hours later, Calli perched on a small porcelain garden stool outside of Linnea's store and watched the ruckus inside through the large glass window. Beside her, Lily sat serenely with her violin and played a woeful song, catching the eye of many passing pedestrians. Calli had to wait until Lily felt she'd done enough inside the store before she could be talked into resting. Even then her daughter couldn't be still and had instead mesmerized strangers with her music. It amazed her how fast Lily had caught on to playing when Benfu had begun to give her lessons. Her natural gift for the violin was astounding.

Surprisingly, a few people had asked them about selling the violin.

"Nai Nai, did you hear that? Sell Viola? That'll never happen," Lily mumbled after the first customer walked away. One man in particular practically drooled over it until Calli had sent him on his way. He'd scribbled down his number and told her if they ever changed their mind, he could get them a great price for it. Lily hadn't wanted to offend the man, so appeased him by tucking the paper into the lining of her violin case, where Calli knew it would probably never be thought of again.

It had been a good day. Calli shook her head in wonder. Linnea was something else. Not only had she negotiated a great profit for the antique snuff bottle she'd found for sale from an old man on a back street, but her designer T-shirts were flying off the shelves. Calli wasn't surprised, as Linnea had always been one of the most independent of all their daughters, but she felt she'd burst with pride each time she'd heard someone compliment one of the vintage shirts that Linnea had worked so hard to create. Her daughter—a designer! Who would have thought it?

Calli had hung around all day, watching shoppers swarm the store in their attempts to be the first to discover new finds and old treasures, until her old knees couldn't hold out any longer and she had to go outside to rest and get some peace from the chaos. She didn't know how, but baby Poppy had slept in the corner of the shop right under all that noise for the last hour.

Calli looked down the street at the other shops. Linnea had picked a good place with lots of foot traffic. It was an old historical street that many locals and foreigners used each day for shopping and many had stopped in to see for themselves what they could find at the new store. Calli didn't think Linnea was going to have to spend any money for advertising—thanks to simple word of mouth.

Earlier in the day, a few other store owners came around to be nosy under the guise of greeting them and stopping to hear Lily play. So far all the neighbors seemed to be thrilled to have Linnea in their midst. The old man from the kite store had even brought over a cup of green tea while she was sitting outside earlier. He was an interesting fellow—a kite maker—who said he was fourth generation and taught by his ninety-year-old grandfather, whose own father had made kites for the imperial family. Calli couldn't wait to hear more of his stories. She also thought she might be able to snag a discount to get the girls a few kites once they got to know each other.

Another shopkeeper from across the way had rushed over and insisted on helping Linnea with her display of vintage shirts in the window. To Calli, he looked like a cartoon character with his rolled-up jeans and huge white sunglasses. She could barely see his eyes through the shaggy hair that nearly covered them.

His store, THINGS OF LING the sign read, was across the road, and from what Calli could see through his front window, it looked like a hodgepodge of homemade jewelry, incense, and Buddha statues. Calli examined the different strands of beads and colorful scarves the fellow had added to Linnea's display from his own stock and had to admit the man—Sky, he called himself—knew how to spark interest. Of course all the borrowed items were tagged with prices, so he was obviously a savvy businessman to take the opportunity to get his merchandise in front of fresh eyes. But it was good that Linnea had someone near her own age to welcome her, seeing how most of the shop owners were older, probably even what the girls would call *ancient*.

Calli looked up from her view of the street as the door opened and another satisfied customer skirted around her, rummaging through the bag hanging from her arm. By the looks of the shape at the bottom, she'd also bought one of the vintage T-shirts that were selling so fast. Calli couldn't believe the fascination with the simple shirts but she was happy for Linnea. She remembered when she was Linnea's age and the stark, unfeminine clothes she was forced to wear during Mao's reign. It was a wonder that Benfu had even seen her for who she was under the masculine clothing, but he had . . . and their love had bloomed despite the lack of what today's generation would consider stylish must-haves.

"Calli, are you okay, m'love?" Benfu poked his head out of the store.

She turned to see his worried look, ironic since he was the one diagnosed with tuberculosis, even if his symptoms had all but disappeared in the last year. But that was the way it had always been, with him taking care of and protecting her. He was the one who'd carried the most physical and emotional scars heaped on him during the Cultural Revolution. And he was the one who'd given up his ties to his old life out of loyalty to her when the biggest tragedy of all had happened—when her own child was taken from her as she slept. But Calli also knew she was so lucky the gods had favored her the night they led a young, starved, and beaten Benfu to seek refuge in her courtyard.

She could still remember that moment, decades ago, when she'd found him outside her home in the middle of the night. He'd been doing his best to bend his beaten body into a position low enough to sneak a drink from their spigot. Before he'd looked up, she'd thought she'd caught a criminal on the loose, a vagrant, or maybe even some sort of lunatic. She'd never forget how frightened Benfu was just before he'd lost consciousness from his injuries. All Calli knew was from the moment they'd locked eyes, they had made a connection that hardship and time had only made stronger. Though many would consider their family to be living on the outside of society because of her husband's profession, Calli was proud to be a scavenger's wife.

She smiled up at him. "*Dui le.* I'm fine. Just tired. You ready to go home yet, Benfu?" She hoped he'd say yes. She was not only drained, but she needed time to start making some of her home-cooked noodles for the evening meal.

Benfu nodded briskly. "Let me tell them we're going. And I'll clean Jasmine up; we kept her busy painting some chipped pottery. I'll just be a minute. I think Linnea is about to lock up for the day."

A smile lit up his face and Calli admired the way his dark eyes still sparkled. "Oh, Calli, it's been quite an adventure! I'm happy for our girl."

With that he disappeared back into the shop. Calli knew Benfu was right. It had been an adventurous year for their Linnea. She'd just about worked herself to the bone trying to save enough money to open her own store. She usually worked six days a week selling shirts at her street stall, and then spent hours on the weekends searching the back markets for antiques to buy. Calli had even combed some of the shops that catered to foreigners and found a few treasures. Watching her daughter work so hard was tough on all of them. Some nights Linnea dropped off to sleep on her pallet without even the energy to eat dinner.

Calli was surprised to admit it, but though they were getting too serious for her taste, she was actually glad Linnea had Jet around to force her to take a few breaks and enjoy some afternoons. It was only with the boy's persuasion she got any rest at all. Calli thought it amusing how protective Jet was of Linnea, reminding her of the young romance she and Benfu had shared.

Yes, Jet had proved to be a valuable friend to all of them. Calli couldn't imagine where they'd be if he and Linnea had not met. Because Jet's father worked in a branch of government and he'd used his connections to step in, they were now getting the financial assistance from the state they needed to support their family. And even Benfu's treatments for tuberculosis were covered. He was feeling better than he had in years. It had been a lucky time for them recently; of that she was sure.

Calli stood and opened the door to the shop. "Lily, you wait until Ivy's ready to go, okay?"

Lily looked so lost in her music that Calli wouldn't have thought anything got through to her, but she gave a quick nod.

Calli pulled the door open and the bell rang loudly. She was going to have to hurry Benfu along after all or he'd never get a nap in before dinner. She shook her head. Her brood of daughters took a lot of energy to keep up with, but it made their life anything but boring. Calli needed to rush home and start preparation for the evening meal.

"Benfu? Where's Poppy? I'll take her and Jasmine with me, and you can follow with Maggi and the others when you get done." With a loud jangle the door slammed behind her and she went to gather their two youngest girls.

Even though she was tired, she wouldn't trade her life for anyone else's. Though fate had taken her child from her so many years ago, it had later brought her many other daughters to soften the grief. She was a lucky old woman and she knew it.

Chapter Four

Qi Jin swallowed to rid herself of the nausea as she maneuvered her moped into the littered lot. She parked it in the middle of a long row of others, some shiny and new, some just as battered as hers. She put the kickstand down, switched off the motor, and glanced at the knockoff Gucci watch Erik had given her and tried to pass off as real. He didn't understand she could tell a fake from a mile away. China had the market on copying name-brand jewelry, clothing, and even shoes. She'd even taken her turn at selling counterfeit watches on the street for a while back before Jojo was born when she had to find creative ways to make money. She'd let Erik believe she thought it the genuine thing, for she appreciated his good intentions back then—but that was before everything had changed.

She was eight minutes early, having allowed extra time to try to calm her nerves. She got off her bike, lifted the seat, and retrieved the padlock and chain. Carefully she looped the chain around the pole and front tire of her bike, then pulled on it a couple times to be sure the lock would stay in place. It would be just her luck to come out and find her moped stolen. Even with the lock it could happen and the thought scared her. She suddenly remembered to check the moped's remaining charge and breathed a sigh of relief that it showed she still had enough juice to get home. She had money for a taxi but didn't want to have to depend on fate to have one ready and waiting if she should need it in a hurry.

She got back on her bike and did her best to keep her head down as she waited three more minutes. She didn't want to attract any attention. She didn't know why she'd been instructed to go into the post office at a specific time, but she knew enough to follow his directions to the letter. At the other side of the area a few men squatted against the wall of the building, smoking and laughing amongst themselves. She didn't look their way, hoping she blended in with the other pedestrians.

When the three minutes had passed, she headed for the door with her head bent as she rustled through her bag to look for the parcel-pickup ticket.

She climbed the stairs and patted the head of the lion statue for luck. This was her last chance to turn around and return the way she had come. Erik would already be back from having coffee with his foreign friends and would be waiting for her. But if she came in empty-handed, there would be trouble. She hesitated, but then she pictured Jojo as he had looked that morning when she dropped him at school. He had walked away grinning, so happy to be a student like the others. Almost the entire term had passed and his glee had not faded a bit. She'd watched his Spider-Man backpack bounce up and down as he'd disappeared through the huge gates, his hand still in the air as he waved good-bye. She was trapped. If she didn't fulfill Erik's commands, he'd make her pull Jojo from school. He knew where to inflict the most hurt to her.

Li Jin took a deep breath and entered through the doors. Inside she was met with no less than what she was expecting—total chaos. All around, people pushed and shoved to get to the counter, all but a few disregarding the tiny uniformed lady as she called out, "*Pai dui!* Get in a line. You must queue up!"

Some people held packages or letters they wanted to mail, while others waved their papers in the air to show they were waiting to pick up something. Despite the pounding in her chest, Li Jin needed to blend in, so she joined the others and began working her way to the front while waving her own orange slip. She coughed and quickly stifled it. The heavy stench of cigarette smoke only made the room more claustrophobic.

To the side, a woman knelt on the floor, packing clothing into a small carton. From what Li Jin could see, the woman needed a bigger box. But a bigger box meant more postage, so she watched as the woman instead used all her upper-body strength to hold down the top of the flaps, while a man beside her taped them closed. It was probably clothing going to her children back home, Li Jin thought. She was lucky; unlike children in migrant families, Jojo got to stay with her. Here it was common for parents to work in one city while their children stayed behind with grandparents in another. But then, her son didn't have any grandparents to stay with. She and her son were alone in the world—except for Erik.

Finally she made it to the counter and slapped her paper down. The woman picked it up and looked at it, then yelled to the parcel picker standing in the doorway leading to the back room. With her orders, the man immediately disappeared and the woman waved at her to step aside for the next person to come forward.

So far so good, Li Jin thought. *I can do this. I can do this.* She concentrated on looking calm on the outside as she quaked inside.

Soon the parcel picker returned with a huge box and Li Jin caught her breath. It had never been that large before. That big a box could get her put away for a long time if she was caught— possibly even executed. She suddenly felt nauseated. The man carried it over and dropped it on the floor next to the clerk at the counter. They said a few quick words to each other, and Li Jin thought she would faint when she heard the woman pronounce the dreaded words.

"Customs check this one."

Li Jin froze. They were going to open it! She'd always known there was a chance this could happen, and so did Erik—which was why he always sent her and had her named as the recipient. Erik had messed up labeling such a large box as office documents, and now his slip was causing a spot check.

Li Jin couldn't help it. She put both her palms down on the counter to support her weak knees. As the parcel picker opened a drawer and pulled out a box knife, she looked around to judge whether she could make it outside before he opened it. She felt sick. It was too crowded and a security guard stood just inside the door. She'd never get by him if she ran now.

The man bent down with his scissors. Li Jin wanted to run. Hide. Anything. What was he going to pull out?

As the man cut through the tape, opened the flaps, and reached in, Li Jin couldn't contain herself any longer. "That's not mine!"

The man pulled out a set of red men's long underwear.

Li Jin froze. *Underwear?* Where was the dope?

With evident irritation, the female clerk beside him grabbed the slip and bent down over the box. She looked from the box to the paper and back to the box. Then she stood, putting her hands on her hips.

"Name?" she asked.

Li Jin looked at the door, wishing she could make a run for it. "Dang Li Jin."

The woman didn't even blink at Li Jin's surname. Most people had something to say or at least snorted in sympathy at the name that branded her as an orphan. But this woman ignored it other than to study the ticket again. "*Aiya!* Wrong number! Take this one back. I said HUW0657, not 0659."

Li Jin breathed a sigh of relief as the sweat ran down the back of her neck. She stood to the side and waited as the woman assisted a few more customers. Finally the squatty man returned with a much smaller box. He carried it in one hand and, with a look of indignation, tossed it on the counter in front of Li Jin, and grabbed the next slip.

This time Li Jin could see the characters of her name on the label but waited as the woman matched the box slip to the paper slip. Once satisfied, she shoved the paper back toward Li Jin.

"Sign for it."

Li Jin hesitated. It didn't look like they were going to open it but she'd never had to sign before. Why was it different this time? She didn't want her signature on file. She looked up at the woman, a question ready on her lips.

"Hurry up, sign. More people are waiting," the woman belted out, slapping a pen next to the paper. Behind her she heard a grunt of impatience from the next customer.

Li Jin was sure everyone around her could hear the thumping of her heart as she bent over the counter and signed her name. But at least the parcel picker had been sent after another package and was ignoring hers. She pushed the paper back.

The woman stabbed the slip over the metal prong beside her register, shoved the package toward her, and turned her attention to the next customer. Li Jin picked up the package and turned to go.

Putting one foot in front of the other without hurrying, Li Jin forced herself to walk out of the post office nonchalantly. She slowly went down the steps and returned to her bike. She put the small box in the wire basket on her handlebars, pulled the keys from her pocket, and with still-shaking hands, unlocked the padlock. Discreetly she looked around to see if anyone had followed her out of the building. When she saw nothing out of the ordinary, she put her lock back under the seat and climbed on. Relieved to be off her wobbly legs, she quickly drove out of the parking lot and headed back to the apartment with only the thought of freedom on her mind.

Six hours later Li Jin straddled her moped as she waited outside the school gates. She adjusted her sunglasses and looked around to see if anyone was watching her. She was still shaky and paranoid from her morning errand and the subsequent fight with Erik. When she'd returned to the apartment she'd thrown his precious package at him and told him it was the last time she'd be his mule. She'd screamed at him that one of these days she was going to be unlucky when the postmaster decided to open and check her package. Then what? She'd be caught and her son would be an orphan.

She reached up and felt the bridge of her nose. The first blow she took that morning was after she told him she knew he was a drug dealer. For months she had pretended ignorance at what was in the packages but how stupid did he think she was? Now that he knew that *she* knew his secret, he'd never let her go. He'd even threatened to implicate her, and with her signature on file at the post office now, they could link the packages to her! She felt a shiver of fear run down her spine. She should've known she was messing with fire by arguing with him. It would have been smarter to just keep her mouth shut and disappear.

Now she'd have to use more of the little bit of money she had stashed away to buy makeup. She wished she'd had time to get it before picking up Jojo but she'd just have to make do with the sunglasses. Now that he was getting older, he was starting to act protective of her and she didn't want him asking questions.

She looked at her watch again. The bell should have rung two minutes ago. She couldn't wait to feel the relief that Jojo brought her with his quick smile and total acceptance. Around her other mothers, fathers, and even grandparents waited for the children, all chattering amongst themselves. As usual, Li Jin stayed to herself. She didn't want anyone asking her questions or looking too closely through the lens of her glasses to see the dark bruise already forming under her eye. She sure didn't want their pity if they should ferret out the truth of who she had become.

Li Jin jumped at the sound of the shrill bell. She started her bike and smiled when she saw Jojo run through the gates in the middle of a pack of excited children. At only ten years old he was the tallest in his group of friends and easy to pick out. She almost chuckled at the way he strutted through the gates. He was trying to act cool for his classmates, but so far he had maintained most of his little-boy innocence.

"Ma! Look what I made you!"

She shook her head and chuckled. Since he'd started school, he'd insisted on trading the endearment of mama for ma. He said he didn't want to sound like a baby. He tried so hard to keep up with the big boys.

From his fingers dangled a string of beads. He handed it over to her, bouncing up and down with excitement as she studied it.

"Jojo, that's so beautiful. You made it for me?" The string of beads was quite colorful with alternating reds and yellows and one pearly white one in the middle.

Jojo smiled and nodded his head. For a second he tried to maintain his macho bravado but then he couldn't contain his excitement. "Yes, the white one is you and the colored ones are the other moms. You always stand out as the prettiest one in the crowd."

Li Jin was relieved she was wearing sunglasses and Jojo couldn't see the tears well up in her eyes. She was also glad that even though he hid it when he was around Erik, he could still show his affection for her when they were alone.

"Thank you, Jojo. I'll wear it forever." She tied the bracelet on her wrist and patted the seat in front of her. "Come on. We're going to go find an afternoon treat. What do you think? Noodles or ice cream?"

Jojo jumped up on the moped, set his backpack on the platform near her feet, and settled himself on the seat in front of her, relaxing against her chest. Sometimes he asked to sit on the back of the scooter, but she was glad he was okay to be in front today. She wanted to hold on to feeling her arms around him for as long as possible. He was her only comfort in a world that so far had done nothing but kick her in the teeth.

"Noodles! Hurry!" He bounced up and down in the seat and made Li Jin laugh. She should've known her boy would want noodles. He was a big eater and was all about filling his ever-aching belly. And they knew if he really wanted it, he'd still get the ice cream later.

She maneuvered the bike carefully out of the school parking area and turned into the bike lane on the street. The other mopeds and bicycles skirted around to make room for one more traveler.

"Let me drive, Ma." He pushed her hands back from the handlebars and Li Jin let them hover over his for a few minutes, then took the steering back.

She knew just where to go. They'd sit down at the corner shop for some of Mr. Wu's best noodles and then she'd find somewhere else for them to spend the evening hours. She knew from experience that it was best she didn't return home until Erik had sufficient time to cool down.

Li Jin leaned back against the tree and watched her son. Beside her, Jojo showed his enthusiasm each time the colors lit up the sky. There had been a wedding party at the park, and they'd watched them pose for photos for over an hour. Now that dusk had come; the people gathered around to cap off the day by watching a fancy show of fireworks.

Jojo was excited they'd found a perfect spot to stay out of the way and enjoy the noisy display. She was happy to have him all to herself where they could both relax and feel free from walking on eggshells as she had to do with Erik around.

"Ma, why do people set off fireworks when they get married?"

"Because, Jojo, the fireworks are supposed to scare off any evil spirits that may be attached to the couple, ensuring a happy marriage full of good luck."

She wanted him to continue to believe that people could be content together. When she'd taken off her sunglasses earlier, he'd noticed the faint bruise around one of her eyes, but she'd told him she ran into the swinging door at the post office. By now he must think he had the most ungraceful mother in the world.

He rubbed at his eyes. With his belly full of noodles and red bean ice cream, he was getting sleepy. He'd already yawned at least a half-dozen times. Li Jin looked at her watch again. It was way past his bedtime, but one more hour and Erik would be out for the evening. Months ago it was her routine to get the *ayi* to stay with Jojo while she went with Erik to the famous Bar Street—a seedy area where the Chinese mingled with the foreigners looking for a good time—but now he went alone. He liked to say he was going to network, but what he meant was *jawl*—which she had learned was South African slang for party. And he was surfing for new customers, too; she was sure of that. But she didn't care anymore. She actually preferred it that way, as she just wanted to be with Jojo. She pulled a few pieces of grass from the back of his shirt.

"Ma, why don't I have a Ye Ye or Nai Nai?" he asked sleepily.

Oh no, not that again, Li Jin thought. In the past year Jojo had started asking questions about why they didn't have extended family, particularly grandparents. So far she had treaded carefully, but sooner or later she knew it was going to get harder to appease his curiosity, especially when it came to who his father was. So far she'd kept him at bay by telling him his father had died in the army, but she dreaded when her son would get old enough to ask for more details.

"Why are you asking me this again, Jojo?" He laid his head on her lap and she ran her fingers through his hair. He loved it when she did that.

"Because Pang's grandfather came to class today and showed us how to do tricks with his yo-yo. Pang asked me what tricks my Ye Ye knew. I told him I didn't have a Ye Ye and he said everybody has grandparents. But you said I don't, Ma."

Li Jin sighed. *How much of your own sad story do you allow yourself to pass along to your child?* The only thing she knew to do was to spin it into some semblance of a fairy tale—even though her childhood had been anything but story-like, and Jojo was getting too old for such babyish tales. Even so, he wasn't old enough for the truth and might never be. She'd told him the story before, but this time she'd add more and hope it would appease his curiosity for a while longer.

"Okay, Jojo. You're big enough now and I can tell you a secret."

Jojo sat up and his eyes widened as he waited. He loved anything considered a secret.

"You *might* have grandparents, but we don't know who they are or where they live. Many years ago when I was but a baby, a dragon snuck into my room and carried me away. Because I cried so long and so hard for my mother, the dragon took me to Beijing and left me in front of a big school that children lived in."

Jojo's forehead wrinkled in confusion as he had another revelation. He was old enough to know that dragons weren't real but he usually played along. Sometimes when it was only them alone together, he just wanted to act like a little boy and that was fine with her. She wanted to keep him that way as long as possible before the harsh ways of the world spoiled his innocence.

"Ma, children don't live in schools. It was an orphanage," Jojo said, his tone stern.

Li Jin was taken aback. They'd never used that word before or even discussed what an orphanage was. So this was part of the whole school experience her son was getting? She wondered what else he had learned.

"But why didn't the dragon just give you back to your mother if he didn't want you?"

Li Jin shook her head. "I don't know, Jojo. Maybe we traveled so far he couldn't find his way back. But anyway, the only thing they knew about me was from a note pinned to my shirt giving them my name." As usual, she allowed him to think that her name was Li Jin. One day she'd tell him the truth, but not today.

"And the tattoo of the flower on your foot!" Jojo said.

"Yes, and someone had drawn the character for flower on my heel. Anyway, the orphanage took me in and I lived in the big school with a lot of other babies until I could walk. I didn't like it there, so I was happy that when I got older they let me stay in a real house with a man and woman."

"Your foster family!" Jojo answered loud enough to turn a few heads.

Li Jin held her fingers to her lips and looked around quickly. "Shh. Yes, my *fuyang jiating*. My foster father was big and round, and laughed like this!" She held her arms out in a big circle and touched her fingers, then let out a jolly laugh. Jojo giggled at her impression.

"And my foster mother was a teeny tiny lady who talked like this." She brought her hands up in front of her to look like little paws, shrunk her head down into her shoulders, and whispered a few unintelligible words through a pretend overbite.

"She was like a little mouse," Jojo added, nodding his head as if he knew every word of the story. And he probably did, Li Jin thought. She'd told him about her foster families before. He always remembered the first one. They were the good family. Some of the ones she'd been in after those she would never tell her son about. Some things a son should never know. She'd also never tell him of the hardship of her times at the orphanage—the dark and cold rooms, and the feeling of isolation even though she was surrounded by at least a hundred others. Sadly she kept a lot of secrets—and they were real ones, not made-up fairy tales.

"Yes, she was like a little mouse. But she took good care of me for a few years. Then she and her husband moved to another place in China far away to help take care of their grandson. I had to go back to the school until they could find me another family."

Jojo reached over and nudged her playfully.

"I don't like the way that story ends. I want you to stay with the fat man and the mousy woman."

Li Jin smiled and rubbed the top of his fingers.

"I know, Jojo. I wish I could've stayed, too. Come on. We need to go; I'll tell you more of the story another time." She

picked up their things and led Jojo to the walking path. She figured they were safe to head home. Jojo would be happy there'd
be no time for a bath. She grabbed his hand as he used the other
one to point up at the final burst of fireworks.

"Dude! Look at that one! It's the biggest one yet!"

"*Dui,* it sure is, Jojo. But please don't say dude." Erik's slang
was really rubbing off on him and Li Jin didn't like it.

"Let me see your tattoo again." He pointed at her foot.

"Not tonight. I'm not taking my shoes off. And we need to
go. Come on." He'd seen her flower many times. It was so cap-
tivating to him for some reason, but to Li Jin all she could think
was how cruel to tattoo a baby's foot. She didn't remember it but
she was sure at one time it must have caused her pain. What sort
of parents had she been born to? It made her angry to think
about.

"Can I get a yo-yo, Ma?" He shuffled his feet, suddenly
looking about five years old as the fatigue really set in. She ruffled
the top of his hair. If all it took was a yo-yo for him to forget
about his lack of a family history, that was a welcome request.

"Jojo with a yo-yo? I guess we can think about that."

She chuckled as she hurried him toward the row of mopeds
and bikes. She loved how he bounced from serious subjects to his
random little-boy thoughts. He'd get his yo-yo and maybe she'd
find someone to teach him how to use it, too.

Chapter Five

Linnea opened the door to her shop and led the way inside with Lily and Ivy behind her. Once again, as soon as she stepped inside she swelled with pride. The store had been open only a month and so far its small success had taken her by surprise. She'd thought it would be much harder to start building clientele but each day had brought in even more people—with many actually parting with their hard-earned money. Just yesterday she was forced to spend the afternoon combing the back streets to find more treasures to stock her shelves. Luckily Nai Nai and Ye Ye had manned the store for her, with the help of Ivy and Lily. Without them she wouldn't be able to keep up with everything.

She hoped she could keep up the momentum and that it wasn't just the curiosity of a new business that was bringing them in. If things kept up the way they were going, she'd soon make enough to rent the second-floor apartment from the building owner. By then she should be able to talk her Ye Ye into letting her move out alone.

"Okay, now how am I going to keep you two busy? And Ivy, you've got some making up to do with Nai Nai when you get home tonight. I bet I can guess who's getting kitchen duty. . . ."

Ivy hung her head only for an instant. Then she looked up and Linnea could see the familiar fire spark in her eyes. "I don't care. If they won't let us go to school together, I just won't go!"

Beside her, Lily grinned in her usual silent way. Linnea knew she wasn't totally innocent in the conspiracy. The girls had staged a revolt against being separated, and once they banded together it was impossible to make them budge. Linnea rolled her eyes at them and answered as she moved toward the back of the store.

"You know they won't let Lily go to your school. But that's fine. Now Lily's tutor will have to give a lesson to both of you, won't she? What do you want to learn today, Ivy? How to button your shirt?"

She didn't wait on a reply as she headed to the back. The girls knew she was just teasing, and Lily could already do most things a sighted person could. And she was getting so good at playing the violin that now it was all she wanted to do. When she brought out her violin in the evenings, it wasn't unusual to see the neighbors gravitate toward her and hang over the concrete gate to listen. Because of the music, their courtyard had become the local hangout.

The violin had obviously changed Lily's outlook on life, but Ivy thought she needed to focus on other things, too, and the tutor was supposed to be teaching her sister new tasks. Since the county had begun to help her family they'd also started sending a tutor once a week to help Lily learn how to function as a blind person. This offer came only after they practically had to restrain her Ye Ye when the county worker suggested massage school. Her Ye Ye made it clear they would have no part of the usual stereotype that all blind people were destined to earn a living by being a masseuse. Even Ivy had almost shown the woman the door at that proposal. None of them ever wanted Lily to spend her life in one room rubbing the hind end of every lazy businessman and perverted foreigner in town. The lady had tried to tell them there were legitimate medical massage clinics, but they weren't going to take the chance that Lily might end up in the wrong place. They'd have to figure out a way for both girls to get an education without separating them.

Linnea stood in the storeroom, surveying her stock, hands on her hips. She had an entire box of wrapped hand-painted vases to go through. She'd found them in various back-alley shops. She needed to find someone with an eye for antiques to help her decide which were truly valuable and which were made only recently to look antique. She'd wait to put them out as she didn't need to get off on the wrong foot with her customers. She wanted to be known as one of the few shop owners who could be trusted. As her Ye Ye had drilled into her, her reputation was everything. Ruin it and she was done. Hopefully a year from now she'd be the antique expert herself.

Moving on, she saw that she had a few more boxes of T-shirts but she was going to have to ask for a rush on her next shipment. She took out her phone and began texting her supplier. She really needed a computer to be able to give a more accurate count but she'd have to make do with a quick appraisal. Hopefully in a few months she'd be profitable enough to afford a laptop. She ought to be happy to finally have a cell phone, as she was probably the only one in China who'd waited until she was eighteen to get one. But still she really needed more office equipment. As it was, she had to make constant trips to the local print shop to scan and e-mail her sketches to the supplier for new designs.

"Ivy, how many of the T-shirts with vintage street signs are stacked up there?" she yelled as she rummaged through one of the boxes at her feet.

She sensed rather than heard someone behind her and startled when she felt a light caress on her hip.

"I think probably not enough."

Linnea jumped up and turned around. Jet stood there, his arms open wide. She eagerly accepted the invitation and stepped into his embrace, breathing in the clean, soapy smell of his neck. An instant feeling of comfort enveloped her. Even after a year of dating, she was always so glad to see him.

"Jet! What are you doing here?" She stepped back and looked up at him, admiring the way his eyes twinkled when he smiled. Sometimes she thought he was just too cute for his own good.

"My father finally gave me some time off. I'm here to see how I can help."

Linnea squinted at him and practiced her most intimidating expression. "Well, you missed my grand opening. Most of the hard work is done."

Jet grimaced. "I know, Lin. I'm sorry about that but Baba wouldn't let me go. He's says I'm earning my stripes. But since all the hard work is done, maybe you and I can sneak away to my apartment and . . ." His roving hands finished the sentence for him.

"No, Jet. I can't leave the store. And stop it—the girls are right in there," Linnea whispered as she slapped his hands away, even though a part of her wished they'd continue their exploration. "Be serious. I need to order some more shirts and get them here fast. You wouldn't believe it but I've almost sold out again. People love my shirts!"

"I do believe it, Linnea. I told you they'd be a big hit. Face it—you have talent as a designer. Aren't you glad now that your old boss fired you from fixing bicycle tires?" He laughed, then sobered quickly at her scolding look. "What can I do? Help you count?"

Linnea pointed toward the front of the store.

"Go keep the girls out of trouble, and tell Ivy to write down exactly how many I have of each style of shirt. I'll get the counts done in here and be up there in a minute to tell you what to do next. While you're here we can do a full inventory."

Jet stood up straight and saluted Linnea.

"*Aiya,* Captain Lin. I'm on it. But I'm taking you to lunch and not taking no for an answer, so you'd better get your work done. And if you're really lucky, I'll let you take me to my place Friday night when my parents are away, and I'll even allow you full rights to do whatever you want to me."

With that he clicked his heels and pivoted around. He marched out of the room to the sound of Linnea's muffled laughter.

Five hours later Linnea closed the door and used her keys to lock it. Jet waited patiently beside her as behind them a woman rattled a can at her, asking for money. The woman had shown up a few days before and, thanks to a few handouts, she'd become a permanent fixture in front of the shop. She was so old that Linnea hadn't had the heart to run her off.

"*Ni hao,*" Linnea greeted the woman kindly, but pushed the can gently away from her face. "I'll bring you back some lunch but no more money."

The woman smiled, showing the gaps in her teeth, and then settled herself down on the curb to wait.

Linnea looked through the door and gave a parting wave to Ivy and Lily, then joined Jet on the sidewalk.

"You sure you want to leave them here?" Jet asked, looking over her shoulder through the glass.

"They don't want to come. They'll be fine. I turned the sign to *Closed* and they'll entertain themselves going through my new stuff in the back. It's just easier for Lily not to have to navigate these uneven sidewalks. We'll bring them back something."

Jet looked down at the rough path in front of them. The sidewalk was made up of small squares of concrete laid six across. The squares bumped up against one another with many meeting to jut upward instead of lying flat like they were intended. "I can understand that. It's even hard for me to walk without tripping. It's a shame that the city can't take better care of this part of town. This is where all the history is."

"History! You want to hear history?" Sky, their neighboring shopkeeper, said as he came up behind them, making quite an impression with his outfit. Today his fashion choice was tie-dyed and in his bright orange and pink shirt he stood out in the crowd of pedestrians mostly dressed in a sea of dark blues and grays. He still wore his huge white sunglasses but today he also wore a funky Mao hat pulled low over his face.

"I can tell you the history of Wuxi from going back three thousand years ago when it was founded by two princes. Ever heard of Taibo and Zhongyong?"

"Oh, *ni hao,* Sky." Linnea waved at him, then gestured. "This is Jet."

Jet gave a slight wave but didn't smile. He didn't look impressed. "Hi."

"Oh, hi! I'll bet you're Linnea's boyfriend. Peony told me all about you."

Linnea blushed and wished her little sister were within choking reach. She wondered exactly what Peony had told him. Sky smiled at her discomfort and fortunately changed the subject.

"Where are we going? Lunch? Great, my grandfather is watching my store," Sky said, not waiting for any answers before moving up next to them and linking his arm through Linnea's.

Linnea had to laugh. Sky was such a character. Quiet, but friendly. Colorful, she'd describe him. She just hoped that Jet didn't mind too much. She looked at him and her laugh faded at the sight of his thunderous expression. He was jealous! But then he showed he could handle it like a gentleman and took her other arm.

"Okay, lunch with Sky it is. But I'm picking the spot," Jet said.

They headed toward the street of small shops and larger restaurants. Linnea didn't care where they ate; she was just glad to have time with Jet and was even looking forward to more conversation with Sky. He was turning out to be the most fascinating person on her new street.

On the way they chatted and all of them stopped when they passed the rock park. In the center of the open area a slight woman had taken over the small pagoda. She was older, that was obvious, but she was still beautiful in her billowing white shirt and loose, colorful pants. The ballet slippers on her feet moved lithely among the scattered flowers on the floor of the pagoda. She was quite a sight and they stopped to watch.

The people in the park stared as the woman leapt around, dancing and singing to the music only she could hear. The cords coming from earbuds tucked into her ears traveled over her chest and connected to a tiny purple iPod attached to her waistband. The woman was oblivious to the crowd, leaping from one side to the other as her long hair bounced around and people either laughed or stared.

"Now *that* is something to see," Linnea mumbled, mesmerized by the woman's total, unbridled joy. It wasn't often she'd seen anyone from that generation singing, or especially dancing, in public. Most people of that age would highly disapprove of that type of behavior. Linnea thought it curious that the woman was so undeterred by the staring. And even with the pace she was keeping, she still moved more gracefully than some half her age could. Linnea shook her head in amazement.

"She reminds me of a butterfly, so free and beautiful."

Jet shook his head. "Someone's been huffing the opium pipe. . . ."

Linnea cleared her throat and when she got his attention, gave him a scolding look.

Sky laughed and began applauding. Then he stepped forward and, holding both hands to his mouth, called out, "Go, Bai Ling, go!"

Linnea sat at the table next to Jet, across from Sky, and listened intently. Her business neighbor was proving to be even more interesting than she had first thought. Bai Ling was not only the namesake for Sky's store; she was also Sky's mother.

Jet snorted. "And that really doesn't bother you that a park full of people are staring at your mother and laughing?"

Linnea elbowed him in the side. "Don't be so rude, Jet. They weren't all laughing. Some of them were clapping. I saw lots of them smiling, too."

Sky nodded. "It's okay, Linnea. Jet obviously comes from a conventional family and doesn't understand freedom of the spirit."

Linnea watched him as he looked over at Jet's crisp buttoned-up shirt and designer jeans, then glanced down at the watch on Jet's wrist that probably cost more than Sky brought in with a week's profits at his store. She felt her ears burn with embarrassment. Jet came off as pretentious sometimes, but she knew that wasn't who he really was.

Sky continued. "Bai Ling lives on a different plane than most people. She doesn't—nor do I, for that matter—care what others think about the way we live. If Bai Ling can make one person feel joy with her dancing, then she has put in an honest day's work and can go to bed with her soul at peace. Bai Ling uses her dancing and singing to escape the bad memories that try to invade her spirit." He brought the bowl up to his mouth and nonchalantly slurped the rest of the broth and noodles from the bottom.

Linnea didn't know what to think. She'd never heard someone call his mother by their given name, and she'd also never met such a different type of family. She wouldn't dare ask any more personal questions about his mother and what memories she was trying to escape. Instead she used her spoon to chase a few stray noodles around the bottom of her bowl.

"So, the jewelry in your store, and the stuff you displayed in Linnea's window, she made all that?" Jet asked.

Sky nodded. "Most of it. But these days she spends more time in the park and I've taken over designing the jewelry. I've been around it all my life, so I can pretty much copy her style exactly. While most of the jewelry makers in Wuxi focus on pearls, we've got the bead market."

Jet shook his head and Linnea hoped whatever he was thinking would come out politely. Her hopes were dashed quickly.

"How can you make a living selling beaded jewelry? Did you even go to school? What's your background?"

Linnea cringed and looked at the bottom of her bowl as if it held the answers to all of life's questions. She wished she were somewhere else. Where had her kind and compassionate boyfriend disappeared to? Jealousy was one thing but outright rudeness she couldn't stand. She was mortified. But Sky didn't seem to be. He went on as if Jet's question were perfectly acceptable.

"School? No, I don't have a worthless piece of paper that tells me I'm allowed to participate in the career a bunch of stuffed shirts has deemed I'm qualified for. I just do it. And how much money do you really need, Jet? Do you think that money will bring you the happiness your heart seeks? Tell me, what is it you have always wanted to do? Work for a pittance for high-browed officials? Is that your destiny?"

Linnea muffled a giggle at the expression on Jet's face. She knew he hated deep conversations like this. To his family, money was the key to everything. And even though Jet had thrown his parents for a loop by choosing a girl of modest means who had no real family tree, the need to aspire to great heights had been ingrained in him from a young age and he'd shared with her many times that he wanted to make his own fortune one day.

Sky continued. "And we have more than jewelry in our store. Like Linnea, I'm interested in bringing back things of the past. Most of your generation is only interested in obtaining the things that foreigners around the world have. They're addicted to the wrong things, like smartphones and computers." He waved his hand dismissively in the air. "They've shut their eyes to what we already have in our own country. I want them to fall back in love with our things and stop coveting everyone else's."

Jet's forehead wrinkled. "My generation? How old are *you*?"

Sky laughed. "We're only as old as we feel. But I can see you are a man who wants real facts. I am just a few months from turning thirty."

Linnea's mouth dropped open. "Thirty? You don't look a day over twenty-two or three!"

Jet waved his hand at the server to signal he wanted the bill. The girl came close and he told her to also wrap up two to-go servings of the noodles.

Sky waited for the girl to leave the table, then nodded. "That is because I haven't spent my life chasing insignificant things. Bai Ling taught me long ago that everything I need can be found right in here." He used his fist to thump his own chest. "Have you ever heard of Falun Gong?"

Linnea cringed as she looked around to see if anyone had heard.

Jet held his hand up and whispered across the table. "Hey— don't start talking about something that's going to get us arrested. I just asked how old you were."

Sky laughed softly. "Jet, Jet, Jet . . . listen, my friend. Falun Gong isn't a cult as the government has led many to believe. It's just a way to cultivate your higher energy using exercise and developing your mind. Think of it as a new way of living life peacefully."

Linnea had heard about Falun Gong but didn't know much about it, certainly not enough to argue one way or the other.

"All the same, tell that to the thousands of Falun Gong followers who are now rotting in prisons and reeducation camps, being tortured for their beliefs," Jet hissed. "I don't want Linnea involved in any part of it."

Sky folded his hands quietly on the table. He looked calmly from Jet to Linnea.

"You're right. This isn't the time or place. Let's talk about more things of the past. Linnea, do you know I have in my store an authentic folding movie chair that was used by moviegoers in the Mao era? It belongs to my grandfather. You have to come see it, and he might even let you use it for your display window."

Linnea perked up at that. It would be perfect as an accessory to her vintage shirts. She wondered if Sky's grandfather would let her buy it from him or possibly trade something.

Through the corner of her eye, she watched Jet stiffen at Sky's offer. She wished that Jet would be more open-minded and realize that Sky was just a harmless nice guy! And a real Mao-era chair? She couldn't wait to see it. She wondered if she could use it to sketch a T-shirt graphic. She'd already thought of a banner to put over it—a quote by Mao would be perfect. If his grandfather would allow it, that was.

"Seriously, Sky? Can I see it today?" She couldn't hide the excitement in her voice, even if it did make Jet scowl. "I'd love to borrow it, if you think he wouldn't mind."

Chapter Six

Calli heard the door open but didn't look up as she wrestled a slippery, soap-covered Poppy in the kitchen sink. The little girl giggled and slapped at the water, obviously happy to be naked, despite the chill in the air. Bubbles and water covered the counter and even the floor around them, but Calli couldn't be cross with her, as the joy on her face and the bubble crown on her head made her quite adorable.

"Sit still, Poppy! I've got to rinse your hair. Benfu, is that you? Come over here and help me. I swear, this little bean sprout is getting so big I can't handle her. I'm too old to keep wrestling these babies." Right on cue, Poppy's butt slid out from under her and Calli had to move fast to keep her from going underwater.

"Oh, Peony, your face! What happened?" Maggi said, behind Calli. And why was Peony already home? It wasn't time yet. Peony attended one of the local schools—but her classes usually let out a bit later than the twins'. Usually she was the last one home, but today she'd even beat Ivy.

Calli held on to Poppy and turned to see what the fuss was about. Peony stood just inside the door and looked a mess. Her hair was sticking out all over, one pigtail down and the other hanging skewed. Her jacket was torn but most shocking was the swelling eye she was sporting.

"Oh my, what happened to you?" Calli asked, already having a hint. Peony was turning out to be one of her most adventurous daughters of all. At only ten, she had a personality that needed no introduction. When she walked into a room, she immediately drew attention. Some of her first battles had been because the other children at school had known she was a part of their family. Peony had been embarrassed to be taunted as a scavenger's daughter until she'd finally settled in with them and become proud of it.

"Feng Ji started a fight and I finished it," she said, her hands on her hips, the fire in her eyes still blazing.

Calli sighed as she finished rinsing the suds from Poppy. Feng Ji again. Would the boy ever stop his bullying? It was going to be hard to discipline Peony when the truth was, she was glad she'd stood up for herself. "Sit down, Peony. Let me finish with the baby, and then I'll fix you up and you can tell me all about it."

Maggi wheeled herself closer to the sink and held up a towel. "Here, Nai Nai. Give her to me."

Calli held Poppy over the water and shook her gently to let the water slide from her little brown body; then she guided her into the towel. Maggi enveloped her with the soft material and hugged her close. Poppy giggled, loving the attention from her big sister.

"Let's get you dressed, Pop Pop." Maggi wheeled them over to the bed where Calli had laid out fresh clothes. Calli was proud that Maggi was taking on many more chores now that her new chair allowed her to be mobile. Besides still doing a lot of work with sorting and ironing out the newspapers neighbors continued to give them to recycle, her daughter had become almost a second set of hands to help with the baby. Still though, she needed to get Maggi to return to school, as she had refused to go since she'd been teased about her disability so much in her first few weeks.

There never seemed to be a quiet or peaceful day anymore, but Calli wouldn't have it any other way. As she looked over her modest home, she felt an unexpected longing for her own mother—or at least a chance to show her what she'd done in her life. She felt her *muqin* would be proud. Even in a time when baby girls weren't coveted, she'd said Calli had been a much-needed burst of colorful affection when she'd arrived. That was how she came to be called Calla Lily, after her mother's favorite flower. The woman would be proud that as a tribute to her, Calli had carried on the tradition and built her own flower garden of daughters.

"Now come over here, Peony." Calli patted the chair at the table, and Peony stomped across the room and plopped down in it, then heaved a loud sigh.

Calli tried not to smile at the indignant look on Peony's face as she went to their tiny refrigerator and pulled out a pack of peas that Widow Zu had given them only the week before. "Tell me what happened."

Peony huffed in exasperation, then started her story. "We were working on our special projects and the teacher called on Feng Ji to answer a question. He got it wrong and then I answered it right. He got mad and called me a melon head."

"Here, hold this on your eye." Calli cringed. Someone from the neighborhood must have spread the story about the growth on Peony's head when she was found. The scar was almost completely hidden now by her hair but before her surgery it had been a touchy subject. Peony was sure it was the reason her mother had left her to be found by someone else.

"Please tell me you didn't start a fight right in class?" She knew Peony's teacher was very strict and she dreaded getting called in to see him. The last time they'd met she'd had to put him in his place when he'd tried to tell her Peony was deficient in intelligence because she was a ward of the state. *Ward of the state, my foot!* Peony was her child as far as she was concerned and just as intelligent as any child in that class!

"No, I waited until we were allowed to go for our break and I got him at the water fountain." Peony set the peas on the table and crossed her arms over her chest.

"Looks to me like he got *you*, Peony. You're going to have a black eye!" Maggi called from the other side of the room. "Wait till Ye Ye hears about it."

"Shut up. You should see Feng Ji's face," Peony answered her sister defiantly.

Calli held her hand up. "Hush, both of you. Peony, I'm surprised at you. You let someone steal your joy and get you all riled up. Why didn't you ignore him? And I can't imagine this all took place without any teachers noticing."

Peony lowered her eyes.

"Peony? Are you in trouble?" Calli really hoped not. Already it was only the first term of the year and Peony had been reprimanded numerous times, usually for her acts of retaliation after being teased. Unfortunately, the teachers never seemed to take her side. There was no compassion involved when it came to disrupting school.

Peony sighed. "I don't know, but I have a letter in my bag. You have to meet with Laoshi tomorrow morning before I can come back to class."

"Peony, you are just determined to live up to your name, aren't you?"

"What do you mean?"

Calli sat down across from Peony. "Well, legend has it that many years ago a famous empress ordered all the flowers in her land to open at the same time. Only the peony dared to disobey and remained closed."

"I would've stayed closed, too! Why should one person be in charge of every flower? What if the flower wanted to open another day instead?"

Calli shook her head. On the bed, Poppy chattered incoherently, oblivious to the stress in the room. Calli wished Benfu would come home from his afternoon errands so he could step in and take care of everything. He was much better at finding words to console the girls than she was. But she could only do what she knew how to do. So she scooted her chair closer to Peony and enveloped her in her arms, holding the tiny stiff body until she finally relaxed and let herself be comforted.

Hours later, after a modest dinner of boiled cabbage and steamed rice had been served and the kitchen was cleaned up, the girls gathered in the living room, some reading and others doing homework. Lily played a low, soft song on her violin, bringing a peaceful and cozy feeling to their evening. Poppy sat on a blanket, happy with the colorful collection of cups and bowls they'd set out for her to play with. Calli felt a sense of contentment fall around her until she looked over at Peony and saw her staring into space, her stack of dog-eared postcards scattered in her lap. *So one of my little flowers is not at peace,* she thought to herself.

"Peony, do you want to take a walk?"

Several heads popped up. They all liked to walk in the evenings when Calli was feeling like it. These days her arthritis flared so much they didn't often get to go with her. Calli shook her head at their hopeful looks.

"Just Peony and me tonight, girls. Tomorrow Ye Ye will take you and if I'm able, I'll join you." She looked at Benfu and he nodded. With that he'd given his thoughts on the subject and would say no more. Peony stood and joined her at the door. Calli handed her a light jacket and they left.

As they moved down the lane between the rows of houses, Calli let the quiet settle between them. She knew her daughter well and Peony would talk about what was really bothering her when she was good and ready.

It didn't take long and they didn't need to venture far. They reached the end of the *hutong* and Peony perched on the low concrete wall of their neighbor's courtyard. Calli settled in beside her.

"Nai Nai, does it mean I'm a bad daughter to you if I think about her?" Peony asked, almost in a whisper she said it so low.

Calli could tell the question was hard for Peony to ask and she wondered how long she had been holding it back. And she needed no detail of who *her* was—it was just known. And all her daughters had these questions swirling around in their minds at different times in their lives; some of them just chose not to speak about it, keeping it close to their hearts instead.

She put her arm around Peony and squeezed her skinny body against her warm, plump one.

"Peony, you could never be considered a bad daughter. We love you so much, girl! And it's perfectly okay to think about your mother. It's only normal, especially for you as you remember her so well." She hoped she was saying the right words. It never got any easier to comfort the girls about the circumstances surrounding how they came to be a Zheng daughter. Poor Peony; her mother had made contact through postcards for a while and given her daughter what could be considered false hope. The postcards had held only a few words and never gave any identifying information about the sender. They were simple pieces of paper, but just enough to keep Peony's emotions on a constant roller coaster.

Using the mail, Peony's mother had dangled hope in front of her for a few years and then suddenly cut off all contact. It had been at least six months since the last card, yet Peony never stopped waiting for the mail to arrive.

Peony turned to look her in the eye. "But I don't want to make *you* sad, Nai Nai."

Calli squeezed her harder. "*Aiya.* You could never make me sad by thinking of your mother! What makes me sad is to see how you get so upset and keep all those feelings bottled up inside. Sometimes it helps to talk with your lips instead of your fists, Peony," she admonished her lightly. Since the postcards had stopped a year before, Peony had really misbehaved at school.

Peony looked away, then down at her feet. She kicked her heels against the wall. "I didn't tell you but Feng Ji also told everyone in my class that I'm not Chinese, that I'm an orphan half-breed. But I know my mother's Chinese because I remember her! But maybe she didn't want me because I have bad blood."

Calli didn't know what to say. They had thought giving the girls their own family name would prevent them from being stigmatized as orphans in school and later in their adult lives. Some children in China grew up with the last names that very clearly marked them as coming from the institutions. Calli and Benfu hadn't wanted that for their girls. But rumors flew in small towns and sometimes it was inevitable that bullies would find the most hurtful piece of knowledge they could and use it to inflict even more invisible wounds.

Recognizing Peony's mixed blood was expected and Calli was surprised she hadn't heard about it earlier. As her daughter grew older, her non-Asian features were becoming more prominent and recognizable to others around her. Even Widow Zu had commented on it to Calli one morning, and she was so farsighted it was a miracle she'd noticed.

"Peony, look at me." She turned her daughter's face and lifted her chin up with her finger. She stared down into her deep brown eyes. "You are so beautiful, you just don't know it yet."

Peony's eyes filled with tears and Calli felt her heart would burst at the sadness she saw. Peony was usually such a brave little girl, always putting on the defensive armor to guard how she truly felt. To see her so vulnerable was tough on an old woman.

"I don't know much about your beginnings but I do know you should never be ashamed of who you are, child. Your mother kept you for as long as she could but she knew she'd have to let you go if you were to get help for your illness. Do you think she would've kept you until you were seven years old if she didn't love you?"

Peony shook her head and the dejected expression on her face reminded Calli of the very day Benfu had brought her home. She could see one lone tear make its way down her cheek, and she wished for the hundredth time that the world was different and such hardships didn't cause the long-standing ripples of consequences her girls had to bear.

"But if I'm not Chinese, what am I, Nai Nai?" She sniffled again.

"Child, you *are* Chinese! The mixed blood that runs through you is only that—blood. Who you are and what you will become comes from your heart. Only you can determine if you will be a true Chinese, not some bully at your school." She hugged her little body close. "Peony, please never think bad thoughts about your first family. You were loved then, and you are loved now. And any time you want to talk about your birth mother, you just come get me and we'll take a walk. *Hao le?*"

"Okay." Peony sniffled. Then she took a deep breath and straightened her shoulders. Calli could see her mentally putting her armor back on. "I'm ready to go back now, Nai Nai."

With that Peony stood and waited for her to join her. Together they made their way back to what Calli felt was the sweetest home on earth. As they walked hand in hand, she thought of all her daughters and hoped that even though she would never want to replace any one of them, she would continue to do all she could to fill the hole their birth mothers had left behind.

Chapter Seven

Linnea stood silently studying the poster while she waited for Sky to bring down the vintage stamps he'd told her about. She'd slowly made her way around the room until she found herself unable to move from the piece of paper tacked to the wall. It was no less than her fourth time in Sky's store in the last few weeks and she never got tired of looking at it. He'd already let her sketch the old Mao movie chair and she'd sent off the design. She planned to start selling the new shirts that Friday when they arrived from Beijing. But now her attention continued to be drawn to the poster.

"Do you know what that is?" the old man called from his perch beside the cash register. Linnea was startled. Usually he didn't even speak to her when she came in. She'd already discounted him as a girl-hater, even though his own daughter still lived under his thumb. She understood now why Bai Ling liked to stay away from her home, as her father was such a cynical old grump.

Of course she knew what it was—he might find it hard to believe but she *could* read after all. The poster, done in stark black and white, pictured a terrified woman running with a child over her shoulder. Behind her a cityscape with huge billows of smoke warned of the impending nuclear war. Underneath, the caption read *Be Prepared. War Is Coming!*

"Yes, I know, but what year was it from?"

The old man stirred more tea leaves into his cup. He took a long swig, then set it loudly on the table. Linnea wondered where all the customers were. Did they have any business at all?

"From 1971. Isn't it amazing how many years the poster survived? So much lost and a flimsy piece of paper withstood it all. In Shanghai back then, everyone was ordered to help build bomb shelters for that impending war. Now those shelters are nothing more than a meeting place for lusty young lovers."

He said the last part with disgust and Linnea tried to hide her grin as she turned to Sky's grandfather. He was old—way older than her Ye Ye. His head was almost bald, save for a few sprigs of gray hair that stood on end. Curiously, he sported a longish gray beard that grew down to a point like in the photos of old Chinese men from ancient times Linnea had found in storybooks long ago. She thought a long dark robe and a sorcerer's wand would be a better fit for him than the baggy pants and frayed blazer he wore. With the thickness of the heavy black glasses perched on his nose, she wondered if he could even see anything. He wasn't a big strong-looking man like her Ye Ye, but perhaps the years had shrunk him. She tried to imagine what he might have looked like before the ravages of age changed every contour on his face. She was sure he knew a lot of fascinating history, and if he was easier to talk to, she'd love to pick his brain. She stared at the sour look on his face and knew he'd be a hard case to break. But she'd just have to win him over.

"*Dui le.* I can't imagine how afraid the people were with posters like these all around. Just look at the panic on that woman's face."

Linnea moved to one of the many racks holding strand after strand of long necklaces made from beads. The store held so many interesting pieces, she could stay all day and just browse if she had the time. She looked down at her watch. She still had almost forty-five minutes before she had to be back. Nai Nai had started coming almost every day to make her step away for a midday break, and if Linnea came back early, she'd have to hear a lot of fussing. Nai Nai kept trying to tell her she needed time away from the store to clear her head or she was going to grow old from worry.

The old man patted the stool next to him. "Come. Sit and wait here. Sky will be down soon enough. It's probably time for one of his three daily wardrobe changes. Might as well relax while you wait."

Linnea spotted the *xiangqi* board on a small table between the two seats. It looked ancient and she'd never played on an antique one before. She looked up at the old man and realized he was lonely. Maybe that was why he was so gloomy. Did Sky spend any time with him at all? Her Ye Ye was lucky; he was always surrounded with girls wanting his attention. Who did the old man have?

"Just wait? We can do more than that. Why don't you let me beat you in *xiangqi*?"

The old man looked taken aback for a moment. Even speechless. Then he looked down at the board and to the watch on his wrist.

"Why not? I've got another eight hours of nothing to do before I can go to bed. Set it up, girl."

Linnea smiled to herself. She'd have Sky's grandfather eating out of her hand in no time. After all, it was obvious the man was starving for companionship and interesting conversation. Linnea would give him both.

Half an hour later Sky had still not appeared, but Linnea was becoming intrigued with his grandfather as he worked carefully to set up the *xiangqi* board. She could've had it ready in minutes, but she sat patiently and watched as the old man examined every piece before placing it in the correct spot. She felt sure he was grateful for the attention and wanted to stretch it as far as possible.

"So, what would you like me to call you, *Laoren*?" she asked, realizing she'd never been formally introduced. Though she was using the universal Chinese title for an old person, she'd like to have something other than *old person* to know him by.

"Mr. Lau will be fine. *Linnea*," he answered gruffly, his sarcastic tone letting her know he already knew her name. He took his pipe from his pocket and after tapping it against the arm of his chair, lit it and inhaled deeply. The smoke swirled around them both, settling like a heavy cloak on her shoulders.

Linnea thought the smell was actually quite nice but it looked like the old man was doing it simply to get a reaction from her. He was a feisty one; she'd give him that.

"Mmm . . . what kind of tobacco is that? Smells good." She smiled at him while continuing to arrange the pieces on the board. She could play both *xiangqi* and the mental game he baited her with.

He shook his head but didn't answer. Linnea could tell he was disappointed that blowing smoke in her face didn't get a reaction.

With the board finally set up, Linnea reached down and made the first move. Mr. Lau frowned, then followed with a move of his own, and the game was on.

"So, girl, what makes you think your store is going to be able to withstand the tough economy around here? Do you know you are the sixth new tenant in that building in as many years?"

Linnea hadn't known that. She hoped she hadn't picked one of those unlucky buildings that some tried so hard to avoid.

"I'm already doing okay. I'm profitable, and that's unusual in the first year or even two of opening a business."

Lau snorted his skepticism. "What's your specialty? Do you have one yet? Something everyone knows to come to you for? Ours is my daughter's jewelry. That's our bread and butter. After all her years of uselessness she is finally doing something to help her family." He pointed at a rack of colorful necklaces next to the wall. "You can't try to specialize in everything, you know."

Linnea nodded her agreement. "Yes, I do know that, Mr. Lau. These days they call it a *signature item* and I've already got one. It's my vintage T-shirts. I sketch designs of old Wuxi and have them printed on the shirts. They're really popular already. I've sold over five hundred since I opened."

Lau's mouth fell open and Linnea choked back her delight at finally seeing something to upset his cocky expression.

"Five hundred shirts? That cannot be. And how do you know anything about what Old Wuxi looked like?"

Linnea didn't care whether he believed her or not. She was confident in her store and the bright future she'd planned. The poor old man, judging by the lack of customers in his store since she'd arrived, was probably struggling to stay afloat. No wonder Sky wanted to display some of the beads in her store. She'd ask him later if there was anything else she could do to help.

"I find ways to bring back the old times. I research postcards, photographs, and even old posters like that one you have back there on the wall. Sky already let me sketch your old Mao movie chair and I'll start selling that design soon. My generation is intrigued with what things were like back in the Mao days."

Lau looked over to the staircase leading up to their living quarters as if he wanted to scold Sky for allowing Linnea to have anything to do with his chair. Sky had already informed her that his grandfather was a die-hard Mao supporter. With Linnea's upbringing by her Ye Ye and his anti-Mao beliefs, Lau's loyalty intrigued her.

She reached down and blocked his chariot with a soldier, much to the dismay of Lau.

"So, speaking of Mao, you and my Ye Ye were both around during his reign. What do you think of the Cultural Revolution? Do you agree that Mao's attempt to destroy educators and the wealthy class was because of his fear that knowledge and money were a power that could lead to his demise?"

Lau sat back in the chair and eyed her suspiciously.

"Who's your Ye Ye? People around here don't talk much about those times." He looked around the store as if someone were waiting in the shadows. "What are you trying to get me to say?"

Linnea laughed. So much paranoia! It still amazed her how the older generation was terrified to speak against a dead man. Did he think she was a reincarnated Red Guard or what?

"I'm not trying to get you to say anything. I'm just interested in hearing about it. My Ye Ye tells us some of his stories and I just wondered if yours are the same." She shook her head. "Mao was something, wasn't he? He thought he could change the way people were educated and dictate how they entertained themselves, and he even demanded to know what their own thoughts were!"

Lau scowled deeper. "How does a mere girl like you know so much about the history of Mao? I asked you once, girl, and I'll not ask you again—who is your Ye Ye?"

They both turned when they heard Sky coming down the stairs carrying an old book. He was indeed dressed in a different shirt, this one shiny silver with huge gold buttons. Linnea thought he looked like he was ready to go to a disco.

"Here're the stamps but what's all this? I hear you getting all gruff, Ye Ye. The man who raised her is Lao Zheng Benfu. I thought I already told you that?"

Lau shook his head. "No, if you'd told me that, I'd remember. I know of Zheng Benfu. His father, Zheng Ju, and I were colleagues. I haven't seen him in decades. I guess I should have gone by his family home before now. But I remember the lad from many years ago before his parents shipped him off to the country."

Linnea wrinkled her brow in confusion.

"Colleagues? You must have the wrong man. My Ye Ye's father was a professor in Shanghai. A very respected one, too." Linnea didn't know a lot about her Ye Ye's family, but she did know that much. She'd assumed, as old as her Ye Ye was, that his own father would be dead by now, but since Lau was still living, she suddenly realized he could be, too.

Lau waved his hand in the air dismissively.

"Yes, I know he was a professor. So was his wife, Feiyan, though she was at a lower tier than we were, more like a grammar teacher. We all taught at the school in Shanghai before the Red Guards blazed through there and demolished everything. I got out just in time but I didn't stick around to see what happened to the Zhengs. But I heard they made it, too."

Linnea remained confused and incredulous that she'd met someone who knew her Ye Ye's parents. She was still skeptical, too. "You were a professor? Sky didn't tell me that."

Sky pulled up a stool next to them. "You never asked and I didn't think it was of importance. Grandfather is long retired and he doesn't like to talk about the past. I can't believe you got him to say as much as he has."

Sky reached over and patted his grandfather on the leg.

"You doing okay? You do remember that they rebuilt that school, right? And now Shanghai has at least a few dozen more just like it—some even have foreign teachers. There aren't any more Red Guards." He reached over and tilted a bowl on the table to look inside at a pile of dried-out rice. "Did you get enough to eat or you want me to bring you another bowl of fresh rice? The cooker is still hot. Or I can bring you some tea?"

"I'm fine. Don't coddle me, boy. I might be close to ninety years old but I'm not senile. Of course I know the Red Guards are long gone. They should've never been allowed to band together anyway. Just a group of folks your age who were given a bit of power and then ran away with it, calling themselves *Mao's personal army*."

"They *were* his personal army, Lao Lau. Even if they were young, they took the same liberties that seasoned soldiers did. The people were terrified to see them coming," Linnea said quietly, trying not to sound disrespectful.

"You think you know so much about it but I bet you didn't know they were only allowed to run amok for two years before Mao stepped in and stopped them. But their reeducation efforts restored calmness and unity to the country, so it wasn't all bad."

Sky grinned and patted the old man's leg again. "Some might beg to differ with you on that. I don't think you'll find too many fans of the Red Guard around here these days."

Lau's face clouded over and he pointed at the door. "I wasn't saying I'm a fan of the Red Guards. Anyway, you'd better go find that crazy mother of yours and bring her in for the day. She gets so caught up in all that silly dancing she won't even come home to eat."

Linnea watched them interact and could see a measure of affection between them. As they bantered back and forth, her thoughts went to the book her Nai Nai kept of their family records, and the entry she wasn't supposed to have read about Ye Ye and Nai Nai's daughter. Just knowing that they had a child who had been taken from them was a secret that for the last year had lain heavily on her heart. But if old Lau knew the family at that time, could he also know something about the girl? Or if he could help her find Ye Ye's father, maybe she could get information about the mysterious baby girl named Dahlia.

She'd bide her time and earn his trust; then if Zheng Ju *was* still alive, she'd get Lau to arrange a meeting. At least he knew where the family home was and that was a start. She needed only a few details and she could search for Dahlia herself if she had to. She knew from reading her Nai Nai's notes in their family book that there was a long-standing chasm between Benfu and his father, but the thought of finding their daughter filled Linnea with hope. If she was successful, it would be her gift to thank Ye Ye and Nai Nai for the love-filled life they had given her when no one else would.

Chapter Eight

Calli filled the pot with water and set it on the stove top to boil. Widow Zu had brought over a dozen eggs and the girls were looking forward to hard-boiled treats later. She looked at Poppy still asleep on their bed, then the clock on the wall, and determined she had just enough time to sit in her chair and rest a bit before beginning preparations for dinner. Linnea was at work but had promised to be home at a decent hour so they could eat together as a family.

Benfu wouldn't be home until right before dark. These days he was finally getting to see what other men his age did in their retirement years. With the increased financial support from the government for each child in their care, her husband no longer combed the streets for trash. Calli was relieved he was feeling better. He'd been through so much over the years; it was good to see him content and able to enjoy life more. She'd never forget those early days when he'd struggled to show her parents he could be an asset to her family and not just a liability. That was how he'd gotten started collecting. Since he was actually hiding from the officials back then, he didn't have a work permit and had begun combing the streets to search for items to sell. He'd gotten good at it and his contributions to the household soon made a huge difference, especially when her father got sick and began failing. And her parents hadn't been blind to the young love blooming right under their noses. They were reserved but finally had allowed it to happen, and soon Benfu had asked for her hand. Oh, the trials they'd been through in their long life together.

She smiled to herself because who would have thought that now Benfu was quickly becoming the neighborhood cards champion. As it was Saturday, he would probably play even later into the day. She would fuss at him but they both knew she really didn't mind.

She glanced at the window. The girls were outside, enjoying the balmy day. They'd all finished their chores in record time so they could get out there. Spring was coming fast and they were all anxious for it to arrive so they could put their outside clothes away for a season.

Even Maggi had wheeled herself out before anyone could help her. She was getting so independent with her new chair and, now that she could do it on her own, liked to go outside often. The other girls teased her about the muscles she had sprouted in her upper arms. They told her they were going to enter her in Beijing's annual arm-wrestling competitions. Calli didn't know if there were any such thing but she went along as it made Maggi beam with joy to hear it.

Every once in a while Calli heard their giggles escalate. Peony, though only ten years old, could be heard over everyone, because she was the loudest. Since she had started school, her personality had become even more outgoing. Even though she was prone to getting into trouble with her classmates, she was a smart one and bragged that her teacher called on her often to answer questions the others couldn't. She was always coming home with entertaining stories of her lessons. Calli felt sure she'd probably be a writer or even an actress one day, she was so spirited.

Calli went to her chair and leaned back, sighing her relief to get off her swollen ankles. She picked up her knitting basket, thinking she might as well get a bit more done on the scarf she was knitting. Jet had brought over the bright red yarn and left it for her. He didn't expect it but the scarf would be his gift at the next Chinese New Year. If Linnea still kept him around, that was.

She dug around in the basket. She knew she'd left the scarf right on top but it wasn't there. Her knitting needles were there, but the scarf and the ball of yarn it was attached to were nowhere to be found. She decided that Maggi might have picked it up. She rose and went to the door. She hoped she could get to her before she had to do too much rework. She wanted the stitches in the scarf to be consistent and knew that her daughter hadn't learned that particular style yet.

She rose and opened the door, poking her head out to call her daughter.

"Mag—"

The scene before her cut off her thoughts of the scarf. She put her hand to her mouth and looked around.

In the middle of the courtyard Lily knelt in the grass, staring straight ahead with a resigned look on her face. In front of her were lines of jagged rocks and around her neck was a piece of paper tied to red yarn. The paper read *I'm the daughter of a counter-revolutionary, an enemy of China.*

Calli looked for and saw Lily's violin sitting to the side of the tree, far from reach. Calli also saw where her red scarf had gone. One of them had unraveled it and the yarn was everywhere. It was used to hold the sign around Lily, wrapped around Peony's arm as a red band, and even used as a noose around little Jasmine's neck as she stood under the tree with the end of her yarn looped over the lowest branch.

"You left Viola on the ground? And what is all this?" Calli felt her cheeks fill with heat when she saw Benfu's extra belt dangling from Peony's hand.

The girls all jumped. Calli was glad they were startled. She knew exactly what they were doing and didn't like it one bit. She put her hands on her hips and readied herself to do some serious scolding, something the girls weren't used to from her.

Peony stepped forward and nervously answered. She hid the belt behind her back.

"Nai Nai, I'm learning about the Red Guards at school. This is a struggle meeting. I'm teaching my sisters about it." She smiled proudly. "Ivy and I are the Red Guards."

Calli remembered struggle sessions well and she was disappointed that the teachers focused so much on the trauma of the past, instead of China's efforts to improve. During the revolution, struggle sessions were used to force normal citizens to confess anything in their lives or family background that might show them to be against Mao's new China. But it was persecution, plain and simple, by bullies who abused people until some of them even made up transgressions just to get it over with.

Calli saw Maggi parked out of the way in her chair, calmly knitting. She didn't appear to be involved. But Peony saw Calli looking that way and corrected her first thought.

"Maggi's knitting socks for Chairman Mao."

Calli sighed. "Socks for a dead man's feet? Hmmm. Yes, I suppose they might be getting pretty cold by now. And what's Jasmine doing with that string around her neck?"

With that question Peony misunderstood and thought everything was going to be okay. She began rambling with her explanation of her well-thought-out drama.

"Jasmine was found guilty of bourgeois ways. She was caught listening to foreign radio shows. Instead of punishment through hard labor, she has chosen to end her life—a common choice during the Cultural Revolution."

Jasmine stood silently under the tree, smiling in her usual serene way, happy to be included in the girls' activities. Calli shook her head. The poor child had no idea what suicide even meant. She just wanted to be a part of anything her big sisters were doing.

Peony pointed at Lily.

"And Lily has chosen to take her punishment. The rocks are supposed to be glass and she must crawl across it one hundred times at each struggle meeting. If she complains or shows pain, I will beat her." She brought the belt around and proudly held it up.

"Peony! You wouldn't dare!" Calli was astonished.

Ivy sat up straight and got off her perch on the low courtyard wall. So far she hadn't said a word but Calli noticed she also wore the red yarn wrapped around her arm. In her hand she held a piece of paper folded in fourths to look like a booklet. Calli assumed it was meant to be Mao's *Little Red Book* of quotations—an item that once no Chinese would be caught without.

"No, Nai Nai. She wouldn't really hit her and we weren't going to make her crawl across the rocks. This is all pretend. I wouldn't have let it go that far."

Calli waved her hand in front of her face, trying to stir up some air. She felt a bit light-headed, but she knew it was from the stress of her girls reenacting a frightening time in her past. It wasn't only the educated who were persecuted, but also land-owners. Her own parents had worked hard to hide the secrets of their family from the ruthless Red Guards. And she didn't even like to think about the pain her own husband had endured during those tumultuous times.

"I should hope not, girls. This is not appropriate; do you realize that the Red Guards actually hurt people? They were a real blemish on the history of China, not something to be taken lightly. Ivy, you are the oldest here—I can't believe you let this go on."

The girls didn't answer. Ivy hung her head. Peony started unraveling the string from around her arm.

Calli pointed at Jasmine. "One of you get that string off Jasmine's neck right now before she really does get hurt."

Calli knew the subject of the Red Guards was becoming more popular again in the current news. So many people who had lived through the atrocities were now coming forward with their stories, whereas for years they were too terrified to speak of it. She'd been a teen when the Red Guards had taken control, and she could easily remember how frightened her parents were that the group would find out they were distantly related to a cousin who owned land. Like artists and teachers, landowners were considered counter-revolutionaries and the Red Guards hunted them down like dogs to punish them. Many nights the local faction had marched up their *hutong* lane as Calli and her parents held their breath, waiting for the knock on their door. They'd really taken a big chance by hiding Benfu, and she'd owe her parents' memory for that gesture until her dying day. The hole they'd dug in the floor was still there; the trapdoor hidden by a colorful rug on the floor. Benfu had squeezed his too-tall body into it too many times to count, spending hours hiding just to be cautious.

But each time it had been another neighbor and not they who'd been pulled out and interrogated, their houses ransacked. And now the latest generation was becoming very curious about the Cultural Revolution and all it entailed. Calli didn't think they saw it for what it really was. But how could they? They'd not seen the horror and devastation with their own eyes.

Calli had a feeling this was going to come up more and more in her own household and she needed to learn how to handle it gently. She was relieved that at least the girls weren't pretending to shave one another's heads in the old Ying-Yang punishing style of shaving only one side. She'd have to watch and make sure Benfu's razor never left the sink.

Lily slowly stood up and removed the sign from around her neck. She shuffled forward until she was directly in front of Calli, then reached out and hugged her.

"Nai Nai, are you sad? We're sorry. We just wanted Peony to teach us what she's learning in school."

Calli hugged her back. Lily was such a sensitive soul. She could always pick up on someone's emotions, without even seeing their face. But Calli supposed it was evident in the sound of her shaky voice as well.

Ironically, even though she was the blind one, Lily led Calli to the bench outside the door and they both sat down. The other girls gathered around, waiting for her to declare their punishment—for real this time. Maggi slowly wheeled herself over until she was part of the circle. Calli took a deep breath.

"Yes, girls, it does make me sad. But I understand it is a part of China's history that is being taught in schools. I just want you all to understand the severity of it. And your Ye Ye would be very upset to see this."

"But why, Nai Nai?" Maggi asked.

"Because the Red Guards were hard on anyone with an education, especially teachers and professors. They thought those who had knowledge could one day revolt against their precious Mao if not suppressed."

"But Ye Ye's parents didn't endure hardship. He's told us that." Peony crossed her arms stubbornly.

Calli shook he head. "No, that's not true. He's told you they didn't endure physical punishments. But they *did* endure hardship. We all did. And that's difficult for Ye Ye to think about. Even though separated from his family, he still felt a responsibility toward them deep in his heart."

At that the girls were quiet. Calli knew they loved their Ye Ye like nothing else in the world and would never want to make him sad.

Peony began running around the courtyard, picking up the pieces of red yarn. "Let's get this cleaned up fast, before he gets home."

Calli looked down at Maggi. The expression on her face was priceless.

"Nai Nai, I'm sorry they unraveled the scarf you were making. I told Peony not to do that because knitting is hard work."

Calli saw her squint her eyes and shoot an accusing look toward Peony.

Peony piped in from across the yard where she was picking up the rocks to return them to their place around the koi pond. "No, you didn't, Maggi! You helped me unravel it!"

"Did not!" Maggi yelled.

"Did, too!"

"Well, this is all your fault, Maggi. I wanted to do a Harry Potter scene—the Red Guards were your idea."

Calli stood up from the bench. The girls were always ready to fuss back and forth and she needed to check on the eggs.

"Come on, Maggi." She got behind her wheelchair and pushed her to the door. "You can help me in the kitchen. Girls, hurry up out here and then come inside to prepare dinner. And no more talk of Red Guards for at least a month. I'm tired of hearing it."

Chapter Nine

As Li Jin walked back from the market, she felt a bounce in her step she hadn't felt in months. At least five weeks had passed since her last post office run and she'd finally made Erik understand her yearning for a real relationship—one without fear of his demands or fists. That morning he'd kissed her before he left, a ritual he'd dropped for the last few months, and with its return she'd allowed herself to feel something again, and to dream of the future once more.

Li Jin realized she was walking with a small smile on her face and people were giving her strange looks. But she didn't care. She was happy again! She hurried along, anxious to get home and get started. She'd told him she'd be gone all day to look for work but after thinking about it, she'd decided to put everything behind her and put some effort into mending things between them. After a lot of heart-to-heart talking the night before, he'd finally relented and told her she wouldn't have to be involved in his unsavory business any longer and could find another job to replace the one he'd made her quit. He also swore he'd never lay a hand on her again. Sure, he'd promised before but this time she felt hopeful that he'd keep his word. It had been difficult, but she'd really made him believe that for the sake of her son, she'd leave if he couldn't let them share a normal life.

It took a lot, but he said he understood and he took all the blame. And he opened up and told her why he was so drawn to her. He told her that her quiet ways and simple beauty were coveted qualities in a wife. Then he held her and once again she remembered what it was about him that was so magnetizing. He was strong, handsome, smart—many things, but most of all when he wanted to, he could make her feel special. And he had said *wife,* which to her meant he wanted to marry her and give her the respectability she craved.

Tonight when he returned home she'd have their apartment spotless, his clothes washed and ironed, and his favorite meal ready. Jojo had laughed that morning when she'd dropped him at school and told him she was making bunny chow for dinner. Erik had taught her to make the South African recipe over a year ago when they'd first moved in together. She didn't make it often, as she definitely didn't care for the spicy curry or the bread dish she'd have to create for it to be served from. But she wanted Erik to know how much she appreciated him compromising. It was all she had to offer, but she'd bring him a familiar taste of his home country to show her appreciation to him for taking care of her and Jojo.

She turned the corner and almost dropped the bags she carried when she saw Erik leaving the entryway from their apartment. He was coming straight at her through the crowd of sidewalk pedestrians, and he wasn't alone. He was with a pretty girl and was holding her hand! It was obvious that they were more than friends.

The girl was at least ten years younger than Li Jin. Blond hair, pale skin—either American or Australian, she wasn't sure. So he'd found his younger and more beautiful girl that he'd always threatened. She felt sick but she would not let them see her pain. She continued walking straight toward them, head held high until she was only feet away and Erik finally saw her through the haze of his midmorning rendezvous glow.

"Li Jin!"

She couldn't believe he had the nerve to sound angry, as if she'd interrupted something important! The girl looked from Erik to her, confused at the sudden tension. Obviously she wasn't aware that her new guy already had a girl. Li Jin skirted around them and continued to walk, barely giving them even a glance. She should have known letting him hang out alone in the clubs frequented by expats would come to this.

She heard his rushed words behind her and then suddenly felt him jerk her around by the sleeve of her jacket. She dropped one of the bags and it hit the sidewalk, tomatoes and other vegetables rolling out of it. Li Jin bent to gather the food. She'd figure out a Chinese dish to make with the supplies and she wouldn't give him the satisfaction of speaking to him.

"Stop! I want to talk to you!" He pulled her to her feet. She looked over his shoulder but the girl had disappeared into the crowd.

"Don't touch me, Erik. I don't want to have this conversation out here for all of our neighbors to hear!" she hissed. "They already hold a grudge against me for rooming with a foreigner. What are you trying to do to my reputation?"

Erik laughed and it sounded cold and hard.

"What reputation? You're an unmarried woman with a bastard son, Li Jin! Do you think they believe you're some sort of saint?"

It was a low blow and he knew it. In one of their more intimate moments, when she trusted him, she'd told him about being raped. Erik was the first person who had ever given her the courage to speak the words aloud. He knew how hard it was for her to do. Now he wanted to brand her as some sort of whore?

She shook her head in disgust and, leaving the bags sitting on the sidewalk, she rushed past him and up the stairs to their apartment.

Hours later she felt the traitorous tears sliding down the sides of her face as she lay quietly, waiting for Erik to finish. He wouldn't consider it rape but she'd told him no. He hadn't listened and to keep Jojo from hearing her, she'd finally stopped fighting. She wanted to say she felt nothing but that wasn't so. She felt trapped. And she felt so alone. She wished she had someone—anyone— to go to for help. For a way out.

His body kept up a rhythmic pace while hers lay motionless beneath him. In the moonlight from the open window the sweat on his body glistened in a way she once thought magical but now just looked sordid. Her body felt bruised and empty. There was a time, before he had begun to hurt her physically and emotionally, that entwining with him had created moments of desire and sweetness. Those nights she had moved along with him, meeting him thrust for thrust. But that was when she had felt wanted. And loved.

But now all she felt was shame and deep—*such deep*— sorrow. She stared at the fan mounted on the ceiling and watched it twirl. She saw a fly riding one of the blades and wondered if it was dizzy. She swallowed repeatedly, trying to keep the sobs from erupting.

Finally Erik rolled off her and onto his back. He nudged her with his elbow and she didn't move. She heard him sigh in frustration. It brought her a sense of satisfaction that he couldn't *make* her want him and she knew he hated that loss of control. Reacting or not reacting to his touch was the only thing she had left and he couldn't take it away.

She hoped he would just go to sleep. She was too tired for more fighting and there was really nothing left to say. If she could just stop the frustrating stream of tears!

"Li Jin. Why are you still crying? I told you I'm sorry. She meant nothing to me. I'm here, aren't I? With you and Jojo—not with her. You said you didn't want to help me anymore—that means I need a new contact to pick up the *dagga*. Get over it already."

Li Jin didn't answer. Anyway, he was lying again. He'd never arrange for packages to be sent to a foreigner; it would cause too much suspicion. And her grief wasn't just a result of seeing him with the girl and his flippant admission of betrayal. It was all of it; the girl, the joy she saw on his face, and even the insult about her son. It all hurt and he had finally broken her. Then as if it were her own fault, he had ranted at her that she was nothing when he found her, and without him she'd be nothing again.

What hurt the most was that he was right. She was nothing. She was so unwanted that even her own parents had discarded her like a piece of trash. She didn't know where she'd come from—or whom she'd come from. A child with no connection to anyone in the world. Now an adult with only one thread helping her to keep it together. Jojo.

He lay right in the next room. Their small apartment wasn't luxurious by any means but it was the nicest place she and Jojo had ever lived in. When she thought of the back-alley hostels and sometimes even parks they'd slept in, she knew that she was lucky. Here Jojo slept on the sofa and was usually lulled to sleep by the sound of his favorite cartoons on the television Erik had bought.

Yes, they were living a better life than they ever had. But at what price? Her dignity? Morals? She was sleeping with what the old-timers called a foreign devil, and doing his bidding. All for a chance at love and a decent home for her child. If she took the love out of it, what was left? Prostitution? At that thought more tears sprang from her eyes. In her lowest moments she'd always had limits but now it felt like that line had been crossed. She was allowing a man she no longer loved to use her body.

Erik threw his pillow at the wall and still she didn't move. He got up and went to the bathroom door, slamming it loudly. Li Jin winced at the noise. Of course he didn't care if he woke Jojo. He only cared about himself. *He* was the bastard—a selfish bastard.

She heard nothing for a few minutes and then she heard him flush the toilet. She turned over quickly and pretended to be asleep, hoping his anger would fizzle out. He opened the door and stomped across the room. She could feel him standing over her and hear his heavy breathing. He stayed that way for a few seconds, then picked up his pillow and climbed into bed. With one yank he took the entire coverlet and left her naked body exposed. She fought her instinct to cover herself and remained still.

"Li Jin, I know you're awake. Just remember what I told you. If you get stupid enough to try and leave, I'll find you. And if I don't find you, I can still make you wish you'd never crossed me." He snorted with contempt and gave his last dig. "I own you."

She didn't answer but oh yes, she knew better than to cross him. How could she forget his constant threats? But he didn't own her—after all her years of being shipped in and out of families and back and forth to the orphanage, being told she was *owned by the state,* she swore she'd never let anyone else own her again.

Chapter Ten

Linnea ran her fingers up Jet's back, making them dance as they traveled the length of his spine. She smiled when he arched, knowing that he loved it when she tickled him. He acted as if he didn't have an ounce of energy left after their lovemaking, and she thought it strange that she always felt the total opposite—as if she were so suddenly full of life she could move a mountain if need be. But Jet had to be brought back slowly, and she'd found that her soft touch on his skin was something he craved after their stolen moments together.

They'd laid out a blanket and made a place in the storage room away from the windows so they could be alone. Linnea had closed the store and told Nai Nai she'd be later than usual but would make it home in time for dinner. With the new demands of running her own business, she was having less and less time for Jet and knew he needed some attention. She grinned. Men—they were nothing but grown little boys.

As she told him about Peony's latest antics, she massaged his shoulders, admiring how wide and strong they were. Her hand finally tired, and she stopped and lay flat on her back. Jet lay on his stomach beside her, quiet now.

A minute later Jet laughed softly, then flipped over.

"What?" Linnea asked. She hated when he didn't let her in on his thoughts.

"I was just thinking of our first kiss."

"So what's so funny about it?" She could feel her face turning red. She remembered acting so immature and she wished he'd just forget it already.

"You only kissed me on the cheek and wouldn't let me move in closer! I'd never had a girl do that before. I acted like it wasn't a big deal, but I really was glad you did that."

"Glad? Why?" Linnea asked.

"I was impressed." He gave her a nudge with his elbow. "Most girls would melt at my feet, but not you—you practically jumped out of the car to get away."

Linnea laughed. "Well, I *didn't* know you well enough, and we parked on the street with about a million other people around. But can we please just forget about that day?"

She waited on him to agree but instead he stared at the ceiling, then took a deep breath.

"Linnea, I have something to tell you."

He sounded so serious that Linnea propped herself on her elbows and looked at him. Was he going to break up with her? Her heart fell.

"What?"

"I'm jealous." He spoke quietly, his eyes still glued to the ceiling above them.

She laughed and plopped back down. She knew exactly what he was talking about. "Oh, Jet. I know you are but you don't have to be. Sky is just a friend. I swear it."

"You say that but I know you go over to his store on your lunch breaks. I came by yesterday and Peony told me where you were. Again. Why do you spend so much time with him?"

Linnea hadn't told Jet about the connection between Jet's grandfather and her family. She'd also never told him about her discovery that Ye Ye and Nai Nai had a daughter taken from them. It was just so personal and she also felt guilty about reading something that wasn't meant for her eyes. She still wasn't ready to share all her secrets, even if she was in love with Jet. She wished she could tell him that her visits across the street had a purpose, but it was just something she wasn't ready to talk about.

She sighed. "I don't even want to take lunch breaks but Nai Nai says I need to get away from the store for at least an hour a day. And I love looking at all the antiques that Sky's grandfather has. Most of the time Sky isn't even there—if that makes you feel any better."

Jet sat up, looking confused. "Then what are you doing when he's not there? Why even go?"

"I talk to his grandfather and we play a lot of *xiangqi*. He's quite good, you know." She laughed softly. "But not good enough to beat me yet."

Jet shook his head. "You amaze me, Linnea. You're spending time with a decrepit old man when you could be hanging out with me."

Linnea sat up, too. He was making such a big deal about things and she didn't get it.

"Jet, you're not around so much, either. You're always working or off on some secret assignment you don't want to talk about." She didn't want to make this into an argument but what did he expect her to do? Sit around and twiddle her thumbs until he was ready to come around? Sky was just a friend. She was building a relationship with old Lau. It was all very simple. As a matter of fact, she was just about ready to ask the old man to help her find her Ye Ye's parents.

"What? It's nothing secret, Linnea. It's just boring. And I'm about finished with my internship. They're going to give me a real job soon. And that means I can finally pay for an apartment. We'll have a nice place to be alone. But are you going to have any time for me? Or do Sky and his old grandfather have all the reservations filled?"

She rolled her eyes. "No, they haven't taken up all the reservations. There's still room for you. But you know what? I might have enough soon to rent my own apartment, too. I want to see if the landlord will give me a deal for the rooms upstairs. I took a look yesterday and it's really nice up there—or at least it could be with a bit of work. If I lived there, I wouldn't have to take that awful bus ride twice a day."

Jet was quiet.

"What? You don't like that idea, either?" she asked. Lately she was beginning to think she could do nothing right in Jet's eyes.

Jet stood up and stretched. "It's not that I don't like it—I just don't know about you living all alone. I don't know that I'd call it a good idea. Would you?"

Linnea did think it was a good idea. Actually, she thought it was a great idea. She loved her family but couldn't wait to have some real independence. She'd always felt older than her years and living on her own had been a dream for a while now. If she'd been born into a normal childhood, she might even be off at college now. Yet fate hadn't wanted her to take that route, so she wouldn't change a thing, and anyway, she couldn't imagine life without her Ye Ye, Nai Nai, and sisters. Even if she did wonder now and then what sort of family had given her up.

"Well, I don't want to talk about it right now, Jet. I've got to get home. Nai Nai will be holding dinner and ready to box my ears." She stood and picked up the blanket, snapping it in the air to loosen any dust.

Jet took it from her and dropped it on the floor again. He put his arms around her and hugged her.

"I don't want to fight, Linnea. You're just moving through life so fast all of a sudden. I miss that girl I met slinging tires on the corner and sketching in her tattered notebook. Sometimes I feel like even though I'm the one with all the connections to get ahead, you're going to pass on by and leave me behind."

Linnea was touched. Jet had never let himself be caught being so vulnerable. She also knew he was proud of her but she hadn't known he was so insecure about her accomplishments. She hugged him back.

"Jet, I'm not leaving you behind. We can both reach success together. And it's only because of you that I was able to do any of this! I haven't forgotten that. I just don't want to slow down and fall into the trap some orphans do. I won't let society brand me as an outcast."

Jet shook his head. "I don't think that can ever happen. You are a born leader, Lin. It won't be long that when people see you coming, they're gonna move out of the way."

Linnea hoped so. The fire in her to succeed and make everyone proud refused to be extinguished. She'd do it or die trying. And one of these days when she was famous or rich, she hoped her birth parents were watching and could see what they'd missed out on.

"Well, we'll see about that. Right now if I don't get my butt home, Nai Nai is going to see me coming and hide my dinner for punishment. This is the third night in a row I've been late."

"I seriously doubt your Nai Nai would let you go hungry. More than likely she'd punish you by stuffing you *too* full." Jet bent down and picked up the blanket to fold it. Linnea watched him and thought over the last year. For him she'd gone against everything she'd been taught and given him what should have been saved for marriage. She didn't know if he understood what a sacrifice it was and how much it took for her to trust him enough to finally relent.

She didn't regret it—at least not most of the time unless she thought about it too deeply—but how long would he stay interested in her, just a poor girl from the wrong side of the city? She knew she was prouder than she had any right to be, but she still resolved herself to put up a few walls to minimize the hurt if and when Jet found someone else more acceptable to date.

Chapter Eleven

Li Jin stared out the window at the passing scenery. She felt carsick but knew better than to voice her discomfort. She'd awoken that morning to Erik standing over her. He'd rushed her out of bed, demanding she take a road trip with him and his South African business partner, Obi. She'd argued but he'd pushed her around until she feared Jojo would hear them, and she finally relented. It was not like she had any choice. The only choice was whether violence was involved. She'd packed a small bag of snacks and a change of clothes quietly, her mind racing. Then she'd woken Jojo long enough to get him into the car, then urged him to go back to sleep.

Now the only thing she knew was they were on their way to Beijing and Li Jin was terrified. She knew it must have something to do with a shipment and she didn't want to be involved. And she sure didn't want Jojo around it. But now obviously Erik didn't trust her to leave her alone for the time it would take him to go and return.

The car hit a bump and Li Jin protectively cradled Jojo's body to keep him from falling off the seat. He lay sleeping with his head in her lap, his arm draped over her legs. They'd been driving all day and he was wiped out. Now he slept soundly and in his sleep he looked younger than he was. She pushed a strand of hair away from his eyes, in case he woke. She was still seething that Erik had called him a bastard. She'd never forgive him for that.

He had warned her to snap out of her pensive mood but she couldn't. He could force her to be there but he couldn't make her talk. When she'd retreated from the conversation Erik and Obi continued to chat in the front seat and left her alone with her thoughts. The words from the day before would not stop playing in her mind. Her son might not have a father, but he was far from being a bastard. The truth was, Jojo's birth was the catalyst that had turned her life around. He had given her a reason to keep living.

They passed a field of wheat, and something about the orderly lines and waving stalks reminded her of the land around her last foster home—the place where her son was created. To be honest, it wasn't so much a foster home as simply a shelter offered to her in exchange for her hard work. After leaving the orphanage at sixteen, she'd ended up on the streets and barely avoiding plenty of dangerous situations. She'd made some friends—albeit ones of the wrong crowd—and had couch hopped around when she could, and huddled in strange places when no one would open their home to her.

Two years later, after one particularly cold week walking the streets, she'd ended up back at the orphanage to talk to Director Wu. It was a humbling moment. She knew if she didn't find a secure place to live, she'd soon be forced to do things she didn't want to just to survive. She could see now how so many of those she'd left behind had resorted to becoming pickpockets and thieves.

She'd shown up dirty, broke, and starving. Though it was the last place she'd ever thought she'd run back to, Li Jin asked if she could stay there and earn her keep, but the director told her she had a better option. She could send her to a foster family near Suzhou. Because of the wife's poor health, the family was no longer willing to foster children but needed some help keeping house and working its small farm. Later she found out the woman was the director's sister and over the years had been given the benefit of many children in and out of the family's home for free labor. This time the family wanted someone older—and Li Jin fit the bill. She didn't know it then but agreeing to that offer would change her life forever.

Erik turned and cleared his throat, jarring Li Jin back to the present. She looked around and saw that they were slowing down to go through a highway toll stop.

"Li Jin, should we stop and let Jojo use the bathroom? We've still got a ways to go."

Li Jin looked down at Jojo and shook her head. Without meeting his eyes, she answered, "He's sleeping soundly. I think he can wait."

Obi glared at her in the rearview mirror. "You tell me if the kid needs to go—this isn't my car and I don't want any accidents!"

"Dude, he's ten. He's bathroom trained, all right?" Erik laughed and fiddled with the radio. Sounds of a popular pop song filled the car. Li Jin zoned it out and went back to her memories.

After a twelve-hour train ride and a frightening taxi trek out of town and into the country, she'd arrived at her new foster home exhausted and hungry. They'd put her to work immediately, without even a chance to rest from her trip. Once settled, Li Jin didn't mind that she was soon taking care of all the cooking, cleaning, and even grocery shopping. She had a room of her own. Even if it was sparse, it was more than she'd ever had, and she was cooking *and eating* three meals a day. It was hard work but she was glad to show her appreciation of being off the street by taking over all the woman's chores. The woman was older, at least fifty, and she suffered from severe arthritis. Li Jin felt sorry for her and was glad to finally be needed. The father was gone working most of the time and Li Jin saw more of his dirty clothes that she washed and ironed than of the person who wore them. Everything was fine until their son came home for a visit. He had a name, but Li Jin would never utter it. She wouldn't even allow herself to think it.

Right away she'd tried to ignore the warning signs she got from the son and put her suspicions to her few years on the street and always having to watch her back. She thought she must be paranoid. Only a few years older than she, the son was in his last year of college. With his fancy clothes and expensive mobile phone he was spoiled; there was no doubt about that. Li Jin even had to cook better foods and more meat while he was there. Mostly he ignored her, treating her like an invisible slave but bragging to his parents in her presence about his life at school and his stellar grade point average, his plan to work as an engineer and buy an apartment in a big city. With his grandiose declarations he made it clear he had a future that she'd never reach, and he wanted her to know it. With his visit Li Jin had been moved out of the house to sleep on the covered porch. She didn't really mind it, other than the relentless mosquitos and the chilly mornings, which she took in stride. She knew she'd be able to move right back inside as soon as the son left.

Li Jin looked at the back of Obi's head as he drove and realized that he was about the same age as the son was back then. She wondered why he wasn't in college and how he had gotten a visa to be in China. All she knew was that he and Erik had come to China at the same time, but they were at least a decade apart in age. Something about the dispassionate way Obi treated Jojo reminded her of the foster son. He'd carried that same cruel look.

Especially the night he came to the porch and took what wasn't his to take.

First she'd put on her tough street act but he'd seen right through that. When he kept coming at her, she'd begged and pleaded with him but to no avail. He was strong and ruthless and had left her battered and scarred. It was the first time she'd been raped, and she'd never forget how he rose from her pallet and told her to have his breakfast ready early the next morning, that he had plans for the day. She'd huddled in the corner, the blanket wrapped around her, trembling from shock. He'd stared at her as if he'd done nothing out of the ordinary, even as if he was entitled to what he took. She'd left the house that night not only without the innocence she'd guarded carefully for so many years, but also without her faith in humanity. With only the clothes she wore and the invisible scars she'd carry forever, she never looked back.

She had known she was pregnant right away. Even before she had begun to show, her body felt different—heavier and special, as if it held a secret.

She was ashamed to admit it now but she'd considered abortion. But she was thankful it was an option quickly discarded. Nine months later in a tiny hostel, the three girls who unfortunately shared the room with her then had to help her through childbirth. That was when she'd laid eyes on Jojo and her lost faith in humanity had been restored.

She'd searched his tiny face so many times those first few months, trying to imagine if he looked like his maternal grandparents, the people she'd never known. But it didn't matter—she finally had a connection to another human being in the world. They belonged to each other and no one could take that away. After all her months of worrying that she wouldn't love him, that perhaps like her own parents she wouldn't want her baby, she'd been relieved to find that instinctively she was a fiercely devoted mother, and that Jojo brought her a peace she had never known could exist. She just wished she could find a way to give back to him all that he had given her. She was trying. That was all she could do—just keep trying.

Li Jin focused on the darkening sky out the window and reached up to wipe away the lone tear that traveled down her cheek. For nine years she had found a way to keep her son safe, most of the time even with a roof over his head. It hadn't been easy as a young, single mother in a country that would hold your sins against you forever, but they'd survived. Without the help of anyone, she had raised an intelligent and compassionate little person.

But she'd not done so well this time. She and her son were headed somewhere that her gut told her wasn't a good place. Just how bad it would be—she didn't know, but she'd soon find out.

Li Jin woke when the door she leaned against was suddenly opened and she had to grab the seat in front of her to keep from toppling out of the car. She looked down and Jojo was still sleeping with his head on her lap. Erik waited impatiently from outside the car, hissing at her to get out.

"What? Where are we?" she asked, trying to clear the fog from her mind. The sky around them was pitch-black, so she knew it was late.

Erik pulled at her arm. "Leave Jojo sleeping—you and I have to make a little trip inside. We'll be right back."

Li Jin struggled to wrench her arm from Erik. She wasn't leaving Jojo anywhere, but especially not out here with Obi. She looked around and saw that they were parked behind a few taxis, at the curb in front of a strip of bars. Even though it was late, judging from the noise and carrying voices, the nightlife seemed to be in full swing. They'd obviously made it to Beijing, despite an accident on the highway that had caused them to spend two hours inching forward.

Around them the music bellowed out of the buildings, creating a circus-like atmosphere. Li Jin looked behind them and saw an arch over the street with the words *Sanlitun Road* engraved across it. A few feet from their car, a trio of men staggered around, the two on the outside obviously trying to guide the middle one down the sidewalk. All of them looked drunk, but the guy in the middle was wasted. Farther down, Li Jin saw a few little street girls, holding flowers they'd try to sell to the bar patrons as they left for the night.

"No, Erik. I can't leave Jojo out here!" She jerked her arm away and Jojo stirred in his sleep. She didn't trust Obi, especially when it came to her son.

Erik bent down next to the car door and put his mouth close to her ear. He grabbed her upper arm and his fingers were like a vise. His hot breath sent a chill down her spine, and not in a good way.

"Li Jin, I'm not asking you. I'm telling you. Jojo will be fine here with Obi. Now you either get out of the car quietly and you'll be back before he opens his squinty little eyes, or I'll pull you out and the little bastard will wake up and be scared shitless. Your choice."

He backed away from her and stood up, glaring down at her. Across his shoulder she saw he carried his familiar yellow Nike bag. It was bulging with something, and she felt sure it wasn't just clothes. The glint in Erik's eyes scared her and she shivered. This wasn't the man she'd fallen in love with. This man—he was evil.

Li Jin resisted the urge to rub away the sting on her arm. She looked down at Jojo and then up at Obi as he watched from the front seat. He winked at her in the mirror and she felt sick. She knew she'd have to do what Erik wanted. He had no qualms about following through and causing a scene, and she didn't want Jojo to be a part of it. She couldn't believe their relationship had come to this and that this same man was the one she'd thought she wanted to spend the rest of her life with.

She gently eased out of the car, pulled her sweater from the floorboard and bundled it up, then slipped it under Jojo's head. She gave him one last look, then quietly closed the door and turned to face Erik.

"Now what do I have to do?" She sighed and crossed her arms over her chest. She prayed it wouldn't involve touching anyone.

Erik put his arm around her and guided her to a small bistro table in front of a bar called Whiskey Jacks. He pushed her into the chair and took the one across from her. At the table next to them, a couple of girls giggled and fed a stray dog a piece of meat off a stick purchased from a street vendor. The smell wafted over to Li Jin and her stomach rolled in revulsion. She realized she hadn't eaten all day, but still she wasn't hungry.

"Now listen very carefully to what I'm about to tell you." Erik spoke in a low voice from across the table. "Tonight you can do this the easy way, and go home with me and Jojo, or you can screw it up and never see your son again."

Li Jin knew by the steely look in his eyes that he was one hundred percent serious. She sighed. It had come to this. So much for believing in happily-ever-afters, because the reality was that life was kicking her in the teeth again. She wondered how she could have misjudged his character so completely. Why hadn't her mother's instinct kicked in to keep her from allowing this man to be a part of her and Jojo's life?

Her shoulders slumped and she looked up at Erik.

"I'm listening. Let's get this over with."

The gleam in his eyes told her that he'd had no doubt she would cooperate with him. His arrogance made her sick to her stomach. With a quick snicker, he leaned in and began giving her hushed instructions.

Inside the dimly lighted bar, Li Jin did as she'd been told and tried to be as inconspicuous as possible while she walked through. Even so, several men had immediately noticed her and given her raised eyebrows or inviting smiles. She'd ignored them all and continued through the room until she found a small table in the corner.

She pulled the Nike bag from her shoulder and set it on her lap under the small table. Her eyes watered from the heavy layer of smoke that filled the room. That, combined with the stench of sweaty bodies and cheap perfume, was enough to make her stomach cramp. She watched as Erik entered and made his way to one of the taller tables and high-fived a few of the standing foreigners.

"*Qingwen,* what do you want to drink?" A waitress bumped her to get her attention, then repeated the question louder to be heard over the music. She set a small bowl of popcorn in front of Li Jin.

Li Jin locked eyes with her and felt a moment of kinship. Dressed in the usual skimpy shorts and high heels, the waitress looked tired and miserable, like she didn't want to be there. Li Jin had worked in bars before Jojo was born and it was far from the glamorous position many girls thought it.

"Oh, *bu yao.* I don't care for anything."

"You have to drink if you want to sit," the waitress insisted, impatience replacing her previously polite tone.

"Oh. Sorry. Please bring me a cola."

"Twenty reminbi. You pay first."

Over the girl's shoulder she watched as another waitress quickly made her way to Erik and placed a tall glass in front of him, then poured from the pitcher on her tray. Li Jin knew what it was. She'd seen before how the bars sometimes provided expats with the rum and bottled tea mixture for free. It was good business to have the foreign devils choose their establishments, and the rich-looking ones were treated like VIPs. In his Chinese tailored shirt and slacks, Erik fit in well at the table full of men who looked like they'd just left an important business meeting. Li Jin wondered whether the other men were married and if so, whether their wives knew where they were. She'd forgotten the hospitality in these parts didn't extend to locals, only to hand-picked foreigners. It was quite ironic that the poor were forced to pay and the rich got so much for free.

The girl nudged her again and Li Jin fumbled in her purse for the money. She couldn't believe they charged twenty reminbi for a Coke when she could buy them in the grocery store for less than five. But she dug the bills out and laid them on the table. The waitress took the money and walked away, tucking the bills down into her apron as she skirted around the crowded room.

Linnea waited on what Erik said would happen next.

Around her the room pulsed with the beat of the music and the bright flashing lights of pink, purple, and blue. Onstage a small Filipino guy stood at the microphone, belting out a strange version of the Eagles' "Desperado" song. Li Jin thought he looked ridiculous with his tight jeans and leather vest over his bare chest. But the crowd seemed to like it—either that or it was the three backup singers dancing behind him in short skirts and hooker boots that got the place so hyped up.

Li Jin jumped when a tall blond guy walked up and put his arm around her.

"*Ni hao,* little China doll."

Though he butchered the dialect, she could understand his greeting and winced at the strong alcohol smell that wafted over her from his breath. He was American, she could see that from his signature big nose, and like most of them she'd met from Meiguo, he looked as if he thought he was the world's greatest catch. She discreetly peeked at Erik and knew this guy wasn't the one. Erik was glaring at her like she'd screwed up. She knew she needed to get rid of the guy fast.

"Uh, hello. I'm sorry, but I'm waiting for someone." She shrugged his arm off her shoulders and resisted the urge to wipe away his invisible germs.

"Well, wait no more, baby. I'm here." He grinned at her and moved closer, putting his arm back around her. Li Jin almost sneezed. His cheap cologne was overwhelming.

She wished once again she were at home on the couch, snuggling Jojo against her. Anywhere but here, with vultures hanging around her, hoping to snag a one-night stand with any Asian girl up for grabs.

Li Jin shivered as she felt the man's clammy fingers graze her arm. She shook him off her again and gave him a steely look.

"*Zhende,* I'm serious. My boyfriend is on his way, and if he comes in and you're over here, there'll be trouble."

The guy sneered at her. "Oh, don't tell me. You have a five-foot-tall Chinese guy that's going to cold-cock me?"

Li Jin rolled her eyes at him. "He's taller than five feet and he's definitely not Chinese."

That got his attention. He obviously wasn't enamored enough to fight another foreigner over her. He jabbed his middle finger in the air and walked away. Li Jin watched him stop at another table where two girls laughed uproariously at a drunken Chinese guy who had jumped onstage and was grabbing the stripper pole as if he knew how to use it. The foreign men egged him on, pumping their fists in the air and yelling their encouragement. Li Jin was disgusted that the local didn't understand he was really being made fun of, not admired.

When she looked up again, Erik had his head bent close to a man beside him, talking seriously. He looked up and nodded at Li Jin, and the man started across the room toward her.

Li Jin felt sick suddenly—so sick she worried she might actually vomit. She fought to get the feeling under control. She knew what she was supposed to do and she'd do it—for Jojo—but she couldn't wait to get out of there and back to her son and eventually far away from Erik. She offered up a silent prayer to the gods that the exchange would go smoothly.

The man was dark skinned and his eyes even darker. Li Jin guessed he was also South African by the way he strutted across the room as if he owned it. Like Erik, he was a snazzy dresser. His outfit looked to be worth more than her entire wardrobe, and it was just a white ruffled shirt and dark black pants set off by shiny biker boots. Unlike when she'd met Erik, she knew right away this man was trouble. He didn't even try to hide the calculating look in his eyes. Li Jin tried to appear nonchalant, just as Erik had told her to do.

He approached the table and sat on the stool next to her. He put his hand on her arm and she fought a wave of revulsion.

"In five minutes I'll get up. Wait two minutes, then follow me to the men's room." He spoke quietly, looking into her eyes as if they were having a friendly conversation.

Li Jin couldn't really hear him over the music, but she read his lips and nodded her understanding.

The man waved the waitress over and ordered a Jack and Coke. The waitress slapped a napkin down in front of him, then scurried back toward the bar. Li Jin watched as she leaned over it and gave the bartender the order, then waited while he sloshed an inch of whiskey into the glass, then popped the top off a can of Coke and added it. He slid the glass over to the waitress, and she put it on her tray and made her way back to their table. She told them she'd start a tab and she sauntered off to the next customer.

He looked at Li Jin and nodded. Then he got up and maneuvered his way through the crowd to the back wall where a short hallway led to the restrooms. Li Jin watched him go and then looked over at Erik.

He still watched her. He laughed along with others at the table and even held his glass up for another *gambei* toast, but all the while his eyes kept darting over to check on her. She had no other alternative. She got up and slung the bag's strap over her shoulder, then headed for the back hall.

In the hall there was a line for the ladies' room. Li Jin ignored the probing eyes of the two girls waiting and instead pushed against the door labeled MEN.

Inside there were two stalls to her right, two urinals on the wall to her left, and two sinks in front of her. The room was filthy and she tried to keep her elbows and hands close so she didn't touch any surfaces as she looked around.

Li Jin at first thought the man hadn't come in but then she saw his shiny boots under the door of the stall nearest the wall. She approached it and tapped lightly as Erik had told her to do.

The man quickly swung it open and stepped around her. Hearing a loud click, she realized he had turned the lock on the door leading out. Then he turned back around to face her.

"Where is it?" he asked coldly, pulling at the bag over her shoulder.

He took the bag over to the sink and unzipped it.

"Wait. Erik said you'd give me the money first." Things were not going as planned and Li Jin felt beads of sweat dot her forehead. Erik would kill her if this guy somehow cheated her.

"I see the goods first. Then I pay." He didn't even look up as he continued to rifle through the clothes in the bag.

Li Jin stood still and watched him. She didn't know what to do. Erik had told her to make sure to get the money first. What if the guy didn't pay? What if someone knocked on the door? Surely someone else would want to use the bathroom soon?

The guy pulled a clear plastic bag out of a sock from the duffel. It was full of tiny squares of folded papers and he looked pleased. He held it up, seeming to weigh it. Then he took it and, pulling his pants leg up, he tucked the plastic bag deep into his boot. Then he pulled another plastic bag out of a different sock and did the same thing on the other side of the boot. Twice more he pulled out socks and plastic bags until both of his boots were full all the way around. He tucked his pants back down over the loot; then he tossed the duffel back to Li Jin. He turned around to wash his hands and grinned at her in the mirror.

Li Jin still stood frozen.

"Now you pay me? Right?" She hoped she didn't sound like she was begging. She was also shocked, as the substance didn't look like *dagga* to her. The tiny square packages showed her it was clearly heroin and Erik had been lying to her. Heroin was a much more serious drug than *dagga*. She thought about Jojo and how if they got caught, she'd never see him again. She felt a rivulet of sweat trickle down her back.

The guy calmly turned off the water and pulled the lever on the paper towel machine. Nothing came out and he rubbed his hands down the front of his jeans, drying them.

"Pay you? I was told that first you'd do me a special favor. Your boyfriend was right—you are quite the looker—much prettier than most I've seen in here. Come on, let's get this started." He moved until his back was against the wall and then he slowly unzipped his jeans, keeping his eyes locked on Li Jin's.

She shook her head, repulsed. "No. That wasn't the deal. Erik would not have me do that. We're a couple." She wasn't going to do it; she didn't care what he said.

"That's not what he told me," the guy said, moving toward her and reaching for her head.

Li Jin moved backward as far as she could go, until she was against one of the urinals. She reached behind her but let go quickly when she realized where she'd put her hands.

"No! I mean it. Let's go ask Erik," she threatened.

The guy was now within inches of her face. Li Jin could tell he'd been eating foreign foods, and by the stench that reached her nose, it smelled like beef.

"Erik and I go way back. We're from the same neighborhood back home. Believe me, he won't care. Let me give you a taste that'll change your mind."

He wrapped one arm around her and with the other he grabbed her hair. He leaned in and began kissing her, pushing his tongue so far into her mouth that she gagged. She pushed against him with all her strength until he let go. She swiped her hand across her lips.

"I swear, I'm going to scream!" She was shaking and she didn't know if her knees were going to hold her up. His assault was bringing back memories from long ago, memories that were ugly.

"Fine." He pushed her and she fell backward, landing in the bowl of the urinal. He pulled his pants up again and buttoned them. He straightened his shirt and looked in the mirror, smoothing his hair back with both hands. "Oh believe me, I don't have to beg. There are about three million girls who look just like you outside that door and they'd love to have these foreign arms around them. You just missed out on the best three minutes of your life."

Li Jin didn't move and didn't say anything. As her heart pounded, she struggled to look tough, in case he changed his mind.

He reached into his pocket and brought out a roll of money. "Make sure you really take this to your boyfriend." He tossed it in the air and she caught it, her heart still pumping so loudly she was sure he could hear it. She tucked the wad into her purse and zipped it up.

He opened the door and stepped out. Li Jin could see a line of guys waiting for the bathroom. He gave her one last look and then with a cocky shrug he pulled his zipper up for all to see.

"Get her, guys—she's good. Cheap, too," he remarked as he left her struggling to get out of the urinal.

Chapter Twelve

"I'm coming for your general!" Linnea declared, indicating she was one away from a win as she scooted her stool closer to the table. Lau watched her quietly, and Linnea knew he was waiting for her to make just one wrong move so he could finally lay claim to victory against her. Sometimes she almost felt sorry for him and thought about letting him win, but then he'd make another of his cutting remarks and she'd regain her senses and show no mercy.

Linnea had tried to talk Sky into staying to play, but he once again declined, even though he told her he thought it was amusing that thus far she remained undefeated. Linnea knew he simply loved that his grandfather simmered over a mere girl being cunning enough to beat someone who'd been playing the game for decades.

Linnea sat back, having used her turn quickly. She didn't need to waste valuable time staring at the board; she was a fast player who could immediately see the moves she needed to make. She didn't even have to think too hard; and good thing because her mind was still on her conversation the day before with her landlord. He'd come to pick up her rent check and before he left he told her to expect some noise because renovations were scheduled for the apartment upstairs. Even though Linnea would love to have it, she didn't ask him more about it. The simple truth was her business was going well, but it wasn't at the point that she could afford anything extra yet. Not only that, but she'd wanted to wait until she had enough saved to buy furniture before she moved out. She dreamed of her own place and especially a bed—it was embarrassing that she was eighteen and had never even slept in a real bed. She would never admit it to him but she daydreamed constantly of snuggling with Jet in the softness of real comfort.

"So, Mr. Lau, do you want to talk today or only play the game?" She was too impatient for his slowness today; the least he could do was entertain her while she waited.

He shot her a grumpy look. "Our hour is almost up. Then we'll talk. Today you will meet my comrade."

Linnea wrinkled her brow. "Your comrade? Who? You know I need to get back to the store soon. I don't have time to meet any visitors."

She looked at her watch and saw she was expected back in less than ten minutes. Surprisingly, her frequent visits to Lau were a high point of her week. Despite his sometimes-surly attitude and his obvious discrimination against the female gender, she really enjoyed his conversation and the history he was able to weave tales around. Her sisters thought she was odd for it, but Linnea didn't care. And she felt like he was getting softer as the weeks went by; he couldn't hide the smile that threatened to erupt when she showed up today. He had been lonely after all, and Linnea felt sorry for the old man. And she was still working toward a more important goal, after all.

Lau nodded. "I know. But today is important. Your little store can wait."

Linnea's next move and the retort on her lips were interrupted by the ringing of the bell alerting them someone had entered. She looked up to see a rare smile on Lau's face. Turning around, she saw an old man standing just inside the door.

"Ni hao." She wondered why Lau didn't greet him.

The man ignored her greeting and instead looked past her to Lau.

"Is this the one?" he asked, nodding toward Linnea.

Lau stood up. "This is her. Be ready, she's a saucy one. But she's also a smart one." He looked at Linnea proudly. "Linnea, we'll finish our game another day. I need to take a walk around the neighborhood and see what's going on. While I'm gone, you be respectful to Comrade Zheng."

Linnea's mouth dried up as she looked from Lau to the other elderly man. Could it be? He did look like her Ye Ye, only smaller and frailer. He had the same thick tuft of white hair, but that didn't mean anything; many old men in China still had a full head of hair. She wanted to deny the resemblance but something about his eyes and the shape of his face settled it for her.

"You mean . . . this is . . . ." She swallowed, trying to remember her words. This was what she had wanted but she didn't know if she was ready for it yet. She'd been taken by surprise. "This is my Ye Ye's father?"

Lau shuffled around her. "I said Comrade Zheng, didn't I? What—are you hard of hearing now, too? Show some manners, girl. And if I get a customer, you know what to do."

With that he pulled his cane from the elaborate ceramic stand and disappeared through the door, the bell once again ringing and breaking the silence as Linnea glared at the senior Zheng.

He had a lot of questions to answer and Linnea quickly collected them in her mind. This might be her only chance and she wasn't going to screw it up.

An hour later Linnea sat back in Lau's rocking chair and crossed her arms. She looked down at the antique pin badge Lao Zheng had brought her. Lau had obviously told him about her vintage store and she guessed the badge was some sort of peace offering. He didn't know her too well if he thought her friendliness could be bought with trinkets. She was much too loyal to her Ye Ye and Nai Nai to be swayed. Even though it had been many months ago that she'd read her Nai Nai's private notes about her daughter, Linnea still remembered the blame had been placed on Lao Zheng's wife for snatching Dahlia away. How a grandmother could do that to one of her own made Linnea's blood boil. A simple pin wouldn't absolve the deed.

"It is real." Lao Zheng nodded as he picked up Lau's pipe from the table, looked into it, then lit it.

"I didn't say it wasn't," Linnea answered, flipping the badge around in her hand. It really was an interesting piece. *If* it was real.

Zheng inhaled from the pipe, then blew smoke rings in the air. "Most of the badges they wore back in those days showed the older Mao, but this was him in 1921. It's to commemorate one of his first attempts to start a revolution, this one with the Anyuan coal miners."

Linnea looked at the drawing of Mao on the front standing at the edge of a cliff overlooking a wide body of water, mountains standing tall in the background. He looked young and slim—even dressed in a long, black Mandarin-collared gown buttoned up to his neck. His chin thrust in the air proudly.

"He looks more like a priest than a revolutionist here," she mumbled.

Lao Zheng chuckled. "Yes, I think he did, too. And you notice, the artist didn't even make his famous mole stand out. They didn't start doing that until later."

Linnea nodded. Before he'd brought out the pin from his pocket, they had talked nonstop and he'd spent most of that time reminiscing about her Ye Ye's childhood and gift for music, an undeniable look of pride in his eyes.

Between his stories of long ago, Zheng asked Linnea questions about her Ye Ye. He had a few blanks he wanted filled in but overall, Linnea was surprised at how much he already knew of their life. Not that he knew her sister's names or any tedious details of that sort, but by other milestones he named, he'd been keeping up to be sure. It also amazed her that in all the years that had passed, he had not even once tried to approach her family and make amends. That in itself showed his guilt was too strong.

"May I ask a question?" Zheng looked hesitant.

"You've asked many—what's one more?"

"Does my son still have the violin?" He leaned forward, waiting for Linnea to answer, his elbow propped on his knee.

She could see the violin was important to him, and something told her the handover of the violin was not something her Ye Ye would want her to share.

She shrugged her shoulders. "I have no idea. You'd have to ask him."

He sat back in his chair and heaved a long sigh, then muttered something about a missed opportunity. Perhaps he thought her Ye Ye should have taken his musical efforts further. Linnea didn't know but she wasn't going to ask him about it; he looked too dejected over whatever it was about the violin, and that could be settled between him and her Ye Ye, if they ever saw each other again.

Now they were both quiet for a moment. Linnea so far had waited for the right moment but she wasn't letting him leave without asking him about the girl, Dahlia. She'd sit on him if she had to. He knew something, she was sure of it. She put the pin on the table and looked back at him.

"So, Lao Zheng—and wow, does that sound strange to call you by that name—where is your wife?"

The old man stared at the floor and when he looked up; Linnea could see a flash of pain in his eyes.

"She died many years ago."

"Oh? What did she die from?" Linnea asked nonchalantly. After all, she'd never known the woman and felt nothing for her but disapproval for what it appeared she had done.

"I believe it was a broken heart. Feiyan never got over losing Benfu. She grieved herself to death when he refused to ever see us again." Zheng shook his head.

Linnea couldn't let that slide. She felt a flush of heat crawl up her neck.

"*She* grieved herself to death? *She?* What about my Nai Nai and Ye Ye who have spent their life grieving for a child taken from them?" She couldn't keep the bitterness out of her voice, just thinking of the pain they'd suffered from the loss of their child. How dare someone say her Ye Ye had caused pain when the old woman was the reason for it all?

Zheng cringed. "I don't know what you mean. What does that have to do with Feiyan? And you don't understand—Feiyan gave up her right to bear more children so she could achieve a higher career status and give Benfu a better life. He was our only child. After he left, we had no one." He shook his head. "I can't possibly know what you mean."

Linnea wasn't going to let him get away with the innocent act or declaring himself and his wife the victims. She stood and pointed her finger at him.

"You know exactly what I mean. And you know that your wife took Dahlia! She was my Ye Ye's only child, too! Now, what I want to know is where she is. Was she killed? Did your wife smother her?"

Zheng paled under the dark stubble on his face and Linnea felt a tiny twinge of guilt. She didn't want to give the old man a stroke, after all.

"*Aiya!* No! Feiyan would never do such a thing to her own grandchild. She only sent her away." With that he covered his face and Linnea felt that he hadn't wanted to admit that much.

Linnea sat back down. She had him now. "So, are you going to tell what you know or not?"

Lao Zheng looked up and squinted at Linnea. "Are you sure you're not his real daughter? You have that same stubborn streak I recognize so well."

Linnea snorted in contempt. "As a matter of fact, I am his *real* daughter. You don't have to be related by blood to have a connection, you know. Ye Ye taught me to read, write, and do all the important things like ride a bicycle and stand up for myself. He and Nai Nai cared for me when I was sick and comforted me when I grieved for my first family. I think if you'd ask him, he'd tell you that I'm his *real* daughter." Linnea took a deep breath and reminded herself he was just a bitter old man. "But maybe you should ask yourself are you a *real* father to my Ye Ye?"

Halfway through her long speech, the old man hung his head. When she finished, he mumbled his response. "You are right, girl. I haven't deserved to be called a father. I let Benfu down and should have made amends years ago. I wish I could take it all back and rewrite time, but I can't."

He looked up at Linnea, his eyes imploring hers.

"Do you think it's too late? If I could die without so much guilt on my conscience, I could rest in peace, and maybe even be allowed a better life in the afterworld. But at this point, is forgiveness even possible?"

Linnea couldn't help it. Compassion seeped in and she felt sorry for the old man. He looked so much like her Ye Ye and even had the same mannerisms. How could she be cruel to someone so like her own beloved Ye Ye? And from what she could see, he'd lived a tortured life of guilt and regret.

"It's too late to rewrite history and take away the hurt you've caused Ye Ye and Nai Nai, but there is something you can do to help right the wrong." She reached over and took Zheng's gnarled hands in hers and leaned in closer. "Listen close and I'll tell you what we're going to do. Tomorrow, you're coming back here."

The old man nodded obediently and Linnea knew she had him. He wasn't saying it but he'd do anything to be able to have a semblance of a relationship with his only son before he died. Anything to help right the wrongs. Linnea hoped with his help she could make a miracle happen—maybe even a few.

Chapter Thirteen

his is nonsense, Linnea. I'm supposed to be watching the store while you're on your break, not gallivanting up and down the street beside you. My old legs are tired, girl." Calli was irritated. Linnea insisted she accompany her to Sky's store and that was the last thing she wanted to do today. She had set her sights on finishing her latest knitted sweater but this would set her back another day at least.

"Nai Nai, I have someone I want you to meet. But first, I want to ask you to keep an open mind." Linnea held the door open.

"Linnea, what is this all about? I've already met Sky's grandfather." Calli walked through, looking around to see who was so important to take her away from getting her work done. The room was darkened by the drawn shade but she saw a man sitting in the corner, crouched over on a small stool. His face was hidden by the shadows.

Calli held her hand up and gave a small wave. "*Ni hao*. Do I know you?"

The man didn't say a word, but he lifted his face and the beam of light from the door shined across and highlighted the deep lines in his face and his dark eyes. Calli could see him clearly then and immediately knew who it was. It wasn't Sky's grandfather as she'd expected. Even though it had been many years, she'd never forget the face that was so like her husband's. She was shocked he was still alive. She did the math and realized he must have already passed age ninety. She looked quickly around the room and was relieved not to see his wife. She wouldn't give him the satisfaction of asking about the old woman. She tried to retreat back out the door but Linnea blocked her way.

"Just talk to him a minute, Nai Nai. He has some things he needs to say."

Calli shook her head stubbornly and turned back to the door. "I have nothing to say to him. He is not a part of our life, Linnea. I don't know how you found him, or how he found you—but he is not welcome in this family."

Linnea took her Nai Nai's hand in hers and squeezed them to her chest. "*Please,* Nai Nai. He wants to talk to Ye Ye. You can help bridge the gap."

Calli finally turned and spoke to the man directly. "Benfu doesn't want anything to do with you. Ever. There—you have your answer and it is not a gap you have between you and your son. It is an endless chasm. He has blamed himself all these years for not protecting our daughter from his own mother. And you stood by and let her commit that evil deed. Tell me, how can you possibly mend that?"

With that she pushed Linnea's hands out of the way and reached for the door.

"What if I told you I could help you find Dahlia?"

Calli froze. No one had uttered her daughter's name in decades. She felt her knees begin to give way and she leaned over the counter beside the door. She clutched her chest and it was a moment before she could speak. Linnea led her to a bench at the end of the counter.

"Dahlia? She's alive?" Her voice had lost all sense of authority and came out sounding weak and embarrassing to her.

The old man lowered his face into his hands for a moment, then looked up and stared Calli in the eye. "She was alive when Feiyan left our home with her a week after she took her."

With that the old man hung his head again. Calli didn't care if his guilt was killing him; nothing he felt could ever compare to what she and Benfu had been through. But she couldn't deny his words sent a piercing streak of hope through her—hope that maybe her daughter was alive after all.

She felt a wave of dizziness as she shook her head from side to side. "I knew it. I *knew* she took her. I smelled her in the house that day. All these years. All the denials and it was her all along."

The old man wrung his hands. "Calli, please. You have to understand. Feiyan was ill in her head. I tried to talk her into bringing the baby back. I begged her! But after everything she'd been through to survive the revolution, she was obsessed with continuing our family name and she was adamant you couldn't keep a girl child. But she regretted it. The guilt eventually drove her to her grave."

Calli's face hardened. "I'm glad; I hope that she suffered with her guilt like I suffered with my loss. But there is no way to compare the two. That was my child, you old fool. Nothing she endured was enough to punish her for what she did."

Linnea crossed the room and put her arms around her. Calli could see that the girl was overcome with emotion.

"Nai Nai, you don't mean that. I think she must have been a very sick old woman."

Calli buried her face in her hands and began to sob. She was ashamed that she was letting a side of her out that most had never seen. A side filled with rage. "Linnea, you just don't know. Dahlia was my little girl. My baby."

"I do know, Nai Nai. I read her page in our family journal. I know she was your baby and she went missing."

Calli felt the tears run down her face. "I've dreamed of her for years. I knew she wasn't dead—I could feel her." She struggled to maintain control and thumped her chest over her heart, then looked up and pointed her finger at the old man. "And you—you and your hateful wife—you kept her from me. You kept her from her father, your only son. How? How can you live with yourself?"

"I'm sorry. I'm very sorry. I know words can't make up for it. But believe me, we never imagined you wouldn't be able to have more children. She thought you'd have a son and then get over the loss of Dahlia."

The memories of her forced sterilization overwhelmed her and Calli wanted to run out the door, but she needed to find out what she could about her daughter. Lately the girl had been on her mind even more than usual and the dreams were becoming more frequent. If he knew anything—anything at all—she wanted to know. She needed that peace.

Now that the old man had gotten started, it appeared he couldn't stop.

"Mao told us all to have many, many children to build a new red China. That is what we thought you and Benfu would do. Then the land couldn't produce enough to feed everyone and Mao decided there were too many children! Who could've predicted the one-child policy? How could we have known what they'd begin doing to women to keep the birth numbers down, Calli? Feiyan was obsessed that Benfu's firstborn be a son. She thought you could have other children, once a son was established. I'm so sorry, but it's Mao's fault."

"Tell me where she is." Calli didn't care to talk about what Mao had done to a nation. She could lament the millions of forced abortions, sterilizations, and abandoned children. *But to what outcome?* Decades of wrongs couldn't be undone in a conversation. She only wanted to know where her daughter was.

The old man sighed. "She was taken to the orphanage in Beijing. Feiyan wanted her far enough away that you couldn't track her."

Calli shook her head. "That's not possible. I traveled to that orphanage, along with at least twenty others just like it. They told me she wasn't there. They all said she wasn't there."

"The director owed Feiyan a favor. One that couldn't be denied. Dahlia's records were hidden so that she could never be adopted. Instead she was shipped from home to home to keep her moving. You know how it is—if they want to keep a child in the system, they do it. We kept track of her, Calli. We know she did okay until she aged out and left on her own accord. Then her trail was lost."

Calli felt a rage well up inside her. Rage like she hadn't felt in decades.

"You kept track of her? And you knew we were suffering but you never told us? Now I might never find her? What kind of monster are you?"

The old man stood, his hand clutching the wobbling cane to try to stabilize himself. He pulled an envelope from his pocket and reached out to hand it to Calli. She refused to take it and Linnea grabbed it instead.

"I've kept track of all of you. I moved here after Feiyan died. I have nothing in Shanghai and I wanted to be close to the only family I have. I've followed your lives. I still have contacts, you know."

Calli felt disgust. "Oh yes, I know. China is all about contacts. Contacts that will hide a child from her mother, connections that will cause a woman to go through hell as her womb is altered to prevent any more children. Those are some amazing connections you have there. Congratulations, Laoren."

He shook his head. "Now, Calli, I had nothing to do with what happened to you after Dahlia was taken. You have to believe that."

She stared at him, standing to meet him eye to eye. She would not let him know how much seeing him had shaken her. She'd end the meeting strong.

He cowered under the brunt of her hate-filled gaze. When he spoke, he sounded as old as every one of his years.

"Calli, I am a guilt-filled and broken man. I have spent these last few years alone, craving the attention of a son or grandchild. Perhaps it won't bring your daughter back, but it might help you to know that my days are short and at least now you have the truth. If it weren't for this girl here"—he pointed his cane at Linnea—"I wouldn't have the courage to be standing here telling you this now. I would have stayed in the background, watching from afar until my dying day. But she is quite the intelligent and persuasive one and now, dear girl, I have kept my word. Good day."

He nodded at Linnea and began to walk toward the back of the room. Then he turned to Calli again. "I had hoped that through you, I might be able to see my son again and tell him how truly sorry I am. But if you are not on my side, I know the effort would be fruitless. Now, I am tired. I aim to go home and rest these old bones."

He opened the door and called out behind him.

"The envelope contains photos of your daughter. Her orphanage name is written on the back. If you find her, you'll know it is her by a flower tattooed on the bottom of her foot. Feiyan did that, too—even though I begged her not to. She said it was just in case. In case of what, I never knew."

With that he waved his hand in the air and disappeared through the back door. He was gone.

With thoughts swirling disjointedly in her mind, Calli slowly walked the ten long blocks to the park and found a bench to sit on. After swearing Linnea to secrecy, she'd told her to go home and tell the family she was visiting Widow Zu. Linnea had agreed immediately as she obviously felt responsible for how affected Calli was to see the old man. Calli didn't want her to suffer, as she knew Linnea had only wanted to help, but she had to get away and think on her own. She needed to decide whether to tell Benfu or not and she feared for what this new revelation would do to his health. Sure, he'd been stable for many months but the doctors had said that any additional stress could trigger a relapse with the tuberculosis, or even weaken his heart further.

A couple and their toddler passed in front of her and Calli saw the proud expressions the parents wore as their son waddled unsteadily on his shaky legs. He was obviously new to walking and he grinned proudly as he grasped the hands of each of his parents for support. She and Benfu had been deprived of moments like those and now all these years later, she'd finally get to see what her daughter looked like. She reached into her apron pocket and wrapped her fingers around the envelope of photos. Linnea had slipped it in there as she hugged her good-bye. Calli was too nervous to look, but too hopeful not to.

In a way, she supposed she and her daughter had been the lucky ones. Her neighbor and best friend had gone through a much worse fate. After Xiao Jodi had become pregnant with her second child, she had been harassed by the Women's Federation group because she had signed the one-child policy and then failed to keep her promise. She'd paid a back-alley physician to remove her IUD and when she became pregnant, and they found out, they'd subjected her to endless persuasion meetings to convince her to take remedial measures—their sterile name for an abortion. Jodi and her husband wanted the baby and could not be persuaded to abort it. They decided to sneak away and hide, back then called *childbirth on the run*. Others had done it and been successful if they could stay hidden. Calli had warned Jodi to avoid shelter from old friends or family but Jodi had thought she was far enough away at her sister-in-law's village. She'd almost made it to term, too.

Sadly, when she hit her eighth month, members from the federation had raided the house and brought her back to Wuxi. After six days of captivity and isolation from her family, Jodi had finally given in. After they injected her stomach with the poisons, the baby had been aborted and Jodi sterilized. In a final gesture of their power over her, the head of the federation had intentionally let Jodi see the remains of the baby and Jodi lived her days with the damaged body of her aborted son engraved in her mind. She had never recovered from it and last Calli had heard, Jodi had left her job, divorced, and returned home to her parents to live out her days secluded from the cruelty of the world.

At least Calli had not been pregnant when she'd been sterilized. But because of the tricks of others like Jodi around the countryside who continued to find ways around the controlled birth policy, she and many others were deceived into signing papers agreeing to sterilization. What else could they do when the officials isolated them and they were told family members were also being kept in custody until they agreed? Calli had relented only when she'd been told Benfu's parents had been seized. Though Benfu's relationship with them was broken, he'd still agonized over their being confined by the officials. He hadn't asked her to, but for him, she'd signed.

It was only after the procedure, which she'd thought was going to be the insertion of a new type of IUD, was she told she'd never have children again. It was a horrific memory but the thoughts of her daughter being returned to her one day had got her through the hazy days afterward. Though she didn't know what happened to Dahlia, she'd always held on to a shred of hope that her daughter was alive somewhere and being treated well.

In front of her the child and his parents continued their stroll and the laughter of the little boy rang in her ears. Calli pulled the envelope from her pocket. She was ready—ready to see the daughter who had remained an infant in her mind all these years.

She opened the flap and removed the photos. She looked down at the first one and the tears began to flow. It was definitely her Dahlia. She'd know those dark eyes and the heart shape of her face anywhere. The photo was only black and white but Calli could still see the sad expression her daughter wore, even at the young age of only a few years old. Dahlia looked a bit wary in the photo, possibly even afraid. In it she wore a dark frog-tied shirt and her hair was chopped off short like a boy's. The wooden chair she perched on had seen better days and Calli imagined the photo was only meant to be placed in her daughter's orphanage file. Nothing about it showed any attempt to make it a nice, friendly snapshot.

She flipped it to the back of the pile and looked at the next one. In it Dahlia looked about seven years old and Calli felt her breath taken away at how much she'd grown to look like her father. Her eyes had changed just a bit, but enough that they looked exactly like Benfu's, even with the sadness they held. Even the shape of her tiny nose mimicked his. Calli suddenly wished she had waited and shared the moment with Benfu, and she felt a ripple of shame.

Two more photos remained. Two more pieces of evidence to what her heart had always known—that her daughter was out there somewhere.

She put the photo in the back of the pile and looked at the next one. At least twelve years old, Dahlia was definitely at the self-conscience puberty stage. Her arms and legs looked long and gangly, her front teeth a bit too big for her head. Her eyes hadn't changed from the first photo; they still held a look of longing. Though her hair was longer in the photo, Calli could tell by the style and the clothes she wore that Dahlia wasn't living a life of fortune. It broke her heart. All that time Dahlia could have grown up with a mother's arms tenderly around her, a father's love guiding her through difficult teenage angst. But she had been deprived of it due to the mental instability of one crazy old woman. It didn't make sense that fate could be so cruel.

She finally looked at the last photo. It completely took her breath away. In this one, the institute had splurged for color and Dahlia had flourished from a gangly duckling to what looked like a graceful swan. She was at least fourteen and beautiful in a sad, pensive way. But through the photo Calli could sense that her daughter was strong—perhaps even stubborn like her father. Her eyes penetrated as if she were looking straight out of the photo and into Calli's eyes.

An old soul, Calli would have described her, someone who had seen too many battles. The expression she used to look at the camera was one of defiance but Calli could also see the same longing, as if she was putting on her best face to encourage someone to love her. Calli stared at her and wished she could have been there to erase the pain from her eyes. She felt the hot tears slide down her face. *I love you, Dahlia!* She wanted to scream it so loud that wherever her daughter was, she could hear her. *I have always loved you. Always.* She felt so helpless, as if with a few photos she'd watched years of neglect happen in an instant. She sobbed quietly and looked up just as the small family returned in front of her. The little boy broke away from his parents and toddled up to her lap. With a concerned look, he searched her face and patted her arm in an innocent and unknowing gesture.

The young mother rushed over to her son, her plastic slippers slapping the walk as she apologized for the interference of what she knew was a private moment. She grabbed him and tried to pull him back as he struggled against her.

"It's okay, it's okay. Leave him be," Calli mumbled as she tried to bring her cries under control. She didn't want to scare the little fellow. The tiny boy looked up at her tears and his lip began to tremble. See? How could such a little soul with no relation to her feel such compassion, whereas Dahlia's own grandmother had been relentless and cruel in her obsession to continue their family line? But if Calli chose not to forgive, wouldn't she be as cruel and void of feeling as Feiyan had been? What was it she had been taught by her own mother? Forgiveness wasn't to benefit the one who'd offended, but to ease the suffering of the one who'd been offended. Oh, how she wished the tangled vines of fate could be undone so that she might see her child again.

Calli stood. She felt an urgency to return home and talk to Benfu. It wasn't too late to find Dahlia but they would need the old man's help. And perhaps forgiving old Zheng would bring her the peace her old heart craved so badly. Either way, she had her first clue about where her daughter had gone and she would not stop until she had done everything she could to pick up where the trail had gone cold. She just hoped her old bones and arthritic muscles would hold up and allow her to do this, give her a chance to tell her daughter she had been wanted.

As Calli carefully tucked the photos back in the envelope and into her pocket, the young mother picked up her son and walked away, her husband beside her patting the back of his son. Over her shoulder the little boy met Calli's eyes with his. *Go,* they seemed to say, *go and find your baby. She still needs a mother.* Calli nodded her good-bye to the tot, then hurried along the path in the opposite way. Her fingers remained in her pocket, protectively grasping the envelope. She couldn't wait to show Benfu what a beautiful daughter they had created. But first she must decide the best way to tell him, for she worried about his weak heart and what news of this caliber could do to it.

Chapter Fourteen

Li Jin stood next to the ironing board in the ray of light flooding through the window. Her shoulders ached. Already that morning she'd cleaned the entire apartment, mopped the floors, done the laundry, and made Erik's favorite home-cooked soup. Even the teakwood side tables were shining from her strenuous polishing and she admired them from her post. She'd had a productive day, hurrying so that she could focus on Jojo when he got out of school. To be honest, she loved keeping house. It made her feel at peace, and if she could only find a job that paid her to keep house and cook all day, she'd be satisfied. But so far no one with the ability to pay had ever wanted to trust someone like her—someone with no background to speak of and no references to give.

She listened to her show and occasionally looked up at the television as she pushed the iron back and forth over Erik's favorite linen shirt. She wished she had the nerve to burn it, as it was the one he usually wore when he went out. She was no longer naive enough to believe it was a night spent with *the boys,* but she also no longer cared. She was planning her escape.

She'd been lucky. So far Jojo hadn't really caught on to the tension between her and Eric over the last few weeks. On the ride back from their impromptu road trip she'd had time to think. She'd realized that she had no choice; she must at all costs get her son away from Erik. Though he'd promised she wouldn't have to be his runner anymore, he'd broken so many promises that she knew not to trust him. It was easy enough for him; if they got caught, he'd point the finger at her and, like thousands of women around the world, Li Jin would be left taking the punishment for her man's crimes. No, she wasn't going to take the chance of leaving Jojo alone in the world. She had to get away.

She sighed. She also didn't want to go back to scouring the streets to find enough work to keep a roof over her son's head and food in his belly. And there'd be no more school. That thought brought a pang to her heart. Jojo loved school and he was so good at it. Only last week she'd received a note from his teacher that his quarterly test scores were in the top five of the entire class.

She flinched as the door flew open.

"Li Jin, I'm starving. Did you make some lunch?" Erik flashed what he thought was an irresistible smile and crossed the room. He stood behind her and put his arms around her waist as she ironed. He nuzzled her neck affectionately.

"*Ni hao.* I have some chicken soup in the cooker," she answered, feeling revulsion at his touch but trying not to show it.

"Mmm, you're great. Can you get me a bowl ready while I wash up? I have a meeting in an hour—just stopped by to eat, then gotta run."

With that he let go and reached over and shut the television off. Right in the middle of the show he knew was her favorite.

"How do you listen to that crap?" he said, and disappeared into the bathroom.

Li Jin set the iron up on end and went to the kitchen cove. She got out a bowl and filled it with soup. Sure she'd serve him up all right, straight to the drug enforcement committee if she could find a way to do it without dirtying her own hands.

Erik returned and took the bowl from the counter and sat on the couch. He slurped it loudly, nodding his appreciation. She followed him and sat down at the end of the couch, relieved to get off her feet for a few minutes.

"Turn it on BBC news, Li Jin."

She rose and switched the television on. She turned the dial until she found the one English channel they could get, then returned to the couch and picked up her bowl.

"Hey, you're getting good at cooking, Li Jin. I'm glad, too; I don't think I can stomach any more Chinese food." He made a face to go along with his sideways compliment.

"*Xie xie.*" Li Jin thanked him, giving him a half smile. She'd been cooking since she was twelve and was known for pulling a fine dish out of almost nothing. That was one thing she could always count on when trying to stay in the good graces of her foster families. She just didn't always cook to *his* specifications. He'd really be upset if he knew it wasn't the chicken breast meat making the soup so good. She'd also put in the chicken feet, what she considered the best part of the bird and necessary to make a good broth. It wasn't much, but knowing he'd be disgusted brought her a bit of satisfaction at her quiet retaliation. He'd told her before to leave the heads and feet behind at the market where they belonged, but disobeying him in small ways felt good, even if he never knew it.

He was so selfish he didn't care that she and Jojo didn't like the strange foods he wanted her to cook. But it was his money, after all. And what he didn't know was that she was squirrelling away a little bit of it each time he sent her shopping or to pay the bills. She wouldn't leave penniless. He'd lose a bit of his money to pay for her being his slave for the last year and a half.

He finished his soup in record time and stood. "Where's my favorite shirt? I'm going out with the guys straight after work." He looked over at the ironing board.

Li Jin jumped up. *Aiya, she hadn't finished the shirt!*

"Give me just a minute, Erik. I'm almost done with it." Behind her she heard him grunt in frustration. She turned the iron on and quickly began to run it over the shirt, even before it was hot enough. She knew even one stray wrinkle could cause him to erupt and she didn't want him to lose his good mood before he got out of there. She was just getting over the latest incident and her body begged for a break, but these days his tantrums came a lot closer together.

"Dammit, Li Jin! You've had all day! What the hell have you been doing? Sitting on your ass watching those damn screeching Chinese operas?"

Li Jin heard a crash behind her but didn't look and restrained the urge to duck. It was probably the soup bowl she hadn't yet washed. With his temper, they'd soon have no dishes left to eat from, but since it was his money that bought them, she'd try not to worry over it. She did hope he didn't reach for the new yellow mugs she'd just purchased, though. Hopefully he was in too much of a hurry to continue his rant. She held her tongue, kept her head down, and ironed faster.

Chapter Fifteen

Hours later Li Jin ran the brush through her hair as she looked in the mirror. Did she really look so old? Erik said she did but she also knew that when she wanted to—and sometimes even when she didn't—she could still turn heads. She just didn't feel the need to look like a raving beauty anymore when nothing she did seemed to impress him. To keep him from nagging her, she'd applied light makeup and even a gloss to her lips. But she would not paint herself up like some of the other local girls hanging on the arms of his expat friends. If he wanted that, he was free to go find it elsewhere.

Erik had insisted they go out for the evening. Li Jin would rather stay home, as it was getting harder each day to pretend everything was normal. It wasn't normal, and she was tired of living in what felt like a prison. These days Erik barely let her go anywhere; his insecurity was high and she knew he could feel her pulling away.

Jojo wasn't happy, either, but he'd agreed to stay with the old woman in the downstairs unit. She heard him in the next room as he thumped out a beat on the coffee table, singing along to some boy band on the television. Recently he'd graduated from constantly watching cartoons to searching the channels for music videos.

She heard the door open and sighed. Erik was home. What used to be her favorite moment of the day now filled her with dread. She put the brush down and prepared to bribe Jojo to go on downstairs. She hoped they'd get home at a decent hour and Jojo could sleep in his own bed.

"Jojo! My main man—look what I got you!"

Li Jin walked in to see Erik hand Jojo a shiny new red yo-yo. Her son's face lit up. It took so little to please him.

"Cool. Thanks, Erik," he gushed as he tried to work the yo-yo.

Erik took it back from him. "Watch me. Do it just like this. Let go of it smoothly; then roll your wrist and bring it back up."

He expertly dropped the yo-yo and brought it back up. Jojo watched him do it a few times. Li Jin stood back and watched from the doorway, not liking that Erik had gotten the yo-yo when she had told him she was going to get it. It was obvious he was trying to win her son over. But Li Jin was torn because she wanted Jojo to be happy, and every time Erik showed him any attention, he literally beamed.

"You try now, Jojo," Li Jin said.

Erik turned around and saw her standing there. He handed Jojo the yo-yo again.

"Oh, hi babe. You about ready?" He rumpled Jojo's head. "Me and your mom are going out on the town tonight, buddy. You gonna hold down the fort?"

Jojo nodded, even as he tried to shrug his way out from under Erik's hand. "I guess."

"He's not staying here, Erik. He's too young to stay alone. The lady downstairs is going to watch out for him." Ironically, the apartment they rented used to be the old woman's second floor of her own home until she sold it to a real estate mogul and he remodeled it into a separate apartment.

"Oh yeah. That's right. Whatever." He moved past her and headed for the bathroom. He'd be ready in a few minutes, so Li Jin needed to get Jojo out the door.

"Come on, Jojo. Let's go down and talk to Ms. Jing."

Jojo was still trying to get the yo-yo to work right and Li Jin could see he was getting frustrated. She stood at the door and waited for him. He tried a few more times but still couldn't get the yo-yo to come back up.

"Jojo. Come on." She was getting impatient. Erik would be annoyed if she wasn't ready to jump in a taxi when he was.

"No! I can't get this stupid thing to work!" Jojo stomped his foot and yelled at her. Li Jin cringed, hoping Erik didn't hear him. She put her finger to her mouth, trying to shush him.

"Jojo, it will take you some time to learn how to do it. Be patient—you just got it."

She heard the bathroom door open and watched Erik come through the bedroom doorway. He held on to the corner of a towel wrapped around his middle and he looked angry.

"Dammit, Jojo. Do what your mom says! We don't have all night to fool around with you."

Jojo used his fist to rub away the start of a tear. Li Jin knew it wasn't just the yo-yo. He didn't want to stay with the neighbor and he couldn't stand Erik scolding him. She crossed the living room and put her arm around him.

Before she could say a word, Erik stomped across the room and shoved her away from Jojo. He snatched the yo-yo and threw it against the wall. The cheap plastic broke into a few pieces.

"Now you've got something to cry about, you little moffie. I should've known you were too much of a baby to have a yo-yo."

Jojo really let the tears come then and Li Jin felt her anger soar.

"Erik! Why would you do something like that? He's just upset because we're leaving him home tonight. You didn't have to break it."

"I'll break more than his damn yo-yo if I hear another freaking sniffle." He turned to Li Jin. "He needs to grow up. And he's ruining my night. You'd better be ready to go when I come out again, Li Jin. I don't want to hear another damn word from either of you."

With that he stomped back to the bathroom and slammed the door. Li Jin held Jojo to her and stroked his head as he cried. His little heart was broken.

"Jojo. I'm so sorry. I promise I'll buy you another yo-yo," she whispered softly.

"I don't even care about the stupid yo-yo, Ma. Why's he so mean to us?" He looked up at Li Jin, tears streaking his face.

Li Jin was surprised. So far other than just now, she'd thought Erik had kept his temper focused only on her. She thought he and Jojo were getting along great lately. He'd even been taking Jojo out on a few afternoon excursions lately. To do *boy things,* he said, telling her Jojo needed alone time with a father figure to teach him right from wrong and make him tough. Li Jin thought he was probably an unlikely candidate for the job, given his unsavory choice of livelihood, but Jojo had been acting more mature and better behaved since their outings.

"What do you mean, Jojo? Has Erik been mad at you before?"

Jojo shrugged and Li Jin moved him toward the door.

"Yeah, yesterday he said I didn't do the drop fast enough and I talked too much. And I did it just like he said but when I finished, he shoved me down the sidewalk and Obi kicked me right here." He pointed at his side. "He was mad at me all the way home."

Li Jin felt a shiver of foreboding. "Drop? What do you mean, Jojo? Where did you go?"

She'd assumed Erik was taking Jojo for ice cream or to the park to hang out. At least that was what he'd led her to believe the few times she'd asked questions. And he had never mentioned Obi being a part of the outings. He knew she didn't like Obi and didn't want him anywhere near her son.

Jojo looked up at her and Li Jin knew that expression. It was his *Uh oh, I'm caught* look.

"Nothing. I'm not supposed to tell you what me and Erik do when we're on our walks. He'll be really mad at me if he finds out." He skirted out the front door and down the steps.

"Jojo, wait!" Li Jin rushed to catch up with him. At the bottom step he waited and turned, looking behind her as if he thought Erik would pop out at any second.

"No, Ma. Let's just go to Ms. Jing's. Please."

Li Jin put her hands on his shoulders and bent down in front of him. She had never seen him look so scared.

"Jojo, you are *not* in trouble. But you have to tell me the truth."

He shook his head from side to side and Li Jin saw his face turn stubborn. She knew she wasn't going to get anything out of him until he'd calmed down.

"Just tell me this, Jojo. Did your drop have anything to do with Erik's yellow Nike bag?"

She felt her heart fall when Jojo nodded solemnly, then turned and quickly went to Ms. Jing's door.

This was trouble—serious trouble. She felt a mother's fury enter her and breathed deeply to bring it under control so she could think logically what to do. Erik had crossed the line this time. He'd endangered the only thing in this world that Li Jin cared about. He had some explaining to do.

Li Jin struggled under his weight as Erik leaned against her, his arm draped around her shoulders. Staggering slightly, she led him toward the line of taxis. The first one waved her away, telling her he didn't want their business. She couldn't blame him, as he was afraid Erik would vomit in his car. She was finally able to reach and wave the one-hundred-reminbi bill that Erik had given her, and the next driver beckoned her over. Just in time, too, as a string of beggar children dashed over to try to pilfer a few coins. Li Jin didn't need them to deal with on top of her drunken boyfriend.

"Li . . . Jin . . . I'm sorry," he slurred, and a string of saliva hung from his chin.

He was so plastered that he didn't even know which way to go. She should just leave him but she couldn't do that. In his state he'd be robbed or even arrested, and even though he'd been nothing less than cruel to her, she couldn't do that to him. But she was disgusted. Not just from his behavior all night, but also from that of his circle of friends she'd been forced to socialize with, including Obi who had been making moves on her for hours. Once they'd brought out the *bai jiu* and Erik had lost all sensibilities, it was all she could do to keep Obi's hands off her. He acted like she was fair game since his best bud was out of commission. To make it worse, every time she looked at Obi, she wondered exactly what he and Erik had made her son a part of, and she wanted to tear him to pieces.

"What are you sorry for, Erik?" She wanted to keep him talking. If he passed out, she'd never get him home. The taxi driver opened the car door and she pushed Erik toward it.

"Duck." She said it a moment too late, when Erik struck his head on the metal door frame. *Oops, too bad,* she thought, shoving him in. She climbed in beside him and shut the door. The driver scurried around the car and got behind the wheel.

Erik grabbed his head and moaned, then leaned his cheek on the glass of the window.

"I'm sorrrrry. . . . I love you baby. . . ." He closed his eyes.

Li Jin told the driver their address, then leaned back and took a deep breath. She was exhausted and infuriated. Erik had tried to make her perform for his buddies as if she were some kind of whore. He'd even picked her up and put her on the stage with the singers! Told her to dance! Li Jin had never been so humiliated as his friends had surrounded her and shoved bills down her shirt and into the waistband of her jeans, copping a feel as she tried to push their hands away. She'd finally gotten out of the circle and run into the bathroom. Once she'd calmed down, she took all the bills off her and threw them into the sink. But then she'd remembered she and Jojo needed that money. It sickened her to have to use it, but she picked it up and folded it neatly, then stuck it down in her purse. It was more money than she'd ever had in her hands at one time and it would be a huge help when she found the guts to run.

Erik moaned again, something unintelligible.

"Okay, Erik. You're sorry. I get it. Now please just shut up." She didn't care what he had to say. She just wanted to get home to Jojo.

The taxi driver kept staring at them in the mirror and it was irritating Li Jin. He was probably wondering how she'd snagged herself a rich-looking foreigner. And with his being from the older generation, he didn't approve. Well, she didn't, either, she thought as she shot him an indignant look. She didn't need his stern looks to tell her she'd screwed up her life by partnering with Erik. But every young woman in China wasn't lucky enough to make only good choices. Some had people in their lives to back them up and lead them straight. Some had the reassurance of a roof over their heads if something went wrong.

Some had parents.

She didn't need him judging her. She'd had enough of that in her life.

"*Kuai yi dian.*" She told him to hurry and shot him another defiant look in the mirror. Then she gazed out the window, ignoring Erik's moans and drunken declarations of love.

Finally the driver screeched to a stop in front of their building. Li Jin nudged Erik to wake him up. He'd have to walk; she couldn't possibly get him up the stairs by herself. This definitely had to be the drunkest she'd ever seen him.

She looked at the driver in the mirror, hoping he'd offer his assistance.

"*Yi bai kuai,*" he said, looking away quickly to let her know there was no room for negotiation.

Li Jin pulled the bill from her purse and threw it over the seat. The driver could have helped her; as he was getting one hundred reminbi for a thirty-reminbi trip. Shooting him a dirty look in his mirror, she opened the car door and climbed out, then came around to Erik's side.

She opened the door and Erik almost fell on top of her. She grabbed him and shook him.

"Erik. We're home. You have to get out and walk." She pulled until he clumsily moved his long legs out of the car; then she helped him stand.

"What time is it?" he mumbled. "Where's my drink?"

Li Jin ignored him and led him to their stairwell. She looked up at the steep stairs and sighed. It was going to be a long climb. As they went, he ranted at her almost incoherently about how much he was doing for her and her son. Li Jin wished she were brave enough to tell him he'd never have gotten the great deal on their apartment if she hadn't put it in her name and helped him avoid the overpriced rent most foreigners had to pay. But he didn't think she was good for anything, obviously.

Half pushing him, half pulling him, she finally got him to their door. She took out her keys and opened it as he leaned against her. Finally, they were in. Out of breath, she led him to the bedroom and to the bed. He dropped, his face buried in the mattress, and didn't move another muscle.

Sweating now from the exertion, she reached down and unlaced his shoes, pulled them off, and tossed them in the corner of the room. She recoiled as she bent over him. He reeked of cigarettes and booze. She looked at her watch. It was after four in the morning. She really wanted to get Jojo but it was much too late to wake up Ms. Jing. She'd just have to wait until morning.

She sighed and went into the bathroom, already planning on taking Jojo's spot on the couch. But there was no way she'd be able to sleep a wink until she got the stench of the bar scene off her. She undressed quickly, dropped her clothes in a pile at her feet, and climbed in the shower, relieved to finally have peace and quiet.

She moaned as the water ran down her back, glad in this moment that their apartment had some of the best plumbing she'd ever known. Most showers in places she had lived consisted of only a showerhead attached to the wall of the bathroom and a drain behind the toilet. But Erik had insisted on a Western-style toilet and shower when he'd moved in and when the owner refused, he'd paid for the renovation himself. Now Li Jin could see why. The added enclosure kept in the steam, making it feel like heaven.

She reached up and touched her hair. It felt awful. She'd have to wash and rinse a few times to get all the smoke out of it.

But first she'd just unwind and let the water cleanse her of the night's insults. She continued to let the hot water soak her hair and run down her back, easing the kinks out of her tired muscles. Finally relaxed, she reached for the shampoo, when she felt something—or someone—behind her. She jumped. She couldn't believe Erik had gotten up!

"No, Erik! You're drunk. Get out!" She pulled away from him and turned around. She felt faint when she saw Obi standing there, completely nude except for a leering grin across his face. The door—she had forgotten to lock it!

"Li Jin. Come on, you know you want me. I saw how you were looking at me at the bar and you've been giving me a show in here for the last ten minutes. You know you want some of this." He reached down and grabbed himself, then moved a step closer, closing the gap between them.

Li Jin backed up until she was completely against the wet wall of the shower stall. She huddled and crossed her arms over her chest, terrified at the look of intent on Obi's face. She didn't know how long he'd been watching her and she felt violated. She looked around, but other than a few bottles of shampoo, there was nothing to defend herself with.

"Obi. Please. Get out. If Erik wakes up, he'll kill you." Her eyes darted around, looking for escape, but there was no way out without him moving.

"Erik won't wake up. He drank more *mao-tai* than any of us. He's lucky he's still breathing. Just be a nice, quiet girl and we can have some fun. He'll never have to know it. I'll be gone in an hour." He reached for her then.

Li Jin couldn't help it. She screamed. In her mind, she suddenly saw the face of her foster mother's son, the way it looked as he had raped her so many years ago. She pushed against Obi and he pulled her to him, pressing his wet body next to hers.

Suddenly his hands were all over her, exploring forbidden places that even Erik had never gone.

"No! Let. Me. Go." She lunged for the glass shower door, but instead of pushing it open, she fell against it. The glass shattered and she struggled not to fall. She couldn't catch her balance and hit her knees, half in and half out of the stall. She jumped up and reached for her towel and saw blood streaming from one of her legs.

"You dumb bitch. I told you to be quiet." Obi moved toward her.

"What the hell is going on in here!"

Li Jin froze. Erik had woken up. Here she was naked in the bathroom with his best friend, but thankfully he would clearly see it was against her will.

"Erik, he attacked me!" Li Jin threw herself against Erik, for once glad that he was strong and could protect her.

Obi calmly climbed out of the shower and pulled a towel from the rack over the toilet. He wrapped it around himself and casually threw his hand in the air.

"Man, you know how it is. She put you to bed and invited me in. I couldn't say no—you get me? Things got a little heated and she fell against the glass." He reached for a towel and began drying himself off. His nonchalant manner made the heat rise farther on Li Jin's neck.

"You're a damn liar!" she spat out, still shaking as she pointed her finger at him.

Erik pushed her away. Li Jin stood against the wall, unbelieving of the accusing look that came into his eyes as he stared her down.

"I knew you were a cheating whore, Li Jin." He slurred his words so much they were barely distinguishable. "Whatcha trying to do? Get another foreigner on your *sss . . . string*? Ain't I rich enough for you?" He staggered out of the doorway, back toward the bed.

He shook his head, then sat down and grabbed the edge of the mattress. Li Jin ran to him and knelt in front of him, holding tightly to the towel around her. She knew he was still drunk but still she hoped he would be alert enough to know Obi was setting her up. She could still hear him in the bathroom, muttering more of the fantasy he'd made up and trying to make it sound even more real.

"Erik, don't listen to him. He's lying." She tried to keep her voice from shaking. "Don't you remember? He didn't help me get you inside. It was just us. I put you to bed and then got in the shower. I forgot to lock the door and Obi came in the house and climbed in with me! I swear! You can't really believe his story, can you?"

Erik reached down and wrapped his hand in her hair. Slowly he stood and dragged her up with him, then pushed her onto the mattress. With one hand he reached behind him and grabbed his own shirt, pulling it over his head. He made a menacing sight, standing over her with only his jeans sagging low on his hips, his expression stone cold.

He jerked the towel from her body and slung it to the floor. He grabbed his already unbuckled belt and pulled it loose from his pants. He suddenly looked more sober and alert. "I've had just enough of you and your lies. Li Jin, you need to learn some respect. And I know just the man to teach it to you."

Li Jin grasped at the coverlet and a pillow and tried unsuccessfully to cover herself. The sticky sweet stench of the alcohol on Erik's breath washed over her and his eyes turned meaner than she'd ever seen before, the whites showing as he glared at her. When the cords on his neck stood out and one began to throb like a beckoning beacon, Li Jin knew she was in for the fight of her life. Before she could react, he threw her down on the bed and towered over her, his face a mask of drunken rage.

Just behind Erik, she could see Obi had come out of the bathroom. She sent him a pleading look but he wouldn't help her; she knew that. He leaned against the wall, his hand disappearing under his towel and a creepy grin on his face as his eyes traveled the length of her nakedness. Her last thought before Erik's belt came raining down was of Jojo and how glad she was that it had been too late to wake him. At least he was safe.

Chapter Sixteen

What felt like hours later, Li Jin opened her eyes and jerked when she saw Erik's face only inches from hers. He lay snoring loudly, breathing his sour breath straight up her nostrils. Moving slowly, she winced at the first streaks of pain. She tried to think back and remembered taking a beating, then Erik raping her as she continued to fight. She must have finally passed out, because everything after that was foggy. Slowly, inch by inch she backed away from him. Her head pounded and she had a hard time focusing her eyes. Strange, she thought, since she hadn't drunk any alcohol.

Finally off the bed, she stood and looked around the room as she struggled to get her balance. Even through her blurry vision she could tell it was a wreck. The colorful red-and-black bedding was on the floor and everything from the bedside table had been wiped off. Even the lamp lay broken on the floor, shards of ceramic scattered around. Li Jin thought about Obi and swallowed the bile that rose in her throat. Where was he? She was too afraid to look in the living room. She felt a shiver of revulsion. After the first few punches everything else was a blur, so she didn't know if Obi had touched her but she prayed not.

She reached down to pick up a sheet to wrap around herself and an excruciating pain shot up her left arm. It didn't want to work properly, so she held it close to her body. With her right arm she got the sheet and clumsily held it against her tender breasts.

Walking softly so she didn't wake Erik, she headed for the bathroom. As she moved, it felt like fire ran through her body, making every muscle contract in pain. She remembered Jojo and frantically looked around. He must still be asleep downstairs but she couldn't believe Ms. Jing hadn't heard the commotion. She hoped she hadn't, at least. She needed to get herself and the room cleaned up before Jojo came home. As she stepped over the items on the floor, she saw the time on the overturned clock said 7:43 a.m. It had only been a few hours since they'd arrived home and her life had literally been turned upside down.

She'd never forgive him this time. The foggy memories were becoming clearer. Erik had beaten her with his belt and then raped her, all in front of Obi.

Li Jin couldn't get Obi's shifty-looking face out of her mind. He'd stood against the wall and egged Erik on, telling him to beat her more and show her who the boss was. Erik had never hurt her so badly before and Li Jin didn't think he would have this time if not for Obi. He probably wouldn't remember much of it, as he was drunker than she'd ever seen him. But that was no excuse. If she wasn't scared for her own hide, she'd go to the police and file a report. But either way, she wished she could kill him—kill them both, actually.

She stepped into the bathroom and closed the door softly behind her. Gingerly she stepped over the broken glass and gasped when she looked in the mirror. She looked like a crazed jungle woman. Her hair was a mess of wild tangles and her left eye was almost swollen shut. A gash across her cheek was open and she wondered if she'd need stitches. The wound was obviously caused from Erik's buckle and it was ugly. She picked up a washcloth and wet it, then held it to her face.

A trail of dark bruises covered her body and now, turning to look at her backside in the mirror, she could see where the burning sensation was coming from. Erik's belt buckle must have caught her a few times there, too, because she saw several open welts sporting beads of dried blood. She looked at the shower stall and wished she could climb in and wash away the dirty feeling she carried, but she knew the moaning of the old pipes could wake Erik. She'd have to wait.

Her heart sank and Li Jin felt the tears spring to her eyes. Why? She'd done nothing wrong. All she'd tried to do was take care of Erik and make him a nice home. Her lip quivered and she shook her head at her reflection. She made herself sick. She was a coward. A failure. Now Jojo was going to come home and there was no way she could hide this from him. He was going to know.

Sinking down onto the closed toilet, she stared at the door. Would Erik still be angry when he got up? Would he beat her more? She couldn't go on living like this. Each time he was getting worse and what if it went too far? And if the next time she didn't get through it, who would take care of Jojo?

She needed to leave, but Erik had threatened her that if she did, he'd find her or turn her name in to the authorities. And now what was he involving Jojo in? It was her responsibility to protect him, wasn't it? And her *hukou* only gave her authorization to live in Suzhou; she'd have to apply for permission to move around China. Frozen with indecisiveness, she didn't hear anyone moving until the door opened. She cringed as the crack became wider. Would it be Erik? Or Obi?

"Ma?" Jojo poked his head around the bathroom door. "What happened in the bedroom?"

No, not Jojo yet! She needed to fix herself.

Li Jin tried to cover more of her body but it was of no use. She couldn't hide from him. She looked up and met his gaze head-on. The door clicked closed behind him and his eyes widened when he saw all the broken glass and then looked up at her. In his hands he held his yo-yo, the pieces taped back together. His eyes widened even more, shock registering at her appearance.

"What happened to your face? Were you in an accident?"

An accident? Of course!

"Yes, baby. I fell through the shower door. But I'm okay." She didn't mention she thought her arm was broken. They'd get to that later. Right now she had to think of what to do next.

Jojo came to her and put his arms around her. She winced as he squeezed her throbbing arm.

"Ma, your face is cut—do you need a Band-Aid? Want me to get you one?"

With that one small compassionate offer and his strong little arms around her, Li Jin couldn't contain her tears any longer. She broke into sobs, her entire body heaving. She was in so much pain—physically and emotionally. She felt more trapped than she ever had in her life, even more so than during her years of being shuttered in and out of the institute at the whims of those who thought they wanted her, then quickly decided they didn't.

"What, Mama? You're scaring me." Jojo pulled away, his eyes wide as he stared at her.

She tried to suck it up and stop crying. Between her sobs she consoled him.

"I'm o . . . kay . . . Jo . . . Jo. . . ." She tried to convince herself. But the truth was, she wasn't okay. She'd never be okay again. Her life was in shambles and that meant his life was in shambles. She was a terrible mother.

She took Jojo's hand and pulled him down to her level. He crouched in front of the toilet on his knees and the stark fright on his face made her more determined than ever.

"Jojo, listen to me. I need your help. We're going to go away on a trip, but I don't want Erik to know." She thought suddenly of her problem of the *hukou* but that issue was pushed aside as she heard something from the other side of the bathroom wall. She froze and listened for a second.

"Jojo, was Obi out there?" she whispered.

Jojo nodded, then wrinkled his nose. "He's asleep on the couch. And Ma, he's naked. I saw his private parts."

Li Jin felt a shiver of fear. Another obstacle. Could they get out without waking either of them?

"Okay, Jojo. Forget about him. We're going to pack some things and sneak out. Do you think you can help me?" She needed to clean herself up and get dressed. That itself was going to be hard. Her body was stiffening up from the pain and every movement she made brought more agony.

"I can do it. You get dressed, Ma. I'll pack us some clothes."

She knew then that her son wasn't as naive as she had thought. By the serious look on his face, he also knew that they needed to get away.

She nodded. "Be *really* quiet, Jojo. I mean as quiet as you've ever been, do you understand? I can pack my things but you use your school bag and pack underclothes, shirts, and jeans. Then go back to Ms. Jing and wait for me on the porch. Okay?"

She was so scared. Leaving was hard enough, but if they woke while she was attempting a getaway, there would be hell to pay. Li Jin didn't know if she could take another beating in the shape she was in, but she had to make a run for it.

"Okay. Don't worry." With that he opened the door and started to slide out.

"And Jojo—if I don't come soon, I don't want you to come back up here alone. Promise me. I should be down in less than a half hour, but if I'm not, you come up and bring Ms. Jing."

"I promise, Ma." His eyes were huge and sad as he shut the door quietly.

Li Jin hoped they would not even have to see Ms. Jing. She didn't want to explain anything. She stood up and dropped the sheet, thankful that her clothes from the night before were still on the floor. They were her only good jeans and she didn't want to have to leave them behind. First things first—she'd work on her face, then tame her hair and get dressed. Pack her bag. Get out. Finally.

Chapter Seventeen

Li Jin fumbled through the linen cabinet, glad it was in the bathroom and she didn't have to try to access it from the bedroom. When they'd moved in and Erik had filled the bedroom closet up with all his designer clothes, she'd been happy just to have a few shelves between the towels for her meager belongings. But that was before she'd realized how selfish and arrogant he was.

Clumsily with only one useful arm, she dressed, then finished packing her bag and slid the lid off the tank of the toilet to the side. The heavy ceramic screeched as it moved and Li Jin froze, listening.

When she heard nothing from the bedroom, she fished out the small waterproof bag of money she'd hung on the inside of the toilet tank. She dried it, then pushed it down into her jeans pocket. She checked her face in the mirror one more time. She'd found a bandage to put over the gash but it wasn't big enough to cover it completely. It would have to do.

Holding her throbbing arm against her, she quietly crept out of the bathroom and paused beside the bed. She stared at Erik and wondered how someone who looked so peaceful in sleep could be capable of such violence when awake. Would he miss her? Even a little? She'd given him over a year of her life and was leaving with nothing but a small bag of clothes and a tiny sum of money she'd been able to save. It wouldn't get her far, but anywhere away from him would be a start.

She looked around the room to see if there was anything else she wanted to squeeze into her sling bag. Living from the streets and bounced around from hostel to hostel, she didn't have much of value when he met her, and still didn't a year later. Then she spotted his jeans lying in a pile beside the bed. Could she do it? If he woke up and caught her, he'd snap once and for all. But he owed her, dammit.

She crept over to the jeans and set her bag on the floor. She had only one useful arm and needed it to check his pockets. She first went through the back pockets but found nothing except his wallet. She knew he didn't keep much in there and what he did have was probably wiped out in last night's partying binge. She felt in the front pocket and found what she was looking for.

Holding the keys tight to keep them from jangling, she picked up her bag and walked to the bedroom door. It stood open and she peeked into the living room. She saw Obi's feet hanging off the edge of the couch and froze. She waited and watched. When they didn't move, she slid through the door and stayed close to the wall while she made her way to the coat closet. Once there, she opened it and bent down. She slid the key into the safe and entered Erik's birth date, praying it was the right code.

The light turned green and the safe beeped. The door popped open and Li Jin held her breath, hoping Obi didn't hear the loud beep or following click. When she heard nothing from the living room, she opened the door the rest of the way and her eyes widened when she saw the stacks of money. *Dare she? Could she?*

Her hands shaking, she pulled one stack out and was surprised to see it was made up of all one-hundred-reminbi bills. She didn't know how much was there but she did know it was more than she'd ever seen. With at least ten stacks just like it, would he possibly miss just one? He owed her that much and she made a quick decision. She stuffed the money in her bag, spaced the other stacks out to cover the empty spot, then closed the door to the safe and stood up.

She heard Obi move and hesitated. She was only a few feet from the door and freedom, but she needed to put Erik's keys back in his pants so that he wouldn't think to check the safe. She waited until all was still, then slowly tiptoed into the bedroom. She returned the keys to his pants pocket and turned to leave.

"Li Jin?"

She froze. He was awake.

Erik turned over with his eyes still closed and felt across the bed. Li Jin knew he was searching for her. Of course he'd think after all he'd done, a few sweet words and caresses and he'd be forgiven. *Not this time.* She looked at the heavy cricket bat propped up in the corner and hesitated. How many hits could she get before he overpowered her? Sighing silently, she realized violence was his thing, not hers.

"Li Jin, where are you?" he mumbled, reaching farther.

Thinking fast, she dropped her bag quietly on the floor, slipped out of her shoes, and crawled in beside him. He reached again and this time made contact with her hair. She held her breath, willing him back to sleep as she fought through a wave of nausea caused by his touch. When it looked like he had nodded off again, she waited five more minutes, silently counting out each second.

With her eyes wide open, she saw the bracelet Jojo had made her sticking out from under Erik's pillow. Slowly she stretched her good arm up and reached the end of the strand of beads. Gradually she pulled it out from under the pillow and closed her fist around it. She prayed Jojo would stay gone and not come up looking for her.

Finally she felt secure enough with the rhythm of his breathing that he was not going to wake up for a while. She scooted away until his fingers were no longer wrapped in her hair and then got up again. Careful not to step on any of the broken pieces of ceramic, she slipped her feet back into the shoes and picked up her bag. She dropped the bracelet into it and quickly this time, she moved out of the room. She paused just outside the bedroom and when she saw Obi was still motionless, she went to the door and opened it quietly. It squeaked like usual and she waited just a second, then slid through and closed it behind her. Almost there.

On the other side of the door she saw Jojo's yo-yo on the floor. It looked like it had been stomped on. Just like her heart, it lay broken into many tiny pieces. Suddenly she knew without a doubt that it wasn't an accident—it was Jojo's way of telling Erik what he thought about his gift. She moved down the stairs quietly and as fast as her aching body would let her, then stepped through the door to the outside sidewalk. She looked around but Jojo was nowhere to be found. Dammit! Where was he?

Sighing with frustration, she pulled her sunglasses from her bag and put them on, then went to Ms. Jing's door and knocked softly.

The door opened and Ms. Jing pulled her in and shut and locked it behind her. Li Jin was shocked; she'd never seen the old woman move so fast. She looked around and saw Jojo sitting at the table in the kitchen cove, eating from a bowl. He gave a guilty wave, then went back to eating.

"*Zao*, Lao Jing," she mumbled, feeling self-conscience about her face.

Ms. Jing stepped back and crossed her arms, a knitting needle still in one hand and a half-finished scarf in the other.

"Don't good morning me, young lady. Why didn't you tell me you were in trouble? I knew something dark was going on up there. I've heard him screaming at you too many times."

Li Jin looked at Jojo and he stared down into his bowl. He'd told her something—that much was obvious. She just didn't know how much he had said.

"I'm not sure I know what you mean," she stuttered, moving toward the table. "Jojo, come on. We've got to go."

She made a move to switch her heavy bag to her other shoulder and cried when the pain shot through her. In the terrifying moments of leaving the apartment, she'd forgotten about it.

"See. Your arm. What's wrong with it? And where did you get all those bruises on you? What's under the bandage? And take off those sunglasses." The old woman acted indignant and Li Jin twirled around to face her, almost fainting from the pain and dizziness that overtook her. She reached out and steadied herself against the wall.

"Look, Ms. Jing. I appreciate your concern, I really do. But my son and I need to go and we need to go fast. Can you understand that?" Her eyes pleaded with Jing to understand without her having to say it out loud.

Jing crossed the floor and came to stand before her. She reached out and put a hand on her shoulder. Squinting her eyes, she looked at the fingerprint bruises running up Li Jin's neck and peered through her sunglasses.

"Oh, you poor girl. I know what's going on now."

Li Jin shook her head. "No, you don't know." Could the woman see right through her? She needed to think fast. "I was in an accident in the taxi last night."

Jing nodded sympathetically. "I know more than you can imagine. I'll let you go, but first, my husband, bless his spirit, was a doctor. Because of him I know how to fix you up. Let me do that much and then if you need a safe place to stay for a while, I can hide you here. Your secrets are safe with me."

Li Jin hung her head. She couldn't talk or she would really lose it. She wished *she'd* known all this time that humanity was so close. She hadn't realized it before but the woman was a gentle old soul—and gave out a feeling of protectiveness Li Jin had not felt much of in her life. The tears came again and though she tried to fight them, they poured from her eyes in a silent plea for more compassion. She kept her back to Jojo so he couldn't see. One good cry in front of her son in one day was already too much. He needed to see her as strong and able, not a blubbering mess.

Fortunately, the old woman saved her. "Come on in here with me, Li Jin. Jojo, you stay there and eat your breakfast."

She led her through the modest living room and to her tiny bedroom. She guided her to the antique wooden bed. Gently she pushed her down to sit and took a place beside her. The woman took a deep breath and began again. While she talked, she examined Li Jin's arm, using her soft fingers to push along the bone.

"The skin's not broken, so I don't think it's a compound fracture, but it is going to need setting. And we're going to have to look under that bandage on your face, in case you might need some stitches." She reached up and carefully slid the sunglasses off Li Jin's face. "Do you have family you can go back to?"

Li Jin shook her head. A mess it was for sure, but the old woman didn't know the half of it. She'd be shocked if she knew what had really gone on in that apartment the night before. She thought of the ways Erik had used her and crossed her legs, feeling the shame spreading across her face. She hung her head.

"Okay, no family. So do you know where you're going?"

Li Jin rubbed at her eyes, wincing at the tenderness. She shook her head again. She really didn't know where to go. Now that she had some money, she could really choose anywhere.

They'd start over. Again. And she was so very tired. But she hoped she would not be stopped by the authorities until she could get some things straightened out.

"Well, I know just the place to take you in. You aren't the only one with secrets—this place is almost invisible except to those who have been dealt a rough hand. My sister runs it and all you have to do is tell her I sent you. It's quite some traveling by bus but once you are there, she'll help you get a new start. She can get you a resident permit, a job, and possibly get Jojo into a local school. At least you won't be on the streets." She patted Li Jin's hand. "Can you trust me?"

Li Jin raised her eyes and looked at Jing. She'd never had anyone to trust before and wasn't sure if she could or not. But for Jojo she needed to start somewhere. She knew they couldn't just run without any destination in mind. Well, they could, but they'd done that before and it was a tough life, one she didn't want for Jojo.

"Okay. I'll trust you." It wasn't like she had any other options.

Jing smiled. "There you go. That wasn't so hard, was it? Now this is what we're going to do. You're so exhausted you look like you're going to fall over. You must sleep for a while."

Li Jin looked up at the ceiling and started to protest, but Jing held her finger to her lips.

"Hush. He'll never know you're here. And you don't want to be falling asleep on the bus when you have to look out for Jojo, do you?"

Li Jin hesitated. The old woman was right about that. If she tried to travel in the state she was in, she'd be worthless to watch over her son. The longer she sat there, the more her body screamed silently in pain. But she really needed to go—she felt an unbridled urge to be far, far away from Erik. Her gut told her the battle wasn't over yet and unfortunately she no longer had the energy to fight.

"Now let's get those shoes off." Jing bent down and gently pulled her shoes off. Then she picked up Li Jin's legs and swung them up until Li Jin was forced to turn and lie back. Li Jin was surprised at the old woman's strength and she lay against the pillows, cradling her throbbing arm. She had to admit, the bed was soft and clean. She looked around the room at the modest decorations and wondered if perhaps her own mother's room might look similar. It wasn't fancy but it was comfortable. Yes, that was the word. *Comfortable.*

Jing arranged her shoes neatly under the bed, then stood up and walked to the window and pulled the curtain closed. Next to her against the wall a wooden rack held a few colorful knitted scarves and Li Jin could just picture the old woman rocking and knitting. Contradicting the peaceful vision in her head, Jing hurried out of the room and Li Jin heard her talking to Jojo.

She sighed. She'd just rest for a little while. It was so quiet there. And safe. Erik would never think she'd be right under his very nose. Or would he?

Jing returned with a cup and sat on the edge of the bed.

"Now I want you to drink this—it will help your injuries inside your body."

Li Jin took the cup and looked in to see a white liquid, with some powdery residue collected around the rim.

"What is it?"

"It's an old tonic called *bai-yao* and will help you rest." Jing beckoned her to hurry and drink.

"But my Jojo, I don't want him to go outside. . . ." She took a long sip from the cup. It wasn't too bad and if it could help ease her pain, she'd drink anything. Her body and her brain fought against each other, as Li Jin needed to rest but wouldn't be able to watch over Jojo.

"*Aiya,* I know that! He won't leave my sight. I promise. I've got plenty to keep him busy. Did I tell you he reminds me of my grandson, Fei Fei?" Jing let her finish the potion, then took the cup and set it on the night table. She pulled a brightly crocheted blanket from the chair in the corner of the room and spread it over Li Jin, tucking it in on each side. She reached up and stroked Li Jin's head for a moment. "Now, I'm going to get some of my garden peas from the freezer and after we get the swelling down, I'm going to set that arm. I'll also mix up some salve for those cuts on you and stitch up your cheek. If your boyfriend comes to my door, I'll tell him I saw you and Jojo get on the bus this morning and I'll act like nothing is out of the ordinary. We'll wait to see him leave before you two set off."

Li Jin lowered her eyes, unable to look at the old woman. She'd realized that this was the first time and the first person to whom she'd ever let go of the secrets of what Erik had done to her. And it was such a blessing that she'd not even had to say the words out loud, that Jing had just known that Li Jin was a victim. Even so, it would take a long time for her to stop feeling it was her fault somehow, to stop examining every moment before every incident to analyze how she could have stopped him.

"Okay. Thank you so much, Lao Jing. For everything. But is it going to hurt even more when you set my arm?" She hated being such a baby but her arm was throbbing so badly. Because of her past, she had a high tolerance for pain but still, she didn't think she could take any more. But even though the aching was strong, her desire to sleep was stronger and her eyelids felt heavier now that some of her worry had been unloaded.

Jing patted her good arm again. "The pain will be nothing even close to what you've already been through. But before we do anything, I want you to rest. You'll be on the road to recovery before you know it. You just wait."

Li Jin hoped so. She truly hoped that this time she was making the right decision with her new path in life.

Jing tucked the blanket around her once more, then reached over and turned off the bedside lamp. The quilt over the window blocked out all the light and any chance of being seen, and Li Jin felt reassured by the dimness.

"Now close your eyes. I'll watch out for your Jojo."

The last thing she saw before she drifted off to sleep was Jing's gentle, wrinkled face smiling down on her, and Li Jin thought finally the gods had sent her some kindness.

For the first time in a long time, she let go of everything and just slept.

Chapter Eighteen

Li Jin awoke to a throbbing headache. As her eyes slowly focused, she looked around the room, trying to remember where she was. The layout looked like her bedroom, but everything was different. Where was she? Slowly she recounted the events in her mind. Erik got drunk. Obi attacked her. Then Erik beat her. Jojo wasn't there. Or was he? But what happened next? And where was everyone?

When she saw the doilies on the dresser and the colorful knitted scarves hanging around, she remembered everything and quickly tried to sit up. The effort made her dizzy and she dropped back against the pillows. She looked down and saw her left arm was in a homemade sling, cradled against her chest. Peeking inside, she saw that her arm was encased in a stiff piece of cardboard and wrapped firmly with tape all around. Also, her bracelet from Jojo was tied back around her wrist. She couldn't imagine why she didn't remember how the sling and bracelet got there.

"Jojo?" she called out, surprised how weak she sounded. She tried again, a little louder this time. "Jojo?"

The door opened and Jing's face filled the frame. She still wore her morning gown but Li Jin could have sworn it was red instead of blue before she went to sleep.

"*Zao*. You are finally awake!" She smiled at Li Jin, showing a toothy smile.

"Where is Jojo? What time is it? How long have I slept?" She struggled to sit up again. She felt like her body was encased in syrup, making every move slow and difficult.

Jing scurried across the room to the side of the bed. She put her hands on Li Jin's good shoulder and gently restrained her.

"Relax, child. So many questions! Your Jojo is fine. He's in there right now watching television. He just finished eating—did you know your son is a bottomless pit?"

Li Jin was confused. Jojo just ate again? He was eating when she got there. She suddenly remembered her bag and the money it held. She looked around frantically.

"Looking for your bag?" Jing asked. She bent and picked it up where it was hidden from view from Li Jin. "Here it is, just like you left it."

She held it up for a moment, then set it back on the floor.

Li Jin tried to speak again but Jing held her finger to her mouth, then pointed at the ceiling. "*Anjing*. Don't speak too loud. Your boyfriend just came home and is upstairs."

With that Li Jin felt a shiver of fear crawl up her spine. She needed to get out of there. But when she tried to swing her legs off the bed, Jing blocked them.

"No, you can't get up yet. You must wait until he is gone before you can go outside, anyway."

"But how long have I been asleep?" She looked down at her arm. "And how did you do all this without waking me?"

"You've been asleep for a whole day and night. It's morning again! I also stitched your face. And Jojo was my little assistant while I fixed you up. He was so good, I think you might have a future doctor in there."

Li Jin reached up and felt rough stitches where the gash had been on her cheek and swallowed back revulsion. She probably looked like a monster.

Jing pointed toward the living room. "He also noticed your bracelet was gone and got quite upset until he found it in your bag. He tied it back on. You were completely knocked out and it made working with your wounds much easier."

"But Erik? Did he come here?"

Jing nodded, a grim look on her face. "Oh yeah, he came. I pretended like I didn't understand his terrible Chinese, but when he said your names, I pointed at the bus stop and yammered off at the mouth in my family dialect until he stomped away. He thinks you left—and he thinks I'm a crazy old woman."

Li Jin thought that was probably an accurate assumption of what he thought. Erik had always ignored the local elderly Chinese grandmothers as too eccentric to bother with. "And Jojo? Did he see Erik?"

"Jojo hid in here with you when we heard the knock. He's scared to death of that man, girl! And I'll tell you another thing— that child knows a lot more than you give him credit for. He knows what's been going on up there."

With the scolding tone of Jing's words ringing in her ears, Li Jin hung her head. She was a terrible mother. All along she thought she'd successfully been hiding Erik's abuse from her son but he knew. She couldn't imagine how scared he was and the thought of him hiding that from her tore at her heart.

Jing patted her hand. "Now don't go getting all sad again, girl. You've made mistakes but we all do. Those trials were put in front of you to help you build your character! But now is the time for your inner mama tiger to come out. Learn from your experiences and you will be strong enough to protect your baby cub. No more tears."

Li Jin swallowed hard and lifted her chin. Jing was right. She wouldn't let her past dictate her plans for a new future. She would get Jojo to a safe place and they'd begin a new life. Again.

"Okay, Jing. I'm ready. When can I leave?"

Jing nodded her head in approval and Li Jin knew it was because of the sudden determined look she could feel spreading across her face. Yes, she was ready. Ready to leave this nightmare behind.

Chapter Nineteen

Calli sat outside her front door, her hand wrapped around the photos of Dahlia hidden in her apron pocket. Her heart still ached at the sorrow she saw on her daughter's face in every picture. Even without them in front of her, she'd already memorized every line and the expressions she wore. Now Calli had to make a big decision and it was the hardest she'd made in decades—maybe ever.

The door opened and Linnea slipped out. "I want to talk to you," Linnea said, looking back and forth between her and the door. Her serious tone let Calli know it was important. She nodded for her to continue.

"Neither you nor Ye Ye are healthy enough to travel. And before you say no, please just listen. You've done so much for me and I can never be at peace until I feel like I have done just as much for you."

Calli shook her head. "Now Linnea, don't be silly. You don't owe us a thing! You're our daughter and the joy you've brought to our lives is more than enough to repay anything you think we've done."

Linnea nodded. "I know that, Nai Nai, but I want to find Dahlia. I am younger and healthy—I can cover more ground faster. You and Ye Ye can look after the store for a week or two, and let me follow up on the leads. I'll start in Beijing and go from there. Jet can come with me."

Calli looked at Linnea, her lips pursed in concentration. She had a point—her arthritis was bad and Benfu's heart was weak. They'd finally gotten control of his terrible cough but any strenuous activity could cause a relapse. That was why she was debating even telling him about their daughter until she had concrete news. She didn't want to chance that he'd suffer a setback. And who would take care of the other girls if they both left? It would be too much for Linnea to mind the store and the house, too.

Calli knew if Benfu was told about Dahlia, he'd want to leave immediately and crush some heads together until they gave up what they knew about his daughter. But she also knew his health was poor and the travel might make it even worse. She wished some of her older daughters lived closer.

She nodded. "*Hao le*. Linnea, you can go if Jet will agree to accompany you. I've decided not to tell your Ye Ye about this until we know more, so that we can protect his health. We'll tell him you are going to visit your shirt distributor. I don't like to tell a lie but when it's over, he'll understand." She pointed her finger at Linnea sternly, "But I want you to check in with us every morning, afternoon, and evening. I want to know you are safe."

Linnea smiled ear to ear. "Nai Nai, you're going to have to finally buy a cell phone then. Unless you think snail mail is sufficient."

"I'll get Ye Ye to buy me one of the blasted things but it's not going to be one of those fancy so called *smart*phones. I just need something simple. And we need to go up to the store and get copies of these photos made. I'm not going to chance these getting lost." She looked down at the photo of Dahlia as a teenager and her lower lip began to quiver again.

Calli rose and stood before Linnea. She put her arms on her shoulders and stared into her eyes. "Linnea, thank you. I know you will do your best to bring Dahlia home."

Linnea nodded solemnly and in that moment, Calli knew she'd raised a daughter she could be proud of. She hugged her close and murmured into her ear, "Please, bring her home. *Please.*" Calli said a silent prayer under her breath that Linnea's tenacity and stubborn streak would be just what they needed to get their miracle before it was too late for either of them to enjoy it.

Linnea hurried out of the house and to the bus stop. She needed to get to her store early to meet Jet before the doors opened to the public. She'd called him and told him she had something important to discuss with him. She just hoped he could get the time off and accompany her on the train to the Beijing orphanage. Maybe on the trip she could finally convince him he had no reason to be jealous, and he could convince her that he was interested in her for the long haul. She thought a trip alone together would take their relationship to an entirely new level.

When Linnea was about to burst with anxiety, the bus finally came and she pushed through to get a seat. Thankfully, she snagged one of the last ones and sank down. She had so much to do before she left at the end of the week and could feel the pressure building in her neck and shoulders. She reached up to rub at it but bumped her elbow into the man standing in the aisle. She didn't bother to apologize as he had a trail of wires hanging from his ears and wouldn't hear her through the beat of his music. This was a popular route and the bus was over capacity with at least twenty or so more commuters standing, swaying back and forth at each turn and lurching forward with every abrupt stop.

First things first; she hoped Jet would agree to go and then they'd need to talk to Lao Zheng to see who his contact at the orphanage had been. If they got the woman's name, that would be their first step. Linnea would also need to talk to her screen printer to see if the next month's orders were processing on time, and let him know to send it on in her absence. She'd need to do some quick antique-hopping to build her inventory before she left. She had to pay her rent—and she had to let the landlord know that Ye Ye would be in charge while she was away.

Linnea wrinkled her nose as she caught a whiff of something unpleasant wafting underneath her nose. The men on the bus were so rude and she wished again that she made enough to afford a car. Jet had promised to teach her to drive when she was ready to go for her license, but that was at least a year in the future, maybe more. And it was a lot harder for females to get licenses in China, so even if she was a great student, it still didn't mean she would pass the exam unless some extra money exchanged hands. Jet could probably help her with that, too, as he knew the people with the clout to get her papers chopped.

Finally they reached her stop, and Linnea stood and pushed to get to the door. She stepped off the bus and immediately saw Jet standing on the opposite corner. Linnea started to wave but then realized he wasn't alone. He was talking to someone who gestured with her hands, flamboyantly trying to describe something.

Linnea squinted to get a better look and saw the young woman was at least a few years older than Linnea and obviously from the same side of town as Jet. She was a picture of perfection with her neat slacks and designer purse, sunglasses propped on her head, and gold bangles on her wrist reflecting the rays of the sun. Linnea noticed that her hair was trimmed neatly in a style that she had recently seen on the cover of a fashion magazine at the corner newsstand. Linnea reached up and felt the long, simple braid that fell over her shoulder. She'd taken about twenty seconds to put herself together this morning. There was no doubt about it; the girl was much prettier than Linnea.

Deflated, Linnea slowly walked toward her store, keeping them in view. She was earlier than he thought she'd be, obviously. But why meet the girl over here? Right in front of Linnea's own store? How cruel could he be?

She stuck her key in the door as she watched them from the corner of her eye, saw Jet kiss her on the cheek, then wave goodbye. She felt sick. Her world had just crumbled right before her very eyes. So it had finally happened. He'd found someone closer to his background to be with. Someone rich and gorgeous—a girl to make his parents proud. Linnea half expected to see the girl climb into a fancy car but she couldn't look any longer.

She felt her knees begin to give out and she leaned on the door. She would not cry. She would not shed one damn tear for him to see. As she stood taking deep breaths, she heard him come up behind her.

"Linnea! Hi—you sure got here fast! What do you want to talk about?"

Linnea opened the door and went in, carefully setting her bag on the counter. She wouldn't bring it up, she told herself. He'd tell her that it was a friend, or something. She knew he would. She turned to face him, pausing to give him time to say who he'd just been talking to.

"Linnea? What's wrong? You look like you've seen a ghost." He reached out and gently took one of her hands.

So that was how he was going to play it. Linnea struggled whether to ask or not. She didn't want to look insecure. But if it had been innocent, wouldn't he have mentioned who she was?

"Oh, everything is fine. I just wanted to tell you that Sky and I are taking a trip." She kept her voice neutral. She wouldn't let him know how much he'd just rocked her world. She might be a poor girl from the wrong side of town, but she still had her pride.

The look that crossed his face was payment enough for the hurt he'd just caused her. While he sputtered with his questions, Linnea pulled her hand away, turned around, and busied herself with counting out the cash for her register. Let him suffer, she thought. He deserved it.

Chapter Twenty

Five days later Linnea slapped a card down and grinned across the table at Sky. They'd been on the train for only a few hours and already she was beating him in his own game. But he didn't seem to mind. He'd been so thrilled that she'd asked him to accompany her to Beijing that she could probably get away with anything on the trip and he'd just smile and nod—but then that was his usual answer for everything in life anyway.

She couldn't say the same thing for his grandfather, though. Old Lau had fussed and blustered about them both leaving. He said it wasn't good for business but Linnea's heart squeezed a bit when she realized he just didn't want them to go. He'd never admit it, though.

Sky glanced at the old man and woman sleeping soundly on the bottom bunks, then whispered to Linnea.

"So, Zheng really gave you all that money? And him having just met you!" he said, shaking his head in disbelief. The train lurched and he grabbed quickly at his plastic bottle of orange juice to keep it from sliding off the table.

"I know! Lao Zheng said that if we found the old director, it would take a hefty sum to loosen her lips. I just hope she hasn't already kicked the bucket. It'll be much harder to find anything without her help. Back in those days, the underhanded maneuvers of the orphanage administration moving children around were never recorded. They kept it all in their heads to keep from being caught."

"It's probably the same way today, from what I've heard." Sky picked up the deck of cards and shuffled them again. "So how mad was Jet that I came with you?"

Linnea looked down at the table. She knew Jet's feelings were hurt more than mad. He'd immediately offered to come instead of Sky, but she had rebuffed him, telling him that she didn't want to take him away from his final months as an intern. She never did tell him that she had seen him with the rich girl. She wouldn't give him the satisfaction of knowing how much it had hurt her.

She smiled brightly and changed the subject. "We can thank Lao Zheng for this first-class cabin! And isn't it nice we don't have to fight for luggage space and somewhere to put our legs?"

Sky nodded and Linnea appreciated that he let his questioning about Jet go.

Linnea was relieved not to be in the general hard seats for once, even if they were sharing a room with a retired couple on their way to see their children. "But he did tell me to book the tickets, so it's not like I'm taking his money for something extravagant without his knowledge."

"I know that, Linnea. Do you think for a moment that I think you'd be that dishonest? You're the most grown-up and responsible girl your age I've ever met."

"Wow, thanks, Sky. I think." Or did he just say she was boring? She wasn't sure. She reached into her bag and pulled out her phone. She checked to see if she had any missed calls. Not a one. The last call she'd received was from her sister, Mari, in Beijing. Nai Nai had arranged for her to meet them at the train station and Linnea was excited to see her.

"So what's the plan when we get to Beijing?" Sky's voice brought her out of her moment of contemplation.

Linnea turned off her phone and slipped it back into her bag. "Well, Mari is going to meet us, and then we'll go to the orphanage and see if they can tell us where to find the retired director. We'll also ask if we can see Dahlia's file. But I'm sure that won't go over well." She didn't mention the letter she had signed by the old man that was intended for the director if they found her.

Sky nodded. "Yeah, they tend to be fairly closemouthed about the kids who grow up there. Are you going to tell them she was abducted and shouldn't have been there in the first place?"

Linnea shook her head. "Not if I don't have to. Lao Zheng asked me not to as it could get him into trouble for what his wife did. If we can avoid stirring up a hornet's nest, I'd rather keep it all calm." What she didn't say was that she couldn't bring herself to get the old man into hot water with the authorities. It looked like he'd suffered for his transgressions quite enough without being prosecuted on top of it.

Sky leaned back on the padded bench seat and crossed his arms. "Wow, I hope you're ready for what we might find. She could be homeless or even emotionally damaged or something. And you said she's about my age—that's a full-grown adult. I can't imagine growing up without my mama. She's always been a bit eccentric, but she's been there for me, you know?"

Linnea nodded, Sky must have forgotten she herself was a true orphan. "Well, I grew up without mine, but I had Nai Nai and there couldn't have been a better mother figure in my life. To think that Dahlia is Nai Nai's biological daughter, and what she missed out on. It's so sad."

Sky sat up quickly. "Chance is a tricky thing, Linnea. Have you even thought about if Dahlia had never been stolen, then

Calli and Benfu may never have begun taking in girls, and you might have been the one to grow up in the institution instead of her. It's strange that you ended up with her mother."

Linnea stared at the window at the blur of passing scenery. No, she hadn't really pieced that together but it was true. What a twist of fate. And now she was on a journey to try to right the wrong, even if she did lose her place in their hearts as a beloved daughter. But she didn't think that would happen. They loved her. Unconditionally. Of that she was sure.

Calli sat on the stool behind the counter and flipped through the *People's Daily* newspaper. She tried to concentrate, but she couldn't stop thinking about Dahlia and wondering where she was, what she was doing, and if she was okay. The photos in her apron pocket were becoming worn at the edges; she'd taken them out so many times to look. She'd also almost slipped up and told Benfu at least a dozen times already. But she'd wait to hear from Linnea before getting his hopes up, just in case. She'd committed to that decision but it was so hard not to share with him, as they usually shared every tiny piece of their lives.

It was only the first day without Linnea and so far business at the store had been steady, but nothing she couldn't handle. Now it was the noon hour and most people here in Old Town were eating or napping, giving her a few minutes to catch her breath. Calli sighed. She was tired and wished for the day to move faster.

Benfu had tried to talk her into letting him take the afternoon shift when he had seen how she kept stopping to rub her hands while peeling potatoes the night before. He'd gone over and taken the paring knife from her to finish the peeling. Her arthritis was flaring and he said he didn't want her wearing herself out at the store. But she insisted and she had the twins to help her there anyway. They were an amazing duo and so far she'd barely had to lift a finger.

Ivy came to stand in front of the counter. "Nai Nai, can I have some of the newspaper to read?" She set her empty rice box on the counter. She had run to the corner shop and gotten their lunch, and Lily still sat quietly picking at hers. Lily ate much slower than her sister, preferring to enjoy each bite instead of racing to the bottom of the carton.

Calli looked up from the paper. "I don't know—don't you have some unpacking to do back there?"

Ivy shook her head. "No, I already got all the new T-shirts sorted and folded." She pointed to the shelves of shirts near the front of the store. "See, we already put them out."

Calli saw the tall stacks of shirts and chuckled. She should have known the girls would have jumped on it and finished the task already. Linnea had promised them both an allowance if they really stepped up while she was gone. They were banking on a good report from her. Even Lily had put away her violin the past few days and did whatever they asked her to do.

"*Hao le.* I guess you deserve a break." She pulled a section from the middle of the paper and handed it to Ivy. "While it's still the lunch hour, I'm going to go back and take a little nap, but let me lock the door first."

Ivy took the section of the paper and went back to her small stool beside Lily. Calli walked to the door and turned the key. She didn't want anyone coming in with just the girls up front. And she looked forward to stretching out for a little while on the thick pallet of quilts she'd arranged in the storeroom.

"Read to me, Ivy," Lily said as Calli walked toward the back, pulling her phone from her pocket. After Benfu had realized how nice it was to be able to talk with all their daughters, he'd stopped by and purchased her a phone, too. Calli wasn't too keen on spending the extra money each month but she had to admit, she was also enjoying the easy communication with everyone.

"Nai Nai! Look!" Ivy jumped up from her stool and barreled toward Calli with the paper.

"What? What is it?" Lily asked, her face a mask of alarm at the urgency in her sister's voice.

"For goodness' sake, Ivy, don't scare us to death. What's wrong?" Calli asked, putting out her hands to steady Ivy as she jumped up and down.

"It's a story about Linnea! Look, here's even a photo of her and the store!"

Calli took the newspaper from Ivy and spread it out on the counter. She read the words and then looked at the photo. "*Aiya!* My own daughter made the paper. Just wait until we tell her about this."

Behind her they heard Lily stomp her feet in irritation. "Read it to me, someone! And tell me what the photo looks like!"

Calli chuckled at her impatience. "Okay, little one. I don't know how they got this photo, but here it is. It's an article under the *Who to Watch in Chinese Fashion* column. It says, '*Artist Zheng Linnea, once a child with no name, is the one to watch as her designer shirts are blazing a fashion trail across the city of Wuxi.*'"

Lily clapped her hands excitedly. "Whoa . . . she's a celebrity!"

"Shh . . . there's more. Read the rest, Nai Nai," Ivy pleaded.

Calli felt her eyes misting over and realized she had a lump forming in her throat. "No, you read it, Ivy. I need to blow my nose."

Ivy smiled up at her sympathetically, then situated herself over the paper. "Okay, listen. It says, '*Major themes in Zheng's work include nostalgic reminders of Old China and landmarks almost forgotten in her hometown of Wuxi. Also in Zheng's new store—Vintage Muse located in Old Town Wuxi Beitang side—longtime collectors will find rare antiques and treasures to be bartered or bought. Want a piece of history? Then Vintage Muse is the place to shop and Zheng Linnea the One to Watch.' "*

Calli stood up and felt the smile spread across her face. Years ago, the *People's Daily* newspaper was only used to promote Mao and his directives to sing praises of the work he was doing across China. Now she was seeing her own daughter's name across the same page. Who would have thought it? She was so proud she thought she'd burst.

"Girls, you know what this means?" she said. Already her brain was buzzing and lists were forming.

"What?" Lily asked. "That Linnea is going to have a big head when she finds out she was written up in the paper?"

She laughed. "Probably. But it also means we're going to be very busy in your sister's absence. We might have to call in the troops. Even Maggi and Peony are going to have to help out. And I'm going to have to place a duplicate order of what just came in and ask them to rush it." She was glad Linnea had left her screen printer's number just in case. So much for a nap—she had a lot of work to do now. If her gut instincts were right, she expected a surge of business in the next few days and she had to be prepared. She didn't want to let Linnea down when she was out there doing something so important for her and Benfu.

"And when we leave tonight, we need to swing by the framer shop. That article is going on the wall before Linnea walks back through that door." She also planned to stop by and spend some money on at least a couple dozen more papers. She would mail a copy to all of Linnea's sisters. This was big news in the Zheng family—*really big news.* She couldn't wait to show Benfu.

Ivy took the paper over to where Lily sat and described in detail the photo of Linnea taken outside her shop. Calli heard Lily ask which of the T-shirts Linnea wore in the picture. Of course, she should have known that design would be the biggest request. Calli smiled as she realized how the newspaper had gotten hold of it. Of course, it was Jet. He'd taken that photo right after the grand opening and he'd alerted the media to Linnea's small success. All that told Calli was what she already knew; the boy was besotted to be sure.

"Girls, I'm going back here to see if Linnea has any hidden shirts. Let's get this ball rolling." With that she disappeared into the storeroom. She pulled her phone from her pocket and dialed the number to Linnea's screen printer in Beijing. She hoped he was ready for a huge order.

Chapter Twenty-One

Linnea stuffed the dirty pair of socks into her bag and zipped it tight. Quickly she stowed her bag under the bunk and out of the way. The train cabin was nice but definitely tight.

She'd awoken feeling refreshed from the ten or so hours of sleep. At first she had struggled to stop thinking of Jet and what he might be doing and with whom, but soon the motion of the train had rocked her like a baby and the soft bunk underneath her felt like heaven. She'd thought Sky was still asleep in the bunk above her but had opened the door to the hallway to find him moving gracefully as he did his morning exercises.

"What are you doing up so early?" she asked.

"This is called the Buddha Showing a Thousand Hands. It is Bai Ling's favorite pose to bring her internal peace," he answered slowly as he stretched his arm all the way to the ceiling of the car.

Jet had warned her not to engage Sky in conversation about the Falun Gong or the supposed exercises that they must do to absorb energy from the so-called parallel universes, so Linnea squeezed past him to the bathroom to wash her face and brush her teeth, luckily beating the rest of the passengers in their car to be rewarded with a moderately clean experience. She'd changed her clothes and returned to find Sky back in their cabin.

And now with nothing left to do, she flopped down beside him and heaved an impatient sigh. Beside her, Sky smiled serenely, his bag also already packed and ready. Still he didn't look in the least bit bored and sometimes Linnea hated how constantly calm he was when her own insides felt like they'd explode with anticipation.

Their cabin mates—the retired couple—sat directly opposite them on the other bottom bunk, watching them curiously. The crinkly faced old man used a soiled cup to spit his tobacco in and kept adjusting the lump it made behind his lip. Both of them were bundled up as if they were taking a trip to the famous icy Harbin and Linnea didn't know how they weren't uncomfortable in the stuffy cabin. As far as she'd seen, they had no plans of changing their clothes from the day before, but Linnea knew that wasn't unusual in the older generation as they thought using too many clean clothes was wasteful.

With only about a half hour until their stop, Linnea was restless and couldn't wait to get going on the search. Waiting in the cramped cabin with strangers had now turned awkward since they'd stopped their snoring and gotten up. After they'd both made trips to the bathroom in their car and the woman had made her husband some green tea, they'd settled down and the silence became heavy.

Linnea flinched as the old woman reached across the few feet between them and grabbed her hand. Her first instinct was to jerk it back, but she hesitated, thinking the woman probably meant no harm.

"So this is your betrothed?" the woman rasped at her, looking from Sky to Linnea as she turned over Linnea's hand and began rubbing her palm with her shriveled finger.

Linnea nodded and tried to hide the smile such an old-fashioned word brought to her lips. She'd never pretended to be engaged before, but Ye Ye had told her it would be best if people thought she and Sky were a couple, and she'd agreed. She didn't want questions about why she was traveling with him or even have to ignore inquiring looks from other guys her age. Better to let strangers assume she was attached, and she was—sort of. Just not to Sky.

"Were you matched by a matchmaker?" the woman asked, her curious black eyes twinkling.

Sky shook his head at the woman and answered solemnly. "No, fate brought us together."

Linnea felt like elbowing him in the side. He was so serious; you'd think they were really engaged. He seemed to like the charade too much for her taste and Linnea couldn't wait until they could drop the act.

The woman flipped her hand over again, then looked at Linnea. "The skin on the back of your hand is firm and healthy." She nodded her head up and down confidently. Beside her the old man removed a small pocketknife from the inside of his jacket and began to clean under his nails. By the bored expression on his face, Linnea thought he was obviously accustomed to his wife reading fortunes for strangers.

"What does that mean?" Linnea asked. Despite her promise to herself not to engage in conversation, she couldn't help her curiosity. Nai Nai had told her long ago that many of the most famous palm readers in the world were in China. Linnea was skeptical because it was her nature, but she still respected their abilities.

"It means you are artistic and energetic. You make the most out of every day, and at the same time you are resourceful and rarely make mistakes. You tend to put the physical before the emotional."

Linnea looked at Sky, her eyebrows up. "And what am I supposed to make of that?"

Sky smiled. "She's right about everything, Linnea. I also see you pushing your emotional needs out of reach in your quest for success."

Linnea shook her head. She didn't believe that and as a matter of fact, she thought her emotional needs were directly linked to her physical needs. Until she was comfortable in the physical sense—especially in regards to her livelihood—she would never relax emotionally.

The woman turned her hand over once again and traced a line across her palm. "You are strong-willed and you don't let anyone stand in your way. But don't let yourself be spoiled by your newfound authority and power. You are about to have a burst of sudden success. Try your best to live with and respect others, because you may be hit by an unexpected downfall."

Linnea gently pulled her hand away and put it behind her. "I respect your predictions, Laoren, but I've already been hit quite enough by downfalls in my life. I'm on the upside now and have no intention of turning the other direction." Linnea did like the prediction of a sudden success and hoped desperately it meant her store would do well.

The old woman nodded. "I understand. Too much knowledge of the future can be a frightening thing." She looked over at Sky, then back at Linnea.

"And he isn't your life partner. I want to tell you that now to save you the waste of many years before you realize it." She smiled apologetically at Sky, then looked at Linnea again. "Some women are saddled with men who have interrupted their true fate and their hearts suffer before they have realized it. But if you would like to tell me your birth date, I could tell you which animal of the moon you should be with."

Linnea shook her head. Even if she wanted to, she couldn't give the woman a completely accurate birth date. So why bother? "Thank you, but I'll pass."

Luckily Linnea was spared any further explanations or discussions as the train pulled into the Beijing station. She and Sky stood and gathered their bags, then made their way into the outside hall and into line with the other passengers hoping to be first off. Linnea looked at her watch and saw it was a few minutes past noon. With any luck they'd find Mari quickly and then get to the orphanage and start their search immediately.

As the taxi weaved through the busy streets, they spent the half hour catching up about Mari's adventures at the Great Wall, and Linnea's new store. It had been over a year since Mari had come to Wuxi and Linnea thought she looked tired, but otherwise the same. She still wore her hair in the unusual long, curly style that went well with her colorful gypsy-looking clothes. And like always, Linnea still thought of her older sister and her husband as somewhat daring for selling their farm to make a career out of dealing with tourists. They'd traded a cow for a camel and set up a photography business at the Great Wall. It was still hard to believe and Linnea respected their courage. Still, though her Nai Nai had asked Mari to take them around town, Linnea didn't need her sister to take charge. This was her moment, not Mari's. But she was still thrilled to see her, and Ivy and Lily had pouted for an hour when they'd heard Linnea would get to visit Mari.

"And little Maggi? Is she still getting around well in her wheelchair?" Mari asked.

Linnea laughed. "Oh yes. She's become an independent little thing. Now that she doesn't have to be carried everywhere, she wants to help Nai Nai in the kitchen, or work in the store—it's just amazing how that chair has changed her life. I just wish the local transportation would catch up with the rest of the world and offer wider doors and lifts for the chair. Getting her to my shop is not an easy thing."

Sky chuckled. "You can't tell that to Lao Calli. She still manages to bring Maggi to Linnea's store at least once a week. That woman is amazing."

Mari nodded. "That's for sure. But what about Peony, is she still getting postcards?"

"It's been a while but it's so sad, Mari. She's constantly looking at or reading the ones she's collected. I think if that really is her mother sending those, it's a cruel way to show her love—staying out of reach and giving Peony false hope."

The taxi screeched to a stop in front of a tall concrete wall, and the driver turned to them and demanded seventy-five reminbi.

Linnea looked at Mari and her sister shook her head. *"Tai gui le."* She whispered it was too much and they both turned to Sky.

He sighed and leaned toward the front seat. It wasn't unexpected; trying to cheat out-of-towners picked up from the train station was a given. Luckily Mari knew the usual Beijing rates.

"Sir, I do apologize for being so forward, but you said the fare would be no more than fifty. So here is your fifty." His voice was so calm and friendly as he held out the money and Linnea had to hide her smile at the puzzled look that came over Mari's face. From what she'd heard, Mari's husband was a tough guy and would've taken a completely different approach.

The driver looked like he didn't know what had hit him. Sky's temperament was so far from the norm for a man his age. The driver had obviously expected a long and loud argument. He reached over the seat and took the bill from Sky's outreached hand, then faced the front again.

Linnea climbed out with Mari and Sky right behind her. She held on to the open door while Sky walked to the back and waited for the driver to pop the trunk. When the lid slowly opened, he pulled both their bags out and set them on the curb. Only then did Linnea let go of the car door and let it shut behind her. Sky came to the front window and bent down and wished the driver a good day. Linnea could only imagine the expression the man wore as he drove away, wondering what kind of weird fellow Sky was since he was being so polite to him.

Linnea turned and looked at the group of buildings over the tall wall. It didn't look inviting in any way, but she wasn't surprised. She'd heard a lot about the various orphanages and knew none of them were any place she'd want to grow up.

"So this is it, huh?" Sky asked.

Mari read the engraved characters on the gate. *Beijing Social Welfare Institute #1*. "Yes, this is it. I can't believe I've lived in Beijing all these years and have never come here."

"Why would you?" Sky asked.

Linnea looked at Mari and they shared a silent thought. If Sky were an orphan, too, he'd know why they might be curious. Both of them had only escaped life in an institution because their Ye Ye had found them. If not for one kind man, things would've worked out differently.

Linnea picked up her bag and headed for the small building and the young guard inside, lounging back in a metal chair with his cap pulled low over his eyes. She hoped he was in a good mood. Behind her, Sky and Mari followed.

"*Ni hao*. I'm here to see Director Long." She cringed as the guard almost lost his balance in his hurry to get his feet off the counter. She'd caught him taking an afternoon nap and he looked embarrassed.

He stood quickly and pulled on his jacket to straighten it. "No, we don't have a Director Long here."

Linnea looked at Sky. Just as they feared, the woman was probably long gone. They'd have to go with the next plan as Lao Zheng had instructed them.

"Well, can we talk to the current director so that we can ask her where to find Director Long? She used to work here many years ago." Obviously the guard wouldn't know who Long was, as he was barely as old as Linnea. Long had probably been gone for a few decades at least.

She saw his face fill with doubt. Zheng had told her it would be difficult to get access to the orphanage and would take strategy and even some smooth talking.

"We have a donation," Linnea added, biting her lip. She pleaded with the gods that they could at least get in. There was no way she was turning back yet.

The guard's expression changed, if possible, getting a bit darker. Linnea could see they weren't winning him over. She turned to Mari to see if she had any ideas, but her sister held her hands up and shrugged.

Sky stepped forward and put one foot on the door frame of the shack, leaning in with a friendly smile on his face.

"Good afternoon, friend. I'm sure you have your orders, but I know they wouldn't want you to turn away any donations, right? I've been here before and can find my way to the administration office. And I'll let the director know you were very helpful."

His calm confidence and politeness, as usual, changed everything. The guard suddenly smiled back and pulled three lanyards with visitor's tags from his drawer. He handed them to Sky and pointed toward one of the shorter buildings among the others.

"Over there you'll find Director Lu's office."

Sky put one of the lanyards around his neck and handed the other two to Linnea. "Let's go."

Linnea shook her head in amazement. She was glad she had brought him and though she missed Jet terribly, knew his way of dealing with those in power would possibly not have been so successful. She knew he wouldn't be rude, but he'd probably use a much less gentle method than Sky had.

"How do you do that?" Mari asked.

"It's all about truthfulness, compassion, and tolerance," Sky answered.

"Please don't get him started," Linnea said. She wasn't up for one of Sky's teaching moments. She quickly changed the subject by pointing out the huge colorful billboard advertising the upcoming Children's Day event. She wondered what sort of experience orphans would have on a day marked to celebrate childhood.

Together they walked through the huge open area that served as a parking lot and a courtyard. Other buildings stood around it in a semicircle and Linnea tried to figure out which one housed the children. The thought of living in the orphanage usually scared but also intrigued her. Though she didn't hear any children's voices, she could see the top of a tall building standing behind the others, starker and less polished than those that stood guard around it, and something told her that was where she'd find the children.

"It's pretty here," Sky said, pointing out a small garden to their left.

In it they saw huge apricot trees and a koi pond. Elaborate benches were set against the borders of the manicured walk, practically begging someone to stop and spend time there to reflect. Next to the area Linnea saw another walking path that led between two buildings and toward the direction of the tall building in the back. She pulled Mari's arm and guided her toward the path. Over her shoulder she beckoned for Sky to follow.

"Sky, before they know we're here, let's go see if that's the children's quarters back there."

Sky looked at Linnea, his brow wrinkled in confusion. "Why? Dahlia's long gone from there, Linnea."

She nodded. "I know. I just want to see what it's like. Please." She continued to walk, her arm through Mari's as she guided her along. When Sky didn't argue, she took that as a positive sign and picked up the pace.

At the end of the path they found themselves in another courtyard in front of the tall building. Sadly, once past all the administration buildings the atmosphere had turned less beautiful and more haunting. Here Linnea saw the true reality of the welfare institute and not the façade that was presented to most of the public.

There was another gate to go through, and a different guard, an older one this time, sat outside it on a bench and shelled peanuts into a pail. Linnea picked up her badge and flashed it at him, then dropped it and kept going with a feigned confidence she hoped would fool him. She felt a hesitation in Mari's gait but dragged her along.

"*Aiya,* Linnea. Look how old this building is. The bars over the windows are even rusted. They look ready to fall off," Mari said, shaking her head.

Linnea agreed. The building was old and years of rain sliding from the pink tiled roof offered a kaleidoscope of pastel colors staining the exterior of the building, bringing the only splash of color Linnea could see. On the third floor there was a landing of sorts and Linnea saw a group of older children hanging clothes on a makeshift clothesline. The children moved awkwardly, making Linnea wonder if they had some sort of disability. She wondered about Dahlia and if she had been like them, working to earn her keep in the orphanage.

She was surprised not to see more kids but then realized it was a school day. There were a few boys and girls standing around outside of the building and they looked up hopefully when they saw Linnea and Mari coming toward them. Linnea could see the children were drawn to Mari's bright outfit, and she let go of her sister. Mari crouched down and began talking softly to the boys and girls as they took turns touching her clothes.

Linnea wandered over to a small girl who used a piece of chalk to draw an endless circle on the pavement. The little girl looked no more than seven or eight and her mismatched clothing was cute in a ragamuffin sort of way. She was separate from the others and Linnea wondered why she had isolated herself. Standing over her, she looked closer at the drawing and saw more than a circle. Inside the drawing were stick figures of a man and woman holding hands with a small child in the middle. Linnea wondered if that was her real family she was remembering, or her future family she hoped for. She bent down beside her and smiled. Sky joined them.

"*Ni hao,* what's your name?"

The little girl smiled at her through the jagged clumps of bangs in her eyes. Her oval face and impish expression reminded Linnea of Peony and she felt a surge of warmth. Another girl a few years older ran over and held her hands up, shaking her head.

"She can't hear! She's deaf," the girl said loudly, pointing at her own ear where a small white hearing aid was visible. Her speech was a bit disjointed but Linnea could understand her fine.

Linnea looked at the little girl smiling up at her, then at Sky, and saw the pity in his eyes. The little girl didn't have a hearing aid. She looked around at the other boys and girls and saw a few of them using sign language with one another.

"So these are the deaf children and I guess they don't go to school." Linnea thought of Lily and wondered if there were blind children there, too.

"Yeah, I wonder why only some of them have hearing aids," Sky said, looking at the other kids. He peered around them into the room they were standing in front of and saw colorful posters of animals and the English alphabet letters pasted to the wall. A young woman sat at a desk, her head bent over her work as she made pencil marks on a paper.

"Some have probably had donations for theirs, while others haven't," Mari said from behind them.

Suddenly they were interrupted when an exhausted-looking nanny came down the concrete stairs from the second level carrying a heavy load of folded clothes. She approached them, a suspicious look in her eyes.

"Who are you?" she asked, setting the clothing down on the walk in front of her. She straightened and used her sleeve to wipe the sweat from her forehead.

Linnea wondered how or why she came to be employed there. Had she been an orphan? Did she even like children?

"I asked who are you?" the *ayi* asked again. "Do you have permission to be back here?"

"Uh-oh, we're about to be kicked out of here," Mari whispered.

Linnea didn't know what to say but Sky stepped forward and flashed one of his winning smiles. "We have a meeting with Director Lu but she said we could stop over here and visit with the children first. Can I help you with that load of clothes?"

Without waiting for an answer, he bent to pick up the basket and turned his head sideways to wink at Linnea. He stood and nodded to the nanny, beckoning her to show him where she wanted the clothes taken.

Linnea was amused to see the nanny a bit flustered but obviously flattered by the attention from Sky. She turned and led the way to a corridor where she and Sky disappeared.

Mari laughed. "That guy is something else. But he probably just bought us a few extra moments. Oh, Lin, why can't we take them all home to Ye Ye and Nai Nai? Just think what they are missing having to live here. It breaks my heart."

"Mine, too, Mari." Linnea put her bag on the ground and dug inside it until she found the bag of dried apricots her Nai Nai had stuffed in there for a traveling snack. At the sight of the bag, all the children came running and surrounded her. Linnea laughed at their excitement while she handed out the fruit to their reaching hands. As they stuffed the treats into their mouths, it was evident their bellies were hungry for food and their hearts for attention.

Chapter Twenty-Two

With the children trailing them as far as the security guard, they all backtracked until they were once again on the way to the administration building. They didn't talk and Linnea used the time to look around and think.

"Are you okay, Linnea?" Mari asked.

Linnea nodded. "Yes—it's just that being here brings up all those questions in my mind I usually try not to think about. Like why my parents didn't want me and where I might have come from. I know you probably feel the same."

Mari didn't answer.

"I can understand how that would be hard to think about," Sky said. "Maybe you should just focus on the good in your lives instead."

Linnea knew he was trying to be there for her, but even though he was sympathetic, she wished for Jet. He would've helped her talk it through instead of telling her to ignore the heavy emotion that had come over her. She reached into her bag and pulled out her phone, looking at the call log.

"Has he called yet?" Sky asked.

"Who?" Mari asked.

"No one," Linnea answered. She didn't want her sister to know she was having boyfriend troubles. It was embarrassing enough that Sky knew it. She flipped through the log and saw there were no missed calls. She checked her e-mail account and there weren't any new e-mails, either. She dropped the phone back into her bag. "Let's hurry up and get to the director's office. I hope she hasn't left for lunch." With that she picked up the pace and led the way down the path and then up the concrete stairs to the double doors. She took a deep breath and pushed through.

"Can you at least check to see if you have a file for her?" Mari stood with her hand on her hip and stubbornness spreading across her face.

Pulling her sweater closer against the chill of the stark room, Linnea waited for the director to answer the question. The woman frightened her—in the fifteen minutes they'd been there she had been nothing less than uncooperative. Linnea was even too afraid to bring out the letter, for she didn't know what the woman would do when faced with such information. Linnea could tell right away the director was a no-nonsense type. She'd met them at the door and quickly shown them to her office, striding ahead of them in her navy dress suit and blocked heels.

The director went to the wall of shelves and, using her finger, traced each label as she went from the left to the right, checking each name on the rows of binders.

"Sorry, no records for a Zheng Dali Yeh," she said, and turned around, crossing her arms over her chest.

"Maybe she wasn't registered under that name. Please check Dang Li Jin." Linnea knew by her attitude and body language the woman wasn't going to find anything under either name.

"Anyway, all records are confidential and I would not be able to share them with you without official permission."

"But we know she was here," Linnea said. "Do you have older records in some other place? She's at least thirty years old now."

The director shook her head. Her assistant, a tall and thin young woman, burst into the room. "Director Lu, is there anything I can do to help?"

Mari smiled triumphantly and Linnea knew her sister thought they might have a chance with someone else present. Linnea was glad to have an interruption to break the awkwardness in the room. The assistant at least looked friendly.

"You can show this couple to the door. I don't have the information they seek."

Sky stood and approached the director. "Director Lu, perhaps we can come to an understanding. We are not saying *you* did anything wrong. This all happened before you took the position here. Director Long was in charge and a girl was mistakenly given up. Her family didn't know what happened to her but they would like to find her."

The director stood with her finger to her mouth, apparently thinking over Sky's request.

Linnea also stood and joined Mari closer to the desk. "And I can promise there won't be any publicity, Director Lu. We only want to meet her and let her know that if she is interested, we'd like to reunite her with her ailing parents. Her father has tuberculosis and his dying wish is to see his daughter." Linnea saw Sky cringe out of the corner of her eye. She ignored him; she'd do whatever it took to find Dahlia.

As she waited, she looked from the director to the assistant. In the younger woman's eyes she saw a hint of compassion and she waited to see if that same spark would transfer to her boss.

Her hopes were dashed when the director pointed at the door. "Sorry, I have no information to help you. My assistant will show you out."

The assistant came around and beckoned for Linnea and Sky to follow her. Linnea felt deflated. They'd come all this way and learned nothing. She thought about Nai Nai and how disappointed she would be. She and Sky stood and reluctantly followed the younger woman out of the office and down the long hall. At the double doors the assistant stepped outside and when they joined her, she shut the door behind them.

"I can tell you where the old director used to live but I don't know if she has passed or not. She was very old and last year I heard she was bedridden." She nervously looked behind them at the door as she whispered.

Mari smiled broadly and threw her arms around the young woman. "Oh, thank you!"

Linnea felt her hopes soar. "Really? You know where she lives?"

"I know where she *lived*. As I said, she may be dead by now. She has a reputation around here as being the most wicked director to have ever retired. Fate may have caught up with her."

"Just tell us what you know," Sky said, putting his arm around Linnea.

"She lived on Liulichang Street, what was once the known academic area of Beijing." She opened the door and stepped through, then turned back one more time. "That is all I can tell you. But my heart has been burdened for these children here for so many years. I do what I can to place them with local families. I do hope even one lost girl can be reunited with her parents and perhaps find peace. Good luck."

Before Linnea could tell her how much she appreciated her kindness, the assistant turned and was gone; only the sound of her heels clicking on the shiny ceramic tiles could be heard as she disappeared down the hall. Linnea had the feeling that she'd just met one of the children's more loving guardian angels.

She smiled victoriously at Mari, then Sky. "All is not lost. We have another lead."

Together they headed to the main road to hail another taxi.

Chapter Twenty-Three

After a long ride to the area of Beijing near the Forbidden City, Linnea and Sky walked down the tight alley the driver pointed out and found themselves on a main street of what appeared to be a tourist area for shopping. All around were various bookstores, supply stores, and trinkets stacked on tables for sale. Old scrolls—which were probably reproductions, Linnea thought—were leaned up against the walls lining the sidewalks. Around them shoppers strolled along at a leisurely pace, taking their time to window-shop as well as stop at the various stands to bicker over prices.

"This can't be right," Sky said, looking around. "This is a shopping area."

"I'm sorry, I'm not familiar with this area. I never have time for just exploring," Mari said.

"Hmmm, well maybe we can ask one of the shopkeepers where the residential area is." Linnea began walking.

A small man sat smoking outside a shop that by the looks of the shelves in the store behind him, sold signature chops. Linnea was pleased to know that she finally had her own chop—for in China to be a business owner, a personalized name chop was imperative to approve transactions or any contract. The day Linnea had chopped her name in the bright red ink on the top of her first agreement with the screen printer, she'd felt like a real adult for the first time.

"Excuse me, sir. Can you tell me where the residential area is around here?" She stopped right in front of him.

He squatted on a small stool, his knobby knees poking high into the air. He squinted up at her through the bifocals perched on the end of his nose. He was a tiny man, shriveled from age and at least eighty years old, so the loud, brash tone of his voice from such a little body took Linnea by surprise. "What residential area? The houses and shops are all mixed in together now. Have been for years, young lady. Who you looking for? Someone who owns a shop? If so, they probably live over the top of it."

Linnea shook her head. "No, I don't believe she owns a shop. I'm looking for Long Ni Xi. Do you know her?"

"She's an old woman who used to work at the children's welfare center," Sky added.

The old man smiled widely, showing gaps where various teeth had taken flight over the years. He nodded his head up and down. "Of course I know Lao Long. She's my sister-in-law—but her husband, my brother, is long dead."

"Great! Where is she?" Mari asked.

Linnea felt a surge of renewed hope. She couldn't believe their luck that the first person they'd run into was related to the old woman, and even luckier was that the woman was still living. Someone—or something—was definitely looking out for them.

The old man pointed down the street. "Why didn't you say so? She lives in the *hutong* behind this line of shops. Go to the end of this road and turn left. Her house is in the next alley. Her granddaughter should be there with her. She can help you talk to Ni Xi."

Linnea looked at Sky and they both raised their eyebrows at each other. So there *was* a separate residential area. The old man must be a bit senile. And she didn't know why they might need help talking to the woman but they'd just have to see.

"Come on, you two. We need to hurry. I've got to be heading home soon. Bolin will be expecting his dinner."

"Xie xie." Linnea thanked the man and they began walking down the busy street. Mari led, staying a few feet ahead of them. A half block or so later, Linnea stopped at a table outside of a bookstore and picked up a copy of Mao's *Little Red Book.* She'd seen many like it over the years, especially since she'd begun treasure hunting to stock her own store, but this was one of the most authentic-looking ones she'd seen.

"You need a lesson in Mao directives?" Sky asked, jabbing her playfully in the side.

Linnea definitely didn't need to learn the words inside. With her own generation of stubborn personalities, it was hard to believe that during the Cultural Revolution, the book was owned and cherished by most every Chinese person. To prove their loyalty, the Chinese memorized—and even believed—all of Mao's words. It still amazed her how so many were fooled by one man and how many thousands of the people who revered him eventually lost their lives early because of his delusions. His vision of a new China not only turned people against their own in an attempt to save themselves, but many families still struggled to overcome the damage done decades ago to their legacies. For Linnea and other lovers of old things, one of the biggest tragedies were his orders to rid the country of antiques and cultural relics. So much history had been wiped out with the command of a few words.

"No, not really. But this book looks really old. I wonder if it's a real antique." The book, unlike others she'd seen in cheap red plastic, was covered in dark red leather. Engraved on the front, it read *Quotations from Chairman Mao Tse Tung.*

She flipped it open and read the characters scrawled inside the cover. *Quotations from Chairman Mao Tse-Tung, first edition 1966.* She closed the book and turned it over in her hands. On the back cover it read *Long Live the Victory of Mao Tse Tung's Thought.*

"Sky, I think this one is real and not a reproduction."

A woman came out of the shop and nodded to Linnea. "You like?"

"How much?" Linnea asked. Even if it turned out to be a fake, her gut told her it wasn't and she usually did well by listening to those inner feelings. She wanted it for her store.

"*Yi bai kuai,*" the woman said.

"One hundred? No way, that's much too expensive." Linnea set the book down and began to walk away. Sky followed.

"You want me to try to get her to go cheaper?" he asked.

Linnea shook her head. "No, she'll call us back. Just wait." Linnea knew with Sky's passive personality, he'd never get a good deal and she'd probably end up paying even more. She wouldn't doubt if with just a few tears the old woman would have Sky handing over all this money.

The woman fell right into Linnea's plan. "Come back! I'll give it cheaper!" she called, her voice taking on a tone of desperation.

Linnea stopped and turned halfway around. She made a look of irritation cross her face. "How much cheaper?"

"You say!" the woman called, waving at her to come back.

Mari nudged her. "You might as well go back and get it. Otherwise you'll be sad you didn't."

Linnea sighed dramatically and began to walk back. She hated the game playing of bartering but knew it had to be done. At the table she picked up the book again, looked at it briefly, and then set it down.

"I don't know. It's kind of worn out. Maybe thirty is all I can go." She looked at the woman, raising her eyebrows. The ball was now in her court. She could take it or leave it, though Linnea hoped it was the end of the exchange.

The woman shook her head. "No, no. Much too cheap. Fifty yuan. Last price." She crossed her arms stubbornly over her chest. Sky joined her.

Linnea smiled. "Okay. Fifty." She pulled the money from her bag and handed it over, then picked up the book and dropped it into the opening. *"Xie xie."*

Sky linked his arm through hers. "Come on, Linnea. Stop bullying the shopkeepers."

She grinned. If she was right and the book was an original, it would be worth far more than fifty yuan. She looked around at the other items peppering the tables and windows and wished she had more time to browse. Sky pulled her and they jogged to catch up to Mari.

At the end of the street, just like the old man had said, they saw the mouth of an alley. They turned down it and found themselves in a tight passage that ran behind the line of stores, separating the businesses from very old dwellings. Linnea felt like she'd been dropped down right in the middle of old China and was captivated by the scene. The houses were made of concrete with row upon row of red curved handmade tiles on the roofs. Each place had a courtyard like hers at home, but these were even smaller. It was evident that the living space had been taken up to make room to build more businesses. Even so, the chickens and small children running around, the colorful clothing swaying on lines in the breeze, and the smells of garlic and onions cooking showed them that the area was still well populated and fighting against the revolution of change as hard as it could.

She bumped Sky in the ribs. "Look at this, Sky! It's hard to imagine that just on the other side of those buildings is such a busy shopping place. This looks like a page out of an old history book."

"You should see one of the old villages close to the Great Wall, Linnea. I wish you could stay longer—I'd show you a lot that you'd find intriguing."

Linnea wished she could, too. History had always been something that fascinated her. But this time she just couldn't linger. Maybe she would have time to come back when they found Dahlia.

They passed a few courtyards before they saw a woman bent over a large wooden bucket, scrubbing her clothes the old-fashioned way, on a washboard. When the woman paused to push the sweaty hair out of her eyes, Linnea interrupted.

"Excuse me. Do you know which house Lao Long lives at?"

The woman was clearly out of breath from her strenuous scouring but she pointed down the lane. "The house with the big tree in the front yard." She went back to work.

They moved along and saw the house with the tree. The branches of the walnut tree were heavy with unpicked walnuts. The house behind it was dark and quiet. They slipped through the gate and went to the door. Linnea knocked.

A young woman at least twice Linnea's age answered. As she propped open the wooden door with her hip, she held a half-empty bowl of congee and a towel lay draped over her arm. She wasn't unfriendly but her tired face told a tale that she wasn't exactly thrilled to have company.

"I'm sorry if we caught you at a bad time," Linnea said, "but is this the house that Long Ni Xi lives at?"

Her curious look turned suspicious. The woman nodded. "Yes, that's my grandmother. I was just feeding her lunch. What do you want with her?"

Linnea and Mari both looked at Sky. This seemed like another moment for his charisma to come in handy.

He returned their look and then seemed to understand. He stepped forward. "*Ni hao*. My name is Sky and we're from Wuxi. Is your grandmother the Long who used to be a director at the local children's home?"

A shadow crossed the face of the woman and she hesitated for a moment. "Yes, that is her. Why?"

Linnea got so excited that she started to answer but Sky put his hand on her arm to stop her. "We have a few questions for her, nothing official, mind you. What did you say your name was?"

Linnea could see he was definitely turning on his charm and she let him go for it.

The woman blushed. "I'm Long Mei Xi. My grandmother is Long Ni Xi. Come in, but I can't promise you she will feel like talking today."

She opened the door wider for them to come in and they entered. They all slipped off their shoes and stepped forward to stand on the plush rug.

It took a moment for Linnea's eyes to adjust to the dim lighting, but when they did, she saw that what looked like a modest home on the outside surprisingly held many expensive furnishings. Amidst the tall vases, lamps, and artwork, an old woman sat up in bed, a bib tucked around her neck. By the sagging look of one side of her face, Linnea knew immediately they might not find out what had happened to Dahlia.

Mei Xi beckoned for Linnea, Sky, and Mari to sit, and they sat around the ceramic table, opposite the old iron bed that held Lao Long. The girl settled down on a stool next to her grandmother.

"I've got to finish feeding her and then we can talk." As she spooned the congee into the woman's mouth and wiped away the streams of it that dribbled out the one side, Long looked at Linnea with an unrelenting stare. Linnea felt uncomfortable, as if they were intruding on a private moment of shame.

"Is she well?" She didn't know quite how to ask what was wrong with the old woman.

Mei Xi nodded. "She's as well as can be expected. She suffered a few small strokes last year but then a few months ago a big one hit her. Her motor skills have suffered but she can understand what's going on around her. She's still as sharp as a tack, and can be a handful. Right, Nai Nai?"

The old woman grunted her answer and with that Linnea was worried. If she couldn't talk, how would they find out what happened to Dahlia?

"Can she speak?" Mari blurted out exactly what Linnea was thinking.

Mei Xi nodded. "She can, but I'm usually the only one who can understand her. I came to live with her full-time after the last stroke." She finished feeding her the remaining congee and wiped her grandmother's face gently. She tucked the cloth into the woman's gnarled hand, then stood and went to the kitchen cove and set the bowl down in the sink. She washed her hands and then turned to them.

"Would you like some tea?" She didn't wait on an answer; instead she opened a cupboard and pulled out three small cups. She filled them with tea from the kettle on the stove and brought them over to the table. Then she returned to the kitchen and plucked an orange from a heaping bowl on the counter. Quickly she sliced it and arranged the pieces on a small plate. She brought the plate over and set it down, then took a seat opposite Linnea.

"Thank you, Mei Xi," Linnea said. "Your home is very nice."

She looked around at the different items. A small cot was arranged on the wall next to the old woman and Linnea assumed it was where Mei Xi slept. Mari nudged her and pointed to a chest that looked antique—and expensive.

"Yes, most of these things were given to my Nai Nai while she worked in the welfare institute. She didn't make much money but over the years many of the items she acquired have paid the bills. Selling one thing at a time has kept us going."

"Has she always lived here in Liulichang?" Sky asked.

Mei Xi nodded. "Yes. Years before she worked in the children's home, she owned a store selling calligraphy books and paper. It was located on the street with all the other shops for scholars. During the Cultural Revolution she lost everything when all the stores were shut down. She was lucky to get a position with the welfare department and eventually was made the director. When that time was over and she could've opened her store again, she chose to stay with the orphanage. It was her passion to continue helping homeless children."

Linnea nodded with feigned sympathy. She'd heard enough of the talk about the woman's history. It was time to get to the heart of the matter. She turned on her stool until she was facing the old woman. "Lao Long, we're trying to find my sister who was at the orphanage you directed. Do you remember a woman named Zheng Feiyan?"

The old woman shifted in bed though she didn't move much. She appeared agitated but she forced out an answer. "Noooo."

"I'm sorry. She doesn't know this person," Mei Xi said. "Perhaps the girl was from the other orphanage?"

Linnea shook her head. "No, Zheng Feiyan wasn't my sister. That was the name of the woman who brought her there about thirty years ago." She turned to the old woman again. Before she could stop it, she felt a burst of irritation and her mouth let loose words that she had meant to keep to herself.

"Lao Long, I know my sister Dahlia was in your care and I know that her grandmother paid you to keep her lost in the system. She was never supposed to be there."

Mari spoke. "Her parents wanted her—she wasn't abandoned. She was stolen."

Mei Xi gasped and covered her mouth. "That's horrible! Surely my grandmother knows nothing about that."

Linnea hoped her sister hadn't ruined things. Sky must have thought the same thing, because he kicked her under the table, making Linnea decide to change tactics. She ignored the grand-daughter and instead drummed up a sympathetic smile for the old woman. She softened her tone. "You were only doing what you thought was right but it was wrong. Now her real parents want to know where she is. Please. You can right the wrong by helping us." She fumbled in her purse for the letter from old Zheng. "I have a letter from Dahlia's grandfather. His wife, Feiyan, is dead but he is releasing you from your promise and asking you to help us find Dahlia."

Lao Long began to wave the dish towel in her hand, back and forth, her hand shaking with the effort.

"Nai Nai, what is it?" Mei Xi got up and went to her grand-mother. The old woman struggled to sit up. A solitary tear made its way down her wrinkled cheek.

"Get me my book . . . ," she moaned.

"What book, Nai Nai?" Mei Xi patted her grandmother's shoulder. She turned to Linnea and Sky. "I don't know what's come over her. She hasn't been this agitated since her stroke. I don't know what to do." She fussed around the old woman, pulling the quilt tighter around her, then using her hand to wipe at the tear.

Linnea looked at Mari, her eyebrows raised. She didn't know what to think, but she didn't feel sorry for her, as she knew Long had deliberately kept Dahlia lost in a maze of red tape for years, keeping her from being adopted or finding her family. Mari shrugged her shoulders.

"No, I'm sorry. I didn't mean to upset her," Linnea lied, hoping it didn't mean the end of the conversation. She still hadn't found out anything.

The old woman began saying one word over and over. Linnea couldn't understand her but Mei Xi leaned in and listened. Then she stood up. "Oh, I know what she's talking about. She's kept a book of records. It must be in her chest of things in the outbuilding."

"Book?" Sky asked.

"Yes, she has a book she kept privately with notes about children she knew over the years. I'll be right back." She patted Long on the arm, then crossed the room and left through the back door.

Linnea looked at Sky. Could the book hold the information they needed? She turned to find Long staring at her again. Though the rest of the woman was ancient, her eyes were unwavering and fixed on Linnea as if trying to read her mind. She was quiet now, waiting for her granddaughter, but still Linnea could see she was very unsettled. She didn't know what to say to the woman, so she held her tongue. Obviously Sky felt the same because he didn't utter one word.

The door slammed behind Mei Xi and Lao Long sat straight up in bed and closed her sagging mouth. She suddenly looked at least a decade younger. The strong voice that came from her was even more startling. Gone was the weak stammering and in its place was a strong, bitter voice. "What do you want from me?"

Linnea and Mari were both too dumbfounded to speak at first. Then Linnea remembered what the assistant at the orphanage had said about Long being wicked, and her temper got the better of her again. "What game are you playing, old woman?"

The woman waved her hand in the air dismissively, without a single tremor. "Show me the letter you have if you want an answer. When my granddaughter returns, we won't find that name in the book and I'll go back to being a failing invalid, so you'd best hurry."

Linnea looked at Mari, then Sky with disbelief. "What the . . . ?"

He shook his head with pity. "She's acting so she can keep her granddaughter at her side is what it looks like to me."

Long nodded. "I'm not faking my illness. I did have a stroke and because of it, for the first time in two decades, I'm not left alone with all the ghosts of the children who haunt me. With Mei Xi here, they stay just out of reach but if she leaves, they'll once again be at my bedside. Hurry! The letter."

Linnea pulled the letter from her bag and opened it, then crossed the room. She held the letter out, and Long snatched it and quickly read it.

"I don't know where this girl is and I cannot help you." She dropped the letter on the bedspread, and Linnea picked it up and tucked it back into her purse. She then pulled the last-known photo of Dahlia out of the inside pocket and held it up for the woman to see.

"This is her when she was younger. You sent this photo and others of her to the Zheng family in Shanghai. And I think you know where she is, and if you don't tell us, I'm going to tell your granddaughter what an amazing actress you are." She crossed her arms over her chest and gave the woman her most stubborn look. Then she looked around at the many expensive trinkets in the room and waved her hand in the air. "How do all these useless items of wealth make you feel now? Do they take away your sense of responsibility for ruined lives?"

Sky joined her at the bed. "Now, Linnea, let's all just calm down here. No need to cause more misery for Lao Long. I think her guilt is burden enough."

"Coming from someone who knew his own parents and was never at the mercy of people like this," Mari whispered.

Sky's face fell.

Long turned her stare to Sky. "I speak the truth. There are a lot of children whose faces I cannot remember, but for those who were in and out of my institute until they aged out and took to the streets to make their own way, I know who they are. That girl— she was one of my most troubled. She would not accept her fate graciously. She went back and forth to many homes."

Linnea felt her temper flaring. "Graciously? You speak of her accepting her fate graciously? What if her fate was to stay with her parents and she was robbed of it by two selfish old women? She *had* a home. But it was taken from her!"

"Despicable," Mari added.

Sky put his hand on Linnea's wrist, urging her to calm down. "Lao Long, if you want us to go away, tell us what you know."

Long stared at Sky for a moment. "Then you will leave immediately? Before Mei Xi returns? I do not want her to know about this. She only knows of the families I helped build through adoption."

"What about the ones you wrecked to pad your pockets?" Linnea couldn't help herself.

The old woman shot her a look of contempt. "Not everything I did was wrong. Mei Xi's not even my real granddaughter.

200

I gave her to my son when she was just a baby left on the side of a street with no one to claim her. She only spent a week in the orphanage before I gave her a home. I gave her an identity when she had none."

"Oh, so now she owes you, right?" Mari asked, shaking her head in disgust.

Linnea was shocked at that confession and infuriated at the flippant way the woman claimed to have *given* a child, as if she owned the baby! But her admission meant that Mei Xi was also one of the lost girls of China and probably didn't know her true beginnings, either. She wondered just how much the young woman did know.

Sky nodded. "That was a noble gesture, Lao Long. And yes, we will leave immediately if you can just direct us where to find Dahlia."

With the salve of Sky's soft tone, an expression of resignation came over the woman. "I can only tell you that the last place she was officially placed was a home in Suzhou. But the foster mother woke up to find her gone one morning. She thinks she may have worked the girl too hard. After that she wasn't heard from again."

Linnea frowned deeply. "Never? How old was she?" To know that Dahlia had lived in Suzhou, only a mere fifty or so miles from her own parents in Wuxi was mind-boggling. So close yet too many miles apart.

Long's brow crinkled in concentration. "I don't know. Maybe sixteen, seventeen—something like that. It was time for her to age out of the system anyway. I didn't bother trying to find her. I had my hands full of enough unwanted children to bother tracking down one more."

"And you have no idea where she went?" Mari asked.

The old woman shook her head.

Linnea didn't want to say another word to her. She saw nothing but pure meanness coming from her eyes. Long would never feel remorse for her part in Dahlia's story, so why even bother? For a second she thought about waiting and telling Mei Xi all that she knew, but then realized it wouldn't help her find Dahlia and might bring the young woman a world of grief to know the truth about where she came from. She quickly decided it wasn't her place to turn another's world upside down.

"Come on, Mari. Sky, we need to get back to the train station and on to Suzhou."

Linnea nodded and continued moving. Sky picked up their bags and followed her to the door. "I don't want you to get your hopes up, Linnea. Suzhou is what they call a big small city. How can we ever pick up her trail?"

Linnea had thought of that and she knew it was a long shot. "Trust me, Sky. I'm not ready to give up yet. Let's go straight to the train station and get our tickets to Suzhou. Then I'll call Nai Nai and tell her what we've found."

"Are you sure you don't want to camp out at my house tonight—get some sleep?" Mari asked, following them out the door. "You know that Mama will have my hide if I don't at least feed you before you leave."

"No, Mari. We need to move on. But thank you so much for coming with us. It's been so good to see you today." She stopped and hugged her sister. Linnea wished she lived closer.

Mari stood back and smiled. "Look at you, Linnea, acting all grown-up all of a sudden."

Sky sighed and Linnea could tell by the slump of his shoulders that he was already tired.

"It's not all of a sudden, Mari. I've been grown-up—you just aren't around. But we can sleep on the train and won't waste any time." She reached out and touched Sky on the shoulder. "I really appreciate you being here with me, Sky. It means a lot."

He gave her a quick smile and picked up the pace, leading them out of the woman's neighborhood.

"Yes, Sky, thank you for looking out for my little sister. She needs someone to keep her out of trouble, that's for sure."

Linnea thought of Jet and then shook her head to clear the thoughts from her mind. She needed to get over him and move on. If he couldn't be honest with her, then he wasn't who she had thought he was. Even so, she still couldn't shake the longing to hear his voice or feel his touch. But with time she knew he'd just be someone she used to know. She'd have a full life even without him, or at least that was what she'd continue to tell herself.

They finally got to the street and a taxi pulled to the curb. "You take this one, Linnea. And please give Mama and Baba a hug from me."

Linnea hugged her one more time. She thought it was interesting that the difference in their ages had given them different names for the couple who'd acted as parents to both Linnea and Mari. But back then, when Mari was taken in, Nai Nai and Ye Ye were young enough to be called parents. Now, they were elderly. The years were moving too fast for them and that thought made Linnea want to try that much harder to find their biological daughter before it was too late.

As she walked away, Linnea looked over her shoulder one last time at Mari and thought her sister looked sad—a tiny colorful waif in the crowd waving at her.

Chapter Twenty-Four

Calli unlocked the door to the store and herded the girls through. It had only been two days since the story in the newspaper, and already Linnea's sales were through the roof and they needed to prepare for a busy Saturday. At the rate they were going, Linnea was going to need to get busy with more designs for her shirts.

She'd thought about hanging a poster outside that said **Designer Linnea will return next week.** She couldn't count how many customers had asked to meet Linnea and you'd think her daughter was a celebrity! Calli felt just a little guilty that so far she'd kept the good news about the article from Linnea on their few phone calls, but she knew her daughter and how uptight she'd be about not being able to be there to supervise. Calli could handle it—she was sure of it. She hoped that when Linnea got home and saw how much profit she'd made, all the secrecy would be forgotten. She pushed away a nagging truth that just maybe she was afraid that Linnea would come back too early, before she'd found news of Dahlia.

"Ivy and Lily, you girls unpack and set up the new shipment of shirts. Peony, I need your little hands to be wrapped around the broom handle." The girls immediately obeyed, and Calli said another thanks under her breath that the screen printer was able to finish and overnight the shirts to them.

Turning around and holding the door open with her backside, she pulled Maggi's chair over the door frame and into the shop. "Maggi, I need you to get the register ready. Here's the money bag."

She pulled the bag out of her deep apron pocket and handed it to Maggi. Only the day before Benfu had come in and built a shorter counter to put the cash register on so that Maggi could reach it. At only nine years old, she'd proved to be very good with ringing out the customers and was perfect as a final friendly touch as they went out the door. All of them instantly fell for the girl's sweet smile and charm, and her efficiency despite her disability. Calli could already foresee many returning customers due in a big part to their interaction with Maggi.

When Maggi began wheeling herself to go behind the counter, Calli shut the door and locked it. They had only an hour to get everything in tip-top shape. Thank goodness Benfu had offered to keep Poppy and Jasmine home with him today. He'd told her the night before they were going to spend the day putting in a tiny garden of vegetables. Calli knew Jasmine was excited about that, as she loved anything to do with nature and the dirt. Poppy was going to be more of a handful than Benfu realized, but she'd told him to set up the playpen in the courtyard and that should entertain her for a while until her afternoon nap.

Calli walked around the store, straightening everything and dusting where needed. She'd told Linnea that to stand out from the other shops on the street, hers needed to be super clean. A neat store with good merchandise would make customers want to return. In front of the window display she stopped to pick up one of Sky's scarves that had fallen off the line. She looked out and saw Jet at the corner, then hurried to the door.

She opened it and poked her head out. "Jet! *Ni hao.*"

He turned and waved, then walked toward her.

"Hello, Lao Calli. How are you this morning?" He crossed the busy street and stood in front of the store, his hands in his pockets. Calli's heart faltered at the look of rejection on his face.

"Come in, Jet, come in. Were you coming by here? What brings you to this side of town?" She held the door open wider for him. She also hadn't told him of the article, since she and Benfu wanted to be the ones to deliver the news. And as far as she knew, Linnea hadn't told him the real reason she was going out of town.

Jet stepped in and as soon as the girls saw him, all work stopped. Peony was on him and wrapped around his legs before a second had passed, her broom forgotten on the floor. More reserved but just as happy, Ivy and Maggi got to him next, with Lily close behind. They hadn't seen him in over a week and, from what Calli could see, had missed him tremendously.

Jet laughed and patted the girls, greeting them and giving each one a small bit of attention. "I had some business to do. I didn't know you all came in this early or I would have stopped by."

Calli could tell he wanted to ask about Linnea but was hesitating, so she beat him to it. "Have you heard from Linnea?"

Jet shook his head, not meeting her eyes. "No, she must really be busy. She hasn't called."

"You should call her, Jet," Peony offered up. "She's stubborn like that."

Jet laughed and Calli smothered a smile. She didn't know what had happened between the two of them but she hoped it didn't last long. They were a good match and she could tell Jet was suffering. The poor boy had probably come all the way across town and walked by, hoping she'd come back already.

"Well, I heard from her for just a minute last night. I think everything is going well and is right on schedule. She should be home in a few days." In truth, Calli didn't know when Linnea would be home. She'd been very stingy with updates and Calli expected her to call this morning.

"Jet, can I play with your cell phone?" Maggi asked.

Jet started to pull out his phone but Calli stopped him. "No, Maggi, you have work to do and I'm sure Jet has some place he needs to be."

Jet slid his hand out of his pocket and held them up apologetically to Maggi.

"Your Nai Nai says no. But I'll see you girls soon, okay? I need to get back across town." He went to the door and opened it, then looked back. "Lao Calli, if you talk to Linnea today, can you please ask her to call me?"

Calli nodded. Young love—she'd been there herself and knew it was hard. She hoped whatever it was Linnea and Jet were going through, it would get settled when Linnea returned. She never liked to see broken hearts and Jet couldn't hide his—it was written all over his face.

"Of course, Jet. I'm sure she's probably been having a hard time getting a signal. You'll probably hear from her today."

Jet waved and was out the door.

Calli picked up the broom and held it toward Peony. "Back to work, girls."

She smiled as they voiced their disappointment at such a short visit from Jet. Calli shook her head. *Linnea better make up her mind about that boy before one of her sisters lays claim to him,* she thought as she went back to dusting.

Chapter Twenty-Five

Linnea and Sky stepped over the doorway of the noodle shop and sat down at a table. After they'd arrived at the train station, they'd gotten a taxi into town and now had been walking the streets of Suzhou for hours. Thus far they'd learned nothing new to help them find Dahlia.

"Do your feet hurt as bad as mine?" she asked Sky as she propped them up in the empty chair opposite her.

He sat up straight. "I'm okay. Just disappointed that we've spent all day here and haven't found out anything. I think it's time you called your Nai Nai."

Linnea sighed. She wanted to wait until she had good news. But the truth was that looking for a girl in a city the size of Suzhou was next to impossible. No one would talk to them. They'd spent four hours at the government building, only to be asked to leave. They'd been treated as if they were nobodies and it stung. Next they'd tried the silk market, asking the old shopkeepers questions, but they'd hit nothing but dead ends.

She took her phone out of her bag and flipped it open. Three missed calls from Jet. In the noise and chaos of the city, she hadn't heard it ring.

"What is it, Linnea?" Sky asked. "You sure are frowning at that phone."

"Nothing." She shut it quickly.

A waiter in a soiled white apron came and took their order and brought them water. Linnea sipped at hers and stared out the window at the people hurrying by. She wondered what Jet had to say. This was the first that he'd even tried to call her. What had he been up to that he was so busy?

"Linnea." Sky got her attention and she retreated from her daydreams.

He reached across and took her hand. "I can see that your heart is still very troubled. Why don't you just call him? It would help to bring you some peace."

Linnea shook her head stubbornly. She wished Sky would stop with his peace talks. "He needs to call *me*. I did nothing wrong."

"But he did call you, right? Isn't that what you were looking at?"

He had a point there. Linnea realized that maybe she was acting immature. She never even gave him a chance to defend himself. He didn't even know what she was mad about! She needed to call him.

"Do you mind if I step out for a minute?" She looked at Sky, smiling at him to show her appreciation. He really was a good friend, even if he was a little weird with all his talk about life and peace.

Sky stood. "No, you sit right there. It's too noisy outside for you to talk. I'll go to the table over there. You join me when you are ready."

He patted her shoulder as he picked up his backpack and walked away. Linnea opened her phone again and dialed Jet.

He picked up before the first ring stopped. "Lin? Where are you? Why haven't you called? I miss you."

Linnea melted.

Then she pulled herself together. "I'm in Suzhou. And it's a long story, but if you want to hear it, I've got time to tell it."

She heard dead silence on the other end for a moment. Then he returned.

"Okay. I've just shut my office door and I'm all yours as long as you need me. Can I just say one more time, I've missed you so much, Lin. When are you coming back?"

Linnea smiled. For some reason her anger at him was buried by the complete comfort his voice gave her. They may still never have their relationship back but in this moment, she needed his confident composure. And his advice. She leaned back in her chair and started talking. Across the room Sky got her attention and gave her a thumbs-up. She winked at him and kept up the chatter.

An hour later Linnea and Sky sat at the entrance to the Humble Administrator's Garden. Jet was due any moment. During their phone conversation, he had convinced Linnea that she didn't need to take a bus or the train home; he wanted to come get her immediately. Linnea had to admit that riding home in Jet's car would be much preferable to another trip on public transportation.

It hadn't been easy but Linnea had spilled everything on the phone to Jet. He'd been shocked to hear all about Dahlia and even more surprised that Linnea had kept it from him. She could tell he was hurt, and they still hadn't discussed why Sky had taken his place on the trip, but Linnea decided she wasn't going to let her pride get in the way of finding Dahlia. And if anyone had the connections to make it happen, it was more likely to be Jet and his father than her, just a girl from the wrong side of town.

Beside her Sky picked at his nails. He had smiled his approval at her when she told her Jet was coming. "Now maybe you two can put the negative feelings aside and go back to the peaceful and loving relationship you had before."

Linnea knew Sky was disappointed that they hadn't been able to find Dahlia but they both agreed that using Jet's family's influence might make more headway. Still, she hoped she hadn't hurt his feelings.

"Sky, are you okay?"

He looked up and smiled. "I'm fine, Linnea. And it'll be nice to sleep in my own bed tonight. I know my mother has missed me—though I doubt my grandfather even realized I was gone."

Linnea laughed. "I'll bet he did. He cares about you more than he shows, Sky. I've seen the way he looks at you with pride. He just doesn't want you to know it."

"Yeah, he's still punishing me for refusing a college education and the pursuit of the Chinese dream of becoming a businessman."

"I don't think so. He's probably glad you are your own man. At least you got a chance to take the entrance exams and pass them, even if you did turn down their acceptance letter."

Sky didn't get to answer as they were interrupted by Jet as he swerved his black sedan to the edge of the sidewalk. He turned off the car and hopped out. Linnea's heart did a little flip-flop at seeing his face.

She composed herself and bent to get her backpack. She lifted it and was almost barreled over when Jet enveloped her in a huge hug.

"Oh man, I've missed you," he whispered in her ear, and she heard him inhale the scent of her hair. She knew it couldn't smell very good after all the time she'd spent traveling but the groan he gave begged to differ.

"Break it up, you two," Sky said. He knocked on the trunk of the car to get Jet's attention. Jet hit his key fob and the lid slowly opened. Sky threw his bag in, then came and took Linnea's and added hers. He shut the trunk.

"Ready?" Jet asked, standing back to look at Linnea as if he hadn't seen her in years.

Linnea was glad for the warm welcome but she could feel her cheeks burning. She wasn't used to such displays in front of everyone else. She looked at Sky, and he rolled his eyes and smiled slightly, then climbed into the car.

"I suppose I've got the backseat to myself," he muttered as Jet opened the door to the front passenger seat for Linnea.

Jet crossed in front of the car and got in. He smiled at Linnea as he clicked his seat belt across his lap. "I stopped by the store and told Lao Calli I was coming after you. She can't wait to see you and wants me to bring you straight there."

"Jet! I'm so tired and dirty. I wanted to go home first," she whined.

He winked at her. "Believe me; you'll want to see what she's been up to. It'll only take a few minutes and then I'll take you home."

He put the car in drive and took off, leaving black marks behind him.

Calli finished washing Poppy off in the sink, then handed her off to Ivy. "Get her dressed and then rock her to sleep. Ye Ye and I are going to take a walk."

"Okay, Nai Nai." Ivy snuggled the little wet bundle all the way to the bed where her clothes were laid out.

Benfu stood up and put on his sweater, then joined Calli at the door. "You girls be good and settle down. When we get back, it's time to go to sleep."

Calli nodded in agreement. It had been a huge day. With only two hours' notice from Jet, they'd pulled together a party to welcome Linnea back as a celebrity. Now she was with Jet but Calli could still remember her expression when she'd gotten out of the car in front of the store. There Linnea had found a line of people waiting for her to autograph shirts they'd just bought. Calli and Benfu had presented the framed article to her and told her how proud they were. Linnea looked like she was in shock the entire time—though it was a happy shock when she found out how much business Calli had done in her absence.

Jet had finally taken Calli aside and told her his ideas on how to find Dahlia in Suzhou. Now was the hard part; confessing to Benfu that she'd been harboring a secret from him. But now she needed him. She needed his strength.

"Benfu, I wanted to talk to you alone." She grabbed his hand as they strolled down the alley of the *hutong*. She looked around one last time but knew Ivy and Lily would watch over the others. Linnea was still with Jet. He had told Calli before they left that he had a surprise for Linnea and wouldn't have her home for a few hours.

"What do you want to talk about?" He turned to her, sensing she was upset.

"I've kept a secret from you. The first one ever." Now that she'd said it, she realized she was wrong to have done it and wished she could take it back. She reached in and felt the security of the envelope of photos.

Benfu chuckled. "What secret, Calla Lily? Have you been skirting around with another gent in the neighborhood? Tell me, is it Lao Yang who has caught your eye? You know, don't you, that he keeps a ready handful of concubines in his cellar?"

Calli led him to the bench at the end of the lane. They sat down.

"Benfu, I'm serious. I can only tell you I regret it and I thought it was for your own good, but I've news of Dahlia."

She felt him freeze beside her. They never talked of Dahlia; it was much too painful. For years each had kept their grief silently to themselves.

"What do you mean, news?" he finally asked without looking at her.

Calli reached into her pocket and pulled out the envelope. "It's a long story but first you have to see something. Let me start with saying Dahlia is alive." She handed him the envelope and watched as he opened it and pulled out the stack of photos. In only a moment she could see he knew it was her.

She'd rarely ever seen him cry, maybe only twice in their entire lifetime together. The first time was when he was finally able to tell her why he'd run from his commune and the terrible things they'd done to him there. The second was when he realized that their moment of happiness as new parents had been yanked away by the selfishness of another. But now to see his daughter's face and know she was alive out there somewhere had broken the reserve, and the tears rolled down his face, some sliding off the tip of his old nose before he could rub them away.

"Benfu, she is quite beautiful, isn't she?" she said softly.

He nodded silently but he wouldn't look up. The tears dropped onto the surface of the photo he held in his hand and his chin quivered as he fought to maintain control.

Calli reached over and put her hand on his knee. "And she looks like you. Those are your eyes, no doubt about that."

He nodded again and Calli swallowed hard, trying to dislodge the lump in her throat. She put her arm around his shoulders. Oh how they had waited for this moment—for some news about their daughter. For years they'd obsessed over it. Then the girls started coming and they had been able to move on in life, but still they had never forgotten Dahlia or stopped hoping.

Finally he cleared his throat and looked at Calli.

"We have to find her," he said. He pulled his handkerchief from his pocket and blew his nose.

Calli saw the intense look in his eyes and knew he wouldn't be deterred this time. She hadn't yet touched on the other news, that his father was the reason for the sudden breakthrough, but she'd cover that later when he recovered from seeing Dahlia's face. He was trying to be strong, but she could see that with this evidence that Dahlia had lived after the abduction, just like her, he wouldn't rest until she was found.

She took his hand and held it to her heart. "There's more. We're very close to finding her. And I have a plan to make it happen. Benfu, we *are* going to find our daughter."

With those words her husband of the last thirty-some years lost control and the sobs tore from him, causing pedestrians to look curiously their way. Calli didn't care; she shooed them away. Together she and Benfu let go of thirty years of grief as they grabbed on to the first piece of hope they'd been given.

"So now that you're selling so many shirts, what's the next step?" Jet asked, leaning across the counter toward Linnea.

Linnea raised her hands and shrugged her shoulders. "I've got to mock up some new designs while the fad is hot. I sketched a few things on our trip. I just need to go downtown and get them scanned in and e-mailed to my screen printer."

Everyone else had gone home and she'd made up her mind that she was going to get a few things off her chest with him, whether she wanted to or not. She couldn't continue wondering about him and the girl. And she'd acknowledged to herself that it wasn't fair to punish Jet for something when she hadn't been mature enough to tell him what it was. But so far she hadn't found a good way to approach it, so here they were making small talk again.

Jet nodded. "Wouldn't it be nice if you didn't have to keep running around to copy, scan, or e-mail?"

"Yes, but that step will not happen until I pay off everything I owe from the start-up of Vintage Muse. I don't want to rack up more debt than I can juggle."

"And what about your idea of renting your own place?" he asked.

Linnea had to give him that—he was persistent. She was glad he was interested in her future but she wanted to get the topic back to them. This was her chance and she wasn't going to let it go this time.

"Jet, we can talk about all that later, but first there's something I wanted to ask you. Can we go sit outside?"

She came around the counter and grabbed her bag and keys. She led Jet out the door and locked it behind her.

"I'll go ahead and lock up—then I can head home in a minute. Nai Nai will be wondering what took me so long."

They sat at the table outside the store and Linnea propped her bag between her feet. She looked up to find Jet leaning back comfortably, staring as if she were the most amazing thing he'd ever seen.

"Lin, I can't tell you how much I missed you while you were gone." He reached over and took one of her hands and brought it up to his mouth, putting his lips on it.

Linnea ignored the streak of pleasure that traveled up her arm and gently pulled her hand away. This was important and he wasn't going to divert her attention.

"I'm sure you weren't *too* lonely," she said, then watched his expression closely.

"What do you mean?" he asked, looking confused.

"Jet, remember the day we met here and I told you I was taking the trip to Beijing?"

He nodded, still acting completely innocent. Linnea knew she was about to sound like a jealous lover but she didn't care; she had to let him know she wasn't oblivious.

"I saw you across the street with that beautiful girl. And you two were acting like you knew each other quite well."

She watched Jet's face as it went from confusion to understanding, then blushed crimson. Why would he be so embarrassed if it was innocent? And now that he was caught, what would he say?

Linnea suddenly wanted to take it back—now would their relationship just crumble? Was that what she really wanted? No way, she told herself. It wasn't.

"You saw us?" he asked, looking crushed.

Linnea nodded and tears threatened to form. She forced them away.

Jet sighed. "I wanted to wait a little while longer until everything was perfect, but I guess it's time to tell you."

Linnea could feel the heat travel up her chest and neck and fill her face. "You wanted to wait until it was perfect? Are you serious, Jet? Then what—break up with me and be exclusive with her?"

Jet started shaking his head, holding his hands up for her to stop. But it was too late to stop now. She wasn't afraid of crying any longer; she was afraid she was going to take his head off! She stood up and grabbed her backpack, struggling to get her arms through the handles. She pointed her finger at him.

"My Ye Ye asked me if I was sure you weren't just playing around with me until you found someone more suited to your background. And I can't believe I defended you! All along you were playing me while you were seeing some little rich girl!"

Jet stood and grabbed her arm. "No—Lin—you don't understand. Let me explain."

Linnea jerked her arm away and stepped back. "Oh, I understand completely, Jet. You don't need to say another word."

She began to walk down the sidewalk, her head down to avoid the eyes of the curious strangers on the street. She felt miserable—and angry—but mostly just very heavy with sadness.

She was only a few feet away when Jet yelled out.

"Linnea, please don't go. I love you!"

She stopped. He'd never said those words before and neither had she. What should she do? An elderly woman strolling down the sidewalk looked at her and raised her eyebrows, as if she were asking, *So, what are you going to do about that?*

Linnea ignored the woman and debated with herself. She realized she should have at least let him give his explanation. It would probably be lame and not make a difference, but she had to admit, she wanted to hear it. She needed to know for sure who the girl was. She turned around and crossed her arms over her chest.

"You've got five minutes, Jet. Then I'm leaving. Start talking."

He came to her and took her hands. "I don't need to talk. Just let me show you something."

She started to protest and he hushed her, putting his finger to his lips.

"For once, Lin, please just do it my way. After you've seen everything, you'll understand."

"Fine. Just hurry up." She couldn't resist but gave up her struggle to keep his hands off her.

He took her hand again and began leading her around the side of the store, into the alleyway. Linnea was confused. What could he have to show her back there? But she held her tongue and kept her questions to herself.

Jet turned to her and smiled, then guided her toward the metal staircase that led up to the second-floor apartment.

"Jet? Why are we going up there? Is that who rented the apartment? That girl?" Now it was making sense. Jet had met the girl because she was the one renovating the upstairs! Linnea stopped at the base of the stairs, refusing to go any farther.

"No, Linnea! The girl you saw does not live up there. You said you'd give me five minutes. Come on." He pulled her up the stairs and she followed grudgingly. At the top he reached in his pocket and pulled out a set of keys.

"You have keys?" Linnea asked.

He ignored her and fumbled until he found the right key; then he put it in the door and turned the knob. He pushed it open and stepped through, then reached over and switched on the light.

Beyond him the room lit up and Linnea was astonished to see the same apartment she'd remembered as dusty, dark, and cluttered was now crisp, clean, and smelling brand-new. It was gorgeous, painted in a soft cream color and accented with dark wooden pieces of furniture, covered in brown and gold silk fabrics. She looked down and under their feet lay what had to be a real silk carpet covering the floor.

"What is all this, Jet?" She couldn't stop her eyes from roving around the room and noticed a few antique pieces. Even the art was exquisite; one scene of a blushing woman on a fainting couch draped in sheer white cloths was the focal point of one wall. Linnea looked at the opposite wall and gasped when she saw a dozen of her first sketches framed and mounted in two rows—the drawings of the first shirts that had become so popular. She blushed. *They looked so professional up there!*

"This is your new apartment, Lin. The girl you saw me with is my cousin and she's an up-and-coming interior designer. She did all this for us—and only charged for materials. But the photos are going in her portfolio." He swung his arm out in a wide arc.

"*My* apartment? What do you mean, mine?" Linnea couldn't comprehend what he was saying. She'd never seen such a beautiful place—except for maybe Jet's own home. But how could it be hers? The landlord had already sold it to someone else.

Jet took her hand and pulled her in, then shut the door.

"I was going to wait a few months to show you. We still have some work to do but I bought this place before anyone else swooped in. It's yours."

Linnea felt dizzy. What was he saying? She moved over to the fainting couch and ran her hand along the smooth mahogany frame. She slowly sank down on it. From her new point of view she saw a small cubby on the other side of the room, complete with a computer and a printer and even a classy filing cabinet.

"Jet, I don't understand."

"That's your office, Lin. You won't have to run downtown for everything now. I want you to stay away from the buses. You need the convenience of living close to your work." He pointed at the other side of the room. "Over there you can take a break and watch television. I haven't bought a TV yet—I was waiting for that. But look at the chair."

Linnea looked and couldn't believe her eyes. It was Lau's antique Mao chair that she loved so much. It sat in the corner and around it, hung artfully on the walls, were vintage movie posters. Linnea recognized Greta Garbo and even a poster from the famous *Gone with the Wind*. "But how?"

"Sky knew what I was doing and he even helped a bit. He's got a lot of style for a guy. His grandfather wanted you to have the chair. He said you were his fiercest opponent in *xiangqi* and you deserved a trophy of some sort."

Linnea smiled. She couldn't believe the old man had given her the chair he had kept safe for so many years. She was touched.

"Jet. This is beautiful, it really is. But I can't take this. It would be weird—like I was your mistress or something."

Jet crossed the room quickly and sat beside her.

"Linnea, don't be ridiculous. I don't want you for my mistress. I want you for my wife."

With those words her mouth dropped open and for the first time ever, she was speechless. Jet laughed at her expression and held his hands up.

"Whoa. I don't mean right *now*. And I was going to have a ring ready for this conversation, but you sort of forced my hand, Linnea."

"I—I—don't know what you mean," she stuttered.

"What I mean is what I said outside. I love you and want to spend the rest of my life with you. I would move in with you today but I know your Ye Ye would throttle me. So, for now, you can live here and if you feel you have to because of your stubborn streak, you can pay a little rent. Then when you're ready and we've made it official, we can move in together."

All Linnea could do was shake her head.

"There's another room I want you to see." He pulled her up and led her past the tiny kitchen and down the short hall. He opened the door and Linnea gasped. She was acting like a giddy schoolgirl and though she didn't want to, she couldn't help it.

Inside was the most gorgeous bedroom she'd ever seen. It had really only two pieces of furniture—but that was all the room needed. Besides an overstuffed chair in the corner next to a table stacked high with books for reading, the room was decorated around an antique Chinese canopy wedding bed.

Linnea knew immediately the piece was one of the few remaining from the Qing dynasty. It was huge and besides the red canopied sleeping area, included an alcove sitting area in the front.

"Jet, this is worth a lot of money." She shook her head in amazement. "I mean, seriously—a *lot* of money."

She crossed the room to get a closer look. She pulled back the delicate silk curtains and peeked inside. It was huge! Looking closer at the wood, she could see the elaborate carvings of garden scenes and birds.

"You said one time you'd never had your own bed. I wanted your first to be one fitting of who you are. This bed has been in my family for decades and my father wanted me to have it. He knows where it is now and agrees. This bed is majestic, proud, and beautiful. It was made for someone like you, Lin."

Linnea truly couldn't find any words to say. She looked at the lush emerald-green silk bedding and piles of pillows and could only imagine how comfortable it was. She turned to Jet and shook her head. He was innocent! And she was an idiot. She felt her face burn with shame.

"You've been very, very sneaky."

He laughed and pushed her back until her knees were against the raised platform holding the mattress. With one more gentle push, she fell on the bed and he joined her. "Want to break it in?"

She playfully hit at him. "No!"

He ignored her and nuzzled her neck. "Mmmm . . . I told you I've missed you, Lin."

Linnea sat up. "Does my family know about this, Jet?"

He shook his head. "Nope. Not a word from me. It's been hard sneaking by them on my way to check on the progress but so far I think I've managed. I didn't know what you'd want to do, and if you turned me down completely, I didn't want to face them."

"Well, tell me this—how did you get this family heirloom away from your mother when she found out it would be something set up for me?" Linnea ran her hand along the silk again, relishing the cool feel of the cover.

"I won't lie—she didn't like it at first. But she's slowly learning to unravel the set plans she had for me and allow me to live my own life. We had a long talk, and she said she's going to try to be easier on me—which means she'll be easier on you. But I don't want to talk about my mother right now, Lin. This is about us, and I want to do this for you. Will you let me?"

"Jet. I don't know what to say." She didn't.

He touched the tip of her nose and traced her profile with his finger, causing more tingles as he touched her lips. "Just say you'll think about it. You could move in here next week if you want to. They only have to finish painting the trim work."

Linnea let herself feel the coziness underneath her and wondered what it would be like to spend every night in a real bed. She wouldn't even let herself think about how it was roomy enough for two—at least. She looked into his eyes and saw the hope there, and she couldn't crush it.

"I just want your life to be easier, Lin."

"Can you give me some time? I need to process all this."

"Absolutely. I'll give you anything—haven't I already proved that?" He leaned in and finally, after weeks of doing without, Linnea allowed his lips to meet hers and she relaxed against him. Maybe she'd spent so much time trying to prove she was more than a scavenger's daughter that she had missed the signs that Jet loved her for who she was. Money, success, looks—all along she'd been thinking she needed all of it to be taken seriously, but now she was wondering if maybe those were just icing on the cake.

She pulled him closer to her, then saw the playful twinkle in his eye. They'd never had a comfortable place to be together and she felt a thrill at the sudden thought of such privacy. As his fingers crept under her blouse, she thought she could get used to such a luxury real quick—she knew that for sure.

Chapter Twenty-Six

Li Jin stared out the window of the bus as the driver careened down the Shanghai expressway and bullied the surrounding cars and trucks to gain prime highway space. Jojo lay sleeping with his head across her lap and his long legs sticking out into the aisle. As the lights of Suzhou had faded behind them earlier, Li Jin felt that same unsettling sense of uncertainty she'd felt before. With only a few clothes to their name—and a decent sum of money, thanks to Erik's stash—they were running again, but at least this time she had a destination in mind. She and Jojo wouldn't be forced to find shelter in the hostels or streets; instead, if everything went as planned, Jing's sister would be waiting for them with a hot meal and a soft bed.

The bus hit a bump and Li Jin was jolted in her seat. She kept her arm wrapped around Jojo's body to keep him from falling forward but he didn't even flinch. Nothing could wake up her son when he was sleeping that soundly. The bus was over-crowded as usual and though Li Jin was already tired of the multitude of strange smells, the incessant chattering of the two old women behind her, and the bumpy ride, she was glad for the feeling of being surrounded.

She felt for her bag with her feet and was relieved it was still there. She wouldn't take the chance of putting it in the overhead with other luggage, instead choosing to keep it in front of her. She moved her head as far to the side as she could without turning around so she could see where the guy was. Just before they'd pulled out of the station, he'd joined the trip and Li Jin couldn't shake the paranoid feeling that he was watching her. When he'd stepped up on the bus and looked for a vacant seat, Li Jin immediately sensed danger. At least twenty-five or so, he wore his pants low and baggy like the gang boys. The black bandana tied around his head only added to his rebellious look. With a small bag draped over his shoulder and an iPod in his hand, he'd swaggered down the aisle and when she had locked eyes with him, his stare bore right through her until she looked away. He'd stopped only a few seats behind hers and without a word, waved at a teen to get out of the way. The teen didn't argue. He picked up his stuff and moved into the seat with another man and gave the gang guy his way. She hoped the ugly stitches holding the gash together on her face would make him stay away.

That made her think of Jing again and Li Jin sighed. Leaving Suzhou behind was a relief like no other, but she wished Jing could have come with them. She'd been such an angel and without her there was no telling where they'd be.

Li Jin knew it wasn't likely but she still couldn't shake the feeling that Erik was after her. She wondered when, if ever, she'd be able to get over her fear of him and his threats to report her to the police for carrying his drugs. But she wasn't stupid. If he pointed the finger at her, then he would be implicated, too. She just hoped he kept his mouth shut so she could make a new life for her and Jojo.

She shifted in the seat to take the pressure from her arm. Jing had done a great job with setting it and despite the original plan for them to leave right away, they'd spent an entire week in her cozy home as she tended to her injuries and Li Jin regained her strength. For a few days even walking was difficult because of the soreness from her beating, but soon with the tender touch of the old woman, Li Jin had felt her instinct to protect her son kick in and she had improved quickly. Jojo was ecstatic when Jing had arranged for her grandson to come visit from Shanghai to keep him company for their last few days, and there were times after a burst of laughter from the boys that Li Jin felt relief that Jing's building and even the interior walls were made from the ancient concrete that would muffle every sound between apartments.

It had amazed Li Jin that the little boy named Fei Fei had been so self-sufficient and got on so well with Jojo, despite being totally blind. As she recuperated, the boys played with cars and even built Lego towers, and never a mention of a disability crossed their lips. Li Jin knew then her son was special, that he could accept someone for what was on the inside instead of judging their outward appearance. Maybe she hadn't done such a bad job as a mother, after all.

Li Jin had tried to leave Jing some money to cover the food and care she had so unselfishly given them, but the old woman had stubbornly refused and told her to save it to rebuild her life. She'd insisted that Jojo call her Nai Nai, and that they come back to visit her one day when the foreign devil had returned to his own country. Jing said she'd keep close watch and keep Li Jin informed if they were lucky enough to see him bid China good-bye. Li Jin felt tears swimming in her eyes as she remembered the firm hug Jing had given her. It was her first from an elderly female and it made Li Jin wonder if that feeling she experienced was what others felt when embracing their mothers. The hug was warm and secure, and Li Jin could have melted into it and stayed forever. She had hated to pull away.

As her eyes got heavier, the memories of years past refused to let her rest. Like a movie, the scenes of the different foster mothers and orphanage nannies she had known scrolled through her mind. Of course she always liked to remember the first family that was kind to her. But along with that memory came the one of the day she was returned to the orphanage.

That was the first time the director told her she wasn't good enough—smart enough or pretty enough—for the family to want to keep her. Over the years she'd heard that plenty more times until she grew old enough to stop caring.

She didn't always want to play the victim and reminded herself that there were good things to remember from her childhood. There were even a few affectionate nannies who passed in and out of the orphanage, on their way to better jobs. Some even took Li Jin under their protective wing during her short visits between homes. But there were also the ones who left scars that would never heal—scars only she knew about because they were on the inside. By the time she'd hit puberty Li Jin had learned what halls to steer away from, what guards to avoid, and which nannies would take their frustration at life out on her. She was considered a long timer, and the other children respected her and came to her for help. They all rooted for her to find a forever family, but it just never happened. No one had ever wanted her. And now, with what would most likely be a horrendous scar slashed across her cheek, no one ever would again.

She leaned her head back against the ratty headrest and let her eyes close. She laid her hand on Jojo's soft head of hair. Life would be different for him. They might not have much, but what he would have was the love and commitment of a mother by his side through thick and thin. He'd feel that sense of protection she'd missed out on. Her son would never have to walk through a long dark hallway with the threat of the unknown chasing him down. She'd see to that if it was the last thing she ever did.

Li Jin stood and leaned against the seat to steady herself from the swaying of the bus, then pulled the matching pillows Jing had sent with them from the luggage rack above their seats. Jojo had wanted something to remember her by and the sweet woman had plucked them right off her couch and pushed them into their arms.

"I embroidered these pillows and something told me I'd be giving them to someone of importance in my life." Jing had pointed to the birds artfully sewn as the main focal point in the center of them. "This is the phoenix and it symbolizes the energy of great strength and resilience. This bird is able to rise from its own ashes to reach greater heights."

Jojo had smiled as he looked down at his pillow and Li Jin had met Jing's eyes over his head. They both knew the message was for her. Jing was encouraging her to be like a phoenix—and that was what she would do. For Jojo.

Li Jin was jarred from her thoughts of Jing by the two elderly ladies behind her. They pointed to the overhead bin and asked her to get their stuff. Awkwardly, Li Jin pulled their bags down, hoping the tape holding the plastic together stayed intact.

"The driver said we'll be there in ten minutes, Jojo! Aren't you excited?" The bus weaved into the fast lane and Li Jin had to grab the seat to keep from falling. With the jarring came more streaks of pain down her arm and to other still-sore places on her body. Strangely, the ladies cackled with delight at her clumsiness, making Li Jin think they led a very limited life. She flashed them a scolding look, then sat back down and stuffed the pillows in front of her feet. She wanted to be ready to be one of the first off when they pulled into the depot.

While she stood, she'd seen Gang Boy in his seat, though she'd pretended not to. Once again he stared at her, a blank expression on his face. Li Jin couldn't quite tell if it was anger or just nonchalance and hoped he didn't get off at the same stop. So far he'd spent his time listening to music or whispering into his mobile phone. As far as Li Jin could tell, he had spoken to no one on the bus.

Trying to shake her paranoid thoughts, she leaned over and kissed Jojo loudly on his eyebrow. He didn't crack a smile. He was hungry and grumpy. The rice cakes Jing had sent were long gone and though they'd stopped at a roadside café earlier, all the passengers had opted to skip breakfast to beat the morning traffic to get farther on their route.

"I want off now, Ma. I need to pee." He jiggled his legs up and down rapidly.

Li Jin ruffled the top of his head. With the hour it took to get to Shanghai and switch buses, they'd been on the road for about six hours, a long time for a kid. "I know you do, Son, just a few more minutes."

"Then where are we going?" he asked. His face was one dark scowl, making him look older than usual.

"Lao Jing's sister is meeting us in Huangshan and she's going to give us a place to stay for a while. Her name is Lao Shuwen."

"But how will she find us? Does she know what we look like?"

"Good question, Jojo. Jing said we'd know her because she'll be the only one holding a bright red balloon to welcome you."

Jojo's eyebrows came together comically. "I'm too old for balloons, Ma."

Li Jin laughed. "I know you are, but just act like you're excited to get it, okay? And it was a good way for us to be able to find each other without our names being posted on a sign."

Jojo nodded and began fidgeting again. Li Jin hoped he could hold it just a few minutes longer.

"After we meet up with Lao Shuwen, she'll take us to our new temporary home." Li Jin was purposely evasive. They wouldn't be staying in Huangshan but instead they'd travel to a nearby village. She didn't want to say it aloud as you never knew who could be listening. She was surprised Jojo hadn't asked more about their destination. She and Jing had discussed most of the plan when he was playing with her grandson, and all they'd told Jojo was they were going to go to a new city and he'd start at another school to make more friends. But Li Jin was sure he knew they were running from Erik. At Jing's place, even unspoken, they were both filled with fear that any moment he would burst in and find them. Even the way he played with Fei Fei, his voice hushed and his moves quiet, showed Li Jin that he was ever aware of just who might be upstairs.

As grumpy as he was, he didn't ask any more questions. Li Jin remembered the small bag of cashews she'd picked up at the station and dug in her bag until she found them. She tore open the package and passed it to him.

"Here, eat these. When we get off the bus, I'll get you something better."

Jojo took the cashews and poured some in his hand, then passed them to her. "Only if you eat half because I know you're hungry, too, Ma."

Li Jin smiled. Despite being exhausted, hungry, and probably even confused, Jojo was still the sweet little boy she'd raised. She took the cashews from him and popped them into her mouth. As soon as the saltiness hit her tongue, she felt hunger and it surprised her. Since the attack from Erik, she hadn't felt like eating anything and even the thought of food had sickened her. Jing had forced her to at least eat congee but it had been difficult. The return of her appetite was a welcome sign that she was on the right track as she chewed and swallowed the salty nuts. A few more minutes and she hoped to be able to add a bowl of steaming noodles to her growling stomach.

Finally they pulled into the station and Jojo popped out of his seat like a jack-in-the-box. With much less enthusiasm because of how drained she felt, Li Jin joined him and handed him his bag and pillow, then nudged him into the aisle to start the shuffle through the narrow space and out the bus door.

Jojo stepped to the side. "You go first, Ma. I'll watch out for you."

Li Jin smiled and squeezed in front of him. It was sweet how protective he was being but she didn't want him feeling that kind of pressure. It was her job to be the protector—not his. But she'd let it pass this once because they were tired, hungry, and ready to get off the bus. Li Jin's muscles, which had felt much better at the beginning of the trip, were beginning to scream in protest after the long ride.

"Okay, but hurry. We need to beat all the old people to the noodle stand and then we'll have more time to walk around and get our blood moving."

Unfortunately her words were lost as the two older women butted in front of Jojo, putting more distance between them. Li Jin struggled to see him around the women but gave up and allowed herself to be pushed up the aisle. Through the corner of her eye, she saw the women let even more passengers in front of them. Now there were at least five people between her and Jojo. Li Jin would just have to get him when he got off the bus.

Finally after being bumped, shoved, and elbowed, she found herself standing on the sidewalk, waiting for Jojo to emerge. Not surprisingly, the bus station was packed and noisy. All around her, other passengers and station pedestrians rushed here and there, and Li Jin started to feel nervous. Where was he?

Li Jin heard some loud laughing and turned to see a group of young guys, dressed similarly to the gang boy, huddled behind her. They all wore black bandanas, some on their heads and some tied around their upper arms. They appeared to be having a great time pointing out people and making fun of them. Li Jin felt sure they were probably waiting for the surly guy who'd been on her bus, and she searched the crowd around them, hoping Jojo didn't fall prey to their bullying antics. She didn't see him and turned back around to watch the rest of the passengers from her bus disembark. More passengers stiffly climbed off until the last ones dwindled out. Everyone but Jojo. Li Jin felt a moment of nausea. She must have missed him. Looking around frantically, she called his name.

"Jojo! Where are you? Jojo . . . ?"

Juggling her bag and pillow, she pushed through the sea of people to the security guard standing against the wall at the entrance to the station.

"*Dui bu qi.*" She pecked on his shoulder to get his attention away from the scene of two passengers arguing over the window seat on the bus parked at the curb in front of them.

He looked at her. "What?"

His tone told her he didn't really want to be bothered.

"My son got lost in the crowd. I need your help," Li Jin answered as she continued to watch the people around the bus she'd just left. He had to be close; there was no way he could have gone too far so quickly.

The guard pointed at the ticket window and spat on the ground in front of her. "Go there and fill out a missing report. Then come see me and I'll start looking."

"A report? This isn't a missing piece of luggage. It's my son and we need to find him right now!"

The guard shook his head slowly. "Report first."

Li Jin stopped in her tracks and felt a rush of heat start in her toes and work its way up to her face. *This couldn't be happening. Hadn't they been through enough?* She thought about the cell phone in her pocket. It was only a lender from Jing but who could she call? No one could help her from so far away. She wished now that she'd gotten Jojo his own phone; at least then she could've called him and found out where he was. But he did have her number! He would ask someone to use their phone! She pulled her phone out of her bag and looked at it. He hadn't called.

She went past the window and into the station. The scene in there was a little quieter but still filled with far too many people. Many stood in line at the bag station, paying a few reminbi to get a checkered plastic carrying bag to put all of their clothes into. Others gathered around in small groups, passing around food and thermoses of hot water for tea. Against one wall a line of food vendors stood behind their stands, hawking noodles and other items. Li Jin had lost her appetite but thought maybe Jojo had been drawn there by the smell of food. She looked but he wasn't anywhere to be found. She ran back out the door and to the window. Ignoring the line of people, she skirted right to the front. It was an emergency, after all, she thought as she heard the grumbling start.

"My son is lost and the security guard said I needed to fill out a missing form."

The night clerk sighed in exasperation but reached into a file stand and pulled out a piece of paper. She passed it through the window, then stared at Li Jin as she began to fill out the short form.

"Can't this be done later after we've searched for my son?" Li Jin couldn't believe the pointless questions on the form that had nothing to do with her or her son. She looked around and saw a woman sitting on a bench, holding the string leading to a red balloon. The woman looked so much like Jing there was no doubt who it was. She dropped the pen, picked up her bag, and crossed the area.

"*Ni hao,* are you Lao Shuwen?" she asked her.

Lao Shuwen stood and a shy smile spread across her face. "That I am. You must be Li Jin. My sister had told me—"

Li Jin held her hand up and saw it was shaking, then put it back down again. "I'm sorry to interrupt, Lao Shuwen, but my son got lost in the crowd getting off the bus and we've got to find him. I don't have time to talk."

The older woman put her hand on Li Jin's shoulder. "Calm down. What's he wearing? Tell me what he looks like."

"He's ten." Li Jin held her hand up to her chest. "About this tall and he's skinny. He has a bag—oh, and he should be carrying a pillow." She turned to search the crowd again.

"What else? We'll need to split up. You go that way and I'll go this way. We'll meet back here at this bench." Shuwen pointed in opposite directions, then at the bench.

"And he's wearing a bright yellow scarf Jing gave him." She thought of the way he had smiled when Jing had given him the hand-knitted scarf; you'd have thought it was worth a lot of money the way he held it to his face. Li Jin knew what he felt in that moment—it was love. It was moments like that when Li Jin felt the loss of grandparents in her son's life. Suddenly she remembered that Jojo had told her he needed to use the toilet.

"Wait! He might have gone straight to the restroom!" She turned in a circle, trying to find a sign pointing to the facilities.

"It's over here. Come on." Shuwen walked quickly to a small shed-like building with two doors. One had a sign of a pipe on it, the other a high-heeled shoe. They both had a place to put a coin.

"These are only one-person stalls and he'd have had to pay to get in there. Did he have any money?" Shuwen asked.

Li Jin shook her head. "No, he didn't."

The door to the men's room opened and a man stepped out, still pulling up his zipper. Li Jin could see the tiny room behind him with the hole in the floor. No one else was in there.

Shuwen pointed down the sidewalk. "Go check over there near the taxi line. He might be waiting there for you. I'll go the other way. If you don't find him in half an hour, meet me at the bench."

She turned and went the other way, still holding the balloon meant for Jojo. Li Jin watched her for one second, then felt the tears burn in her eyes. No longer feeling hunger or exhaustion, she took off at a jog toward the taxi line.

Chapter Twenty-Seven

Li Jin struggled to stay awake. She held up her watch and squinted through tired eyes to try to see the time.

"Four o'clock," Shuwen said from beside her. "Do you think we could go to the house now? Get some rest?"

Li Jin shook her head. She wasn't leaving. This was the last place she knew for sure that Jojo had been, and what if he came back? It would soon be daylight and they'd spent the last six hours searching the same places over and over. The security guard had finally gotten involved, even bringing in two more officers to help. Shuwen had called her driver and he'd also searched until he felt it was useless and had retreated back to the van to wait. The guard called the police and an officer arrived and took a quick report, but he told her she'd have to file a formal one the next day. Despite all efforts, Jojo was nowhere to be found.

"No, but please, Lao Shuwen, you go on ahead." Li Jin stared straight ahead at the empty place the bus they'd come in on had left when it took off. She was exhausted and weak, but so far none of the tragedies in her life could compare to the pain she felt at losing Jojo. It wasn't even just mental—she truly felt a physical ache throughout her entire body. Where was he? Was he hurt? Hungry? Had whoever took him let him use the bathroom? Silly questions for such a serious predicament, she thought to herself. She at least hoped he knew that she was looking for him and would never give up until she found him.

"Li Jin, I know you don't want to leave here but you have to get some sleep so tomorrow you can keep up the search." Shuwen reached over and picked up Li Jin's limp hand. She held it and patted the top of it. "We've searched every corner, my dear. He is not in this station. Tomorrow's a new day and the police department will help us."

Li Jin shook her head. She could feel the hot, silent tears begin to run in rivers down her cheeks. Why? What had she ever done to deserve this? Jojo was the only piece of her life that wasn't a total disaster. With him gone, she had no reason to live. None.

Around them the station had quieted to a dull hum. People slept on benches and propped on their bags on the floor. Li Jin couldn't understand how they could just sleep like nothing was happening when her life had just been turned upside down.

She had called Jing in Suzhou around midnight and though the woman tried her best to comfort Li Jin, she didn't have anything to say that helped. It was hopeless. And Shuwen, her sister, had stayed and helped in the search, despite being old and obviously tired. When she saw the woman prop one of her feet up on her other knee and rub it again, Li Jin felt a rush of pity and knew the woman needed to get home and go to bed. She stood up.

"You promise we can come right back here in a few hours?"

Shuwen nodded and stood up. "Of course, child. We'll go by the police department first and then come straight here." She gathered up her bag and umbrella, then waited for Li Jin.

Li Jin looked at the wilting red balloon tied to the bench behind Shuwen. They'd put it there hours earlier, hoping Jojo would see it. "Can we leave the balloon?"

Shuwen nodded, then dug in her bag and came up with a black marker. She handed it to Li Jin. "Here. Write your number on it, just in case."

Li Jin pulled the phone from her bag and flipped it open. She punched a few keys until her number came up, then copied it onto the side of the latex balloon. Underneath she wrote, *Jojo, I'll be back here soon. If you come, don't move. Wait here. I love you. Ma.*

She hesitated, debating her decision, but Shuwen pulled her along. She led Li Jin through the parking lot to a blue Buick van and she pecked on the window. The driver, stretched out sound asleep on one of the seats in the back, jumped up and opened the door. Li Jin saw her bag and pillow on the floor where he had stored it earlier and she thought again of Jojo clutching his pillow to his chest as he beckoned for her to go first down the aisle. If she'd only made him step out in front of her so she could've kept her eyes on him. She was so stupid!

"Did you find him?" His hair stood up all over and Li Jin felt a flash of guilt for being the reason he hadn't been able to return home to his family.

Shuwen shook her head and guided Li Jin up and into the van. "No, but we'll come back tomorrow. Let's get Li Jin to the house and to bed for a few hours."

Li Jin moved over close to the far window and sat down. Shuwen sat beside her, then pulled a pack of crackers from the console. She handed them to Li Jin. "Nibble on these. You must be weak by now."

Li Jin took them from her and held them in her hand. She was past the point of arguing. She felt strange, as if she were moving through a dream. She knew she looked like a madwoman, her hair wild around her face and her clothes filthy from being in the station all night. She had run through there, sweating and crying as she called his name over and over. People had moved out of the way immediately and Li Jin didn't even care about the fear she saw in their eyes at the way she looked. Her mind raced to come up with reasons why someone would take Jojo. Her biggest fear was that he'd been taken for child trafficking, as it was a common crime within China. Or he could've been taken to serve as a pawn in a beggar ring. She looked out the window, still searching for him at every corner, every streetlight.

She'd spent years on the streets and had met children who'd been stolen only to be forced to beg for their captors. She didn't know where or why he was gone; she just wanted Jojo back.

Li Jin awoke when the driver stopped the van and Shuwen reached over and shook her.

"We're in Hongcun now," she said. "We made record time, too. This early in the morning the traffic was so light it only took us a little over an hour."

For a minute Li Jin forgot where she was and looked around for Jojo. He was usually right beside her. When she saw only Shuwen there, it all came back and Li Jin felt nauseated. It had really happened; someone had taken her son. She leaned her head back on the headrest and closed her eyes again. She just wanted to shut everything out.

"Come on, Li Jin. We'll go inside, and I'll make you some strong tea and a bowl of congee. You need to get something in your stomach before you go back to sleep."

Li Jin stared down at the pack of crackers still in her lap, untouched. She got up and climbed out of the van behind the old woman, then turned around and picked up her bag and pillow.

"I don't want to sleep. Jojo is out there somewhere," she mumbled, so tired she knew her words sounded unintelligible.

Moving clumsily with her sling, she gathered the pillow against her and welcomed the jolt of pain that ran up through her body. She wouldn't even flinch. She deserved much more than that for being such an incompetent mother. She turned to follow Shuwen.

They were parked behind a two-story brick building in a very run-down lot. The lot was full but the space the driver had pulled the van into had a sign at the front stating RESERVED FOR OFFICIAL. WILL TOW VIOLATORS. Li Jin assumed Shuwen was the supposed official since her van was parked there.

"Follow me," Shuwen said as she led Li Jin through the vehicles and to a covered walkway. The path led into a small walking bridge over a large pond. At the other side of the bridge walkway was a quaint building with a large, red round door. On the door, large gold characters read MOON HARBOR INN, with OPEN FOR RENTING posted on a small sign beside it.

"Moon Harbor Inn?" she asked.

"Yes, we run a small inn here for tourists. But my girls live in the converted attic. Most people don't even know there is anyone living here other than me and my housekeeper. The customers think the girls they see are just hired help, in and out."

Li Jin watched silently as Shuwen unlocked the door and held it open for her. She walked through and stood, waiting for Shuwen to lead. The woman locked the deadbolt and then found her place in front again. They walked down a long empty hall until they entered a large kitchen.

"Take a seat, Li Jin. Let me find Wan."

Li Jin pulled a chair from the long table and sat down, letting her bag settle at her feet. She put the pillow on the table and traced the shape of the phoenix. For some reason, it gave her comfort and hope that somewhere Jojo was doing the same with his own pillow. She looked around the quiet room. The wooden table she sat at had nine chairs—four on each side and one at the head. Li Jin assumed that one was reserved for Shuwen. Each place at the table had an inviting bamboo place mat with a set of chopsticks resting on a tiny ceramic holder. A large bowl in the center held a variety of oranges and other fruit. Li Jin ran her hand over the surface of the table; it was old and scarred, but, unlike the modern furniture that Erik preferred, it had character and probably years of memories. Actually, the entire room felt homier than any room Li Jin had ever been in. She felt a pang of longing, wishing she could provide something similar for Jojo.

Her eyes wandered to the middle of the room where a huge embroidered rug of red and gold circles lay. It was clean and obviously meticulously cared for. Beside the large industrial sink was the biggest stove top Li Jin had ever seen and above it hung a stainless steel rack of pots and woks. She thought they must do a lot of cooking and felt a small rumble in the pit of her stomach. She knew she needed to eat or she'd be useless to find Jojo the next day. She was still tired but most of all she was weak. She didn't even know how many hours it was since she'd had a meal—maybe a day? She remembered Jojo sharing the cashews with her and felt a lump rise in her throat again. *Where was he? Was he okay?* She looked at her watch. It was almost five in the morning and they had been apart for seven hours. A lot could happen to a little boy in seven hours. Horrible visions filled her mind; visions she didn't want any part of.

She laid her head on the pillow and closed her eyes. No more tears would come; she'd cried herself dry.

She rested for a moment, then raised her head when she heard Shuwen returning with another set of footsteps behind her. Before she could even make a judgment on the woman called

Auntie Wan, the petite woman moved behind her and began pulling her hair back. She produced a brush from somewhere and Li Jin felt it move through her hair.

"Um . . . *ni hao?*" she said, looking up at Shuwen with raised eyebrows. She fought the urge to jerk her head away. She heard a sudden grunt from the woman behind her and felt her head tugged back as Wan began gathering her hair to form a braid.

"The woman behind you is Auntie Wan. She's in charge of the kitchen and thinks she's in charge of the girls. Wan thinks to feel a sense of calm, one must look calm. I told her about Jojo and she is here to get you settled." She chuckled. "She insists on mothering everyone who walks through that door. Next she'll make you wash up, then feed you until you feel like popping."

Li Jin thought washing up sounded enticing, but even though she knew her stomach was empty, she wasn't sure if she could keep anything down.

"Can I just go wash up and catch breakfast later?"

Auntie Wan finished tying off the long braid and came to stand in front of her. She crossed her arms over her chest. "No."

Well, Li Jin thought, she sure gave a simple and straightforward answer. She finally got a good look at the woman and despite her extremely short hair and ruddy full cheeks, she had a certain charm about her. She'd obviously climbed straight out of bed, as the petite woman still wore a long pink—and ratty—housecoat over a nightgown. Her feet disappeared in her bulky slippers and her face still showed faint crease lines from her sleep.

Shuwen chuckled. "Come on, I'll show you to the washroom while Wan starts cooking. The other girls will be up soon anyway, so she'll just get an early start on breakfast. We eat an hour before the customers—then Wan will do it all again and feed the masses."

Li Jin got up to follow Shuwen while behind her Wan began to clatter the pots and pans. Shuwen led her back into the hallway but this time she opened a door Li Jin hadn't noticed on the way in.

"Here's the bathroom. You'll find clean towels in the cupboard. Just find your way back to the kitchen when you finish."

With that Li Jin stepped into the small room and Shuwen closed the door behind her. Li Jin heard her soft footsteps retreat down the hall. She turned to the sink and leaned in to see her reflection.

She looked awful. Her hair was now neat, but it felt strange as she'd never worn it in a braid. As she studied her sudden frown lines she thought she looked as if she'd aged ten years in a few hours. And the gash—there was no way it was going to heal as Jing had told her it would. What little beauty she'd once held was gone. But perhaps it was best. Beauty wasn't needed when one never intended to love again.

She turned on the water and used one hand to bring it up and splash it against her face. That made her feel a little better and she splashed some more. She saw a bar of soap on the sink and used it to scrub at her hands and as much of her arms as she could reach without taking off her sling. At least now she smelled better. She grabbed a small towel from the cupboard over the toilet and used it to pat herself dry.

Leaning in again, she stared at the woman in the mirror. There she saw the obvious anguish present, but she also saw her old strength fighting to come through. It was that inner strength that had got her and her son through many hard years. She had survived terrible things before without help from anyone. Not anything this terrible—*but she could do it.* Jojo needed her to stop being a sniveling, weak mother and let her inner tiger out of the cage. She whispered under her breath. "Pull yourself together, Li

Jin. Be as fierce on the inside as your scar makes you look on the outside and you will find your son."

She folded the towel and placed it on the sink. She raised her shoulders and straightened her spine. Not caring who heard her now, with a louder and stronger voice she said it again. "Pull yourself together, Li Jin. You *will* find your son."

She opened the door and stepped out, ready to eat something and sleep for a few hours before she would make her first appearance at the local police station. They might not know who she was now, and they might not have any concern for her child, but by the end of the day tomorrow they would help her. Whether they wanted to or not.

Chapter Twenty-Eight

Four days later Li Jin was trying not to show how drained and upset she was that she'd left the bus station yet again without Jojo. That first morning after she'd slept about five hours, Shuwen had woken her and taken her to the police station. They'd filled out a report and after the police had been no help, she and Shuwen had gone back to the bus station and searched again. They spent all day there and a few locals had even joined the search. With the five of them working together, they'd covered the station and the several blocks around it with still no sign of him. Jojo was still out there somewhere and Li Jin hadn't wanted to leave, but Shuwen talked her into coming back to the shelter to rest up and make plans for their next move. The next days were the same. They started with the police and moved on to searching around the bus station, then came home. She didn't know how, but Shuwen had kept up with her and was still going strong, not even showing the first sign of exhaustion. The woman was at least twice her age but was a machine!

Tonight they'd finished dinner with the rest of the women and then Shuwen invited Li Jin to go out and see Moon Pond with her. It was beautiful, and they stood and watched the people around it. Some scrubbed their laundry in the murky water and others sat around it, enjoying the peaceful scene. The local shopkeepers and kiosk owners were busy shutting down for the night. It was almost dark and most of the tourists had left town on the last buses, so more of the locals were out and about, free from the invasive curiosity and constant picture taking from visitors to their town.

Shuwen gestured toward her building. "Years ago when I opened the shelter, the only way for someone to get approved to come here was if they put in an application to their local neighborhood committee. Then the committee would approve it—or sometimes not—and send it on to the Women's Federation. If that group stamped it approved, the woman was allowed to come to the shelter for one week. Then they had to find another place to go."

Li Jin didn't understand. Why was that a bad thing?

Shuwen continued. "But some women can't wait for the application process. Sometimes they have to flee immediately or they jeopardize their lives. And many can't find a new place to go in only seven days."

"How do you maintain your inn and take care of the women? Does the government give financial assistance?" Li Jin asked as she strolled along around the large pond arm in arm with Shuwen. Surprisingly, she'd felt an immediate connection with the woman but thought perhaps it was because Shuwen was almost a carbon copy of her sister, Jing. Even their compassionate spirits were the same. Like her sister in Suzhou, Shuwen worked tirelessly to help everyone around her. It amazed Li Jin.

"Not any longer they don't." Shuwen guided her toward the center of the village. She'd already showed her the grounds of the inn, which looked more like a boutique hotel to Li Jin with the immaculate rooms and their private patio areas manicured to perfection. Li Jin could imagine living there forever, it was so pretty. She wished Jojo could have seen it with her.

"Why don't they help you?" She couldn't imagine the woman kept up the entire inn and shelter for the women all alone but for the spry little Wan. It had to be expensive to care for so many people.

"Bureaucracy. Government regulations. It's a tangled vine better left untouched."

"Well, that's not right," Li Jin said. She didn't mention that she was wondering where places like this were the many times she was out on the street. She didn't know such a thing even existed.

"It's worked out okay. I converted the bottom floor to an inn for tourists and business is steady. All the girls pitch in to keep the inn going and do some work in town during the day to bring in additional income. We're not rolling in it but we manage." She reached down to pull up the nylon that was rolling down her swollen ankle. Such a simple woman, yet Li Jin could sense that she was much more intelligent than she appeared. This was a woman who had everything under control at all times, in all circumstances.

She looked Shuwen straight in the eye. "I've been so wrapped up I haven't told you how appreciative I am that you made a place for me here. I know when I find Jojo, this will be the perfect place for us to get back on our feet. Thank you, Lao Shuwen." She hoped the woman didn't catch on how hard it was for Li Jin to say thank you. It wasn't that she wasn't grateful; it was just that she wasn't used to people helping her, so the words didn't come easy. Li Jin reminded herself to slip some money to Shuwen out of Erik's stash. So far she hadn't had to spend any of it and it sat locked in her trunk at the end of the bed.

"Oh, never mind that. My sister said you were a good woman and we're glad to have you. Now look out over there. I'll tell you some history." Shuwen guided Li Jin to a bench, and they say while she pointed to the line of buildings behind the pond. "Hongcun Village is known for being shaped like an ox."

Li Jin squinted to see how the village looked like an ox. Shuwen sounded convincing, so she knew she must be missing something.

"Over there is Leigang Hill, and it's supposed to be the head." She pointed again. "See the two tallest trees on either side? They are the horns. Under that are the houses—they're the body. And the winding stream that goes around the village is the intestines—and the stream by the way was man-made after the entire village burned to the ground many years ago. And obviously Moon Pond is the stomach and the four bridges are the hooves."

Li Jin could see it now and the serene atmosphere was bringing her a sense of peace she hadn't felt all day. She was still terrified about Jojo, but she was determined. She'd find him and she wouldn't give up until she did.

"So, what do you think of my current little family?" Shuwen asked. She pulled her feet back just in time to avoid being run over by a boy on his bike. The girl who followed directly behind him apologized on his behalf and Shuwen waved her away.

Li Jin wasn't sure how to answer. She still felt like she was in a fog—that she'd wake up to find it was all a bad dream and Jojo would still be with her.

But Shuwen waited for an answer. What did she think of the other women? She'd shared the dorm room with them but other than pointing out her bed in the long line of bunks stretching across the large attic on the first day, no one had spoken to her. So honestly she hadn't felt welcomed by them and had actually recognized a current of resentment toward her at dinnertimes. So far no one had asked her any questions about why she was there.

Li Jin didn't even know if they knew the story about Jojo. And at this point she didn't think they'd care.

"Well, they seem really nice. And quiet."

Shuwen nodded. "For the most part they are pleasant, once they get to know you."

Li Jin shuffled her feet under the bench and kept her eyes hidden. She didn't know what to say to that but obviously Shuwen wasn't going to let her get away with staying silent. "They're hard workers. As soon as breakfast is over they all scatter." She felt that was a safe-enough reply. She didn't want to get into discussions of how they were treating her.

"Yes, they are hard workers. And the reason you aren't doing the evening cleanup and prep right now is because I wanted to talk to you first. You haven't been able to really think logically these last few days, you've been so frantic. I know you're tired and you're focused on finding Jojo, and starting tomorrow I'll still loan my driver to take you back to the bus station for a few hours, but when you return, you'll have to pitch in. That is how you'll earn your stay here with us. There are plenty of tasks you can do, even with your arm in the sling."

Li Jin was taken aback. "Of course, Lao Shuwen. I'm so sorry if you thought I didn't want to work."

Shuwen reached over and patted her hand. "No, I thought no such thing. I'm just telling you how it will go. But I also wanted to explain to you that when new people come in, it takes a while for the others to trust them. These women—like you— have been hurt badly. Some only emotionally, but others physically as well. Many times they never again trust anyone else, but while they are here they are very fragile and frightened. I don't want you to take it personally."

"Oh. Okay. I won't then," Li Jin said. She was the last person to fault anyone for putting up walls for self-preservation.

She'd been doing it her entire life. And as far as she was concerned, she didn't need to make any friends. She just wanted to find Jojo and get on her feet to build a new life for them.

"They all have unhappy stories that affect the way they interact with others, but you probably noticed Sami more than anyone."

Li Jin looked at Shuwen, shaking her head.

"She is the youngest one there—she has a purple streak dyed in her hair," Shuwen said.

"Oh yes. I saw her." Li Jin didn't add that the girl, even though she looked at least twenty or so, could have passed for much younger because of the immature way she acted. But there was no doubt that she was a beauty. Her hair, even with the purple streak, hung silky straight and soft to her tiny waist. Every feature on her face looked as if it had been carved from pure porcelain. But because of her icy expression she had stood out among the others. At her first dinner with them, Li Jin had mistakenly sat down in the girl's chair, causing her to stand silent and sullen behind her until Li Jin realized what was wrong. She'd finally gotten up and moved to another seat. Still she had not said a word to her, even though their beds were right next to each other. It was awkward, to say the least.

"Sami has been with us over six months and she's still very angry. When she turned thirteen, her father sold her to an uncle for his massage shop. They didn't have the money it would take to send her to school, so he took the next option. Unfortunately for Sami, it wasn't only massages she was expected to perform. She refused at first but her uncle beat her until she eventually obeyed. She spent years in a room on her back."

Li Jin was shocked. "Sold her into prostitution? You mean families are still selling their daughters? I thought that was abolished decades ago?"

Shuwen shook her head. "Unfortunately it still goes on today in the poorest regions. Sami was willing to sacrifice her future for her family, but she wasn't willing to lose her life in the process. One of her clients got possessive and jealous. He came in one night when she had someone else in the back room, and he busted in and beat her. No one stopped him because they didn't want the police involved. Right now she's angry at her uncle, her father, and I think just about everyone else in the world. She told Wan what had happened to her and that is the last time she has spoken of it. She even refuses to cry. Sami is so full of bottled-up bitterness and shame for the life they made her lead that it is poisoning her spirit."

Li Jin stared at a young couple strolling around the park. The girl looked close to the same age as Sami, yet they were worlds apart. The girl laughed and flirted with the boy, batting her eyes at him as he spoke to her with his head bent to hers. It was so sad that Sami's family intended for her to miss ever knowing that feeling of new love and infatuation, instead sending her to a fate that could only have ended badly.

"How did Sami get away?" she asked. She couldn't even picture the tiny girl being beaten by a grown man; it was a horrible vision to contemplate. She was barely more than a child! And forced to give sexual favors? It wasn't fair.

"Her uncle was also fond of the *bai jiu* and after weeks of handing out beatings during his binges, he got drunk enough—and stayed passed out long enough—for Sami to get away. She escaped with nothing but the clothes on her back and Wan found her sleeping under a bridge in Huangshan. She brought her here when the girl said she had nowhere else to go. So far everyone avoids her because she is so angry."

Li Jin thought that Wan must truly be an angel, just like Shuwen. She had no words but the feeling of being insulted by the girl slipped away. Now she only felt sympathy for her—the girl had no one, and at least Li Jin had Jojo.

Shuwen stood up and yawned, stretching her arms over her in a Tai qi arc. "Come on, Li Jin, it's time for you to get settled in for the night. You have a big day tomorrow. And if the gods are watching out for you, maybe we'll be lucky enough to find your son."

Li Jin followed her down the path toward the inn. She certainly hoped the gods would indeed show her favor.

The women in the room were all dressed in their nightclothes. Because their living quarters were right above the inn rooms, everyone naturally moved and spoke in hushed tones. Some wrote in their journals while others gathered in the tiny family area around the small television. A cartoon played quietly and the few mothers who had brought their children to the shelter chatted while the kids watched. So far Li Jin had tried to avoid looking at the children—especially the little boys. It hurt too much.

"His father took him."

"What makes you think that?" Li Jin responded to Sami's remark as she hugged her pillow close. She knew the girl was trying to goad her into an argument; she could tell by the nasty tone of her voice. Li Jin wouldn't bite—she was still a guest here and wouldn't insult Shuwen that way. She took a few deep breaths, reminding herself the girl had a lot of hurt inside her. She pulled the coverlet up over her legs and noticed a few girls shooting her looks and whispering. They were probably shocked she was even having a conversation with Sami.

She was finally in bed, after waiting for all the other girls to finish and allow her time in the bathroom. As the newest resident, she was last on the rotation. By the time she'd gotten her shower, the water was ice-cold. She'd climbed the stairs to the attic with a towel wrapped ineptly around her head, to find a group of giggling grown women who thought it funny that she'd had to be last. She hadn't cared; at least they were talking to her now—just a little but it was something.

In the bed next to her Sami sat cross-legged while she pulled a brush through her long hair. Li Jin had noticed that Sami didn't join any of the other activities and had never seen Sami even talking to anyone else. She was usually alone, oblivious to everything and everyone around her.

Beside her Sami stopped, holding the tip of the brush to her mouth. "It only makes sense. You say your son doesn't know his father, but what if the father has been following your lives and finally decided he wanted his son? So he waited until you were in a busy place before he took the opportunity to snatch him. If I had a son, I have no doubt his father would turn over every rock and climb every mountain to find him. Men are obsessed with sons."

Li Jin didn't answer. Sami's explanation of what she thought had happened to Jojo was so far out of reality it didn't even deserve a reply. Jojo's father didn't even know Jojo existed; she'd left that morning after he'd attacked her and never looked back. As far as she was concerned, Jojo didn't have a father. And it couldn't have been Erik, for he didn't know she was on that bus and why would he want the responsibility of Jojo anyway? It had to be random. Little boys were taken every day in China and given or sold to families who needed sons. Because of one distracted moment, Jojo was lost somewhere.

"He'll find a way to get word to me. He has the number to my cell phone. He just has to find it." She remembered before they'd left Jing had scratched the number on a scrap of paper and stuffed it into the small zipper of Jojo's bag while he was still sleeping.

"Just in case," Jing had said, smiling at Li Jin. Had she known something even then? But why hadn't Jojo used it? He wasn't a baby; if he saw the paper, he would know to call the number. Maybe whoever had him had taken his bag? She prayed nonstop that he would find the number and call it. She kept her phone in her pocket at all times, sneaking looks at it to make sure it was still working. But so far nothing.

She was brought out of her thoughts when Sami threw her brush over at her and it landed with a heavy thud on her knee.

"Want to use this?" she asked, laughing at Li Jin when she jumped.

Li Jin felt sorry for the girl but not so much she was going to let her get away with acting like a brat. She'd already put up with days of the silent treatment from her, and now this?

"That hurt, Sami," Li Jin said. "Be careful. I have a broken arm. You could've made it worse." She picked up the brush and tried clumsily to pull it through her hair. It was amazing how much in life required two hands, things she'd never thought about before. So far since her arm had gotten hurt, she'd only used the fingers of her good hand to pull the tangles out of her hair.

Sami got up and crossed the small space between them. "Here, let me have it."

Li Jin handed her the brush and Sami jerked it out of her hand, then climbed on the bed and sat behind Li Jin.

Li Jin tensed, expecting the girl to be rough. She was surprised when Sami began brushing her hair gently, so gently in fact that Li Jin closed her eyes and savored the moment. Sami still acted as if she didn't quite know what to think of her new bunkmate, but she was softening, Li Jin could tell.

"So how did you get your broken arm? And the scar on your face?" Sami asked in a whisper as she gathered up Li Jin's hair and began to separate it into three parts. It felt heavenly and Li Jin could feel the frustration and fatigue of the day slipping away. At least she could until Sami asked that question. She wouldn't admit it but she had craved conversation, though talking about Erik wasn't something she was ready to do.

She hesitated. To speak about it out loud would make it feel so much worse—so much more humiliating. But with the one nice gesture, she realized she'd never really had someone she could call a true friend. She knew that, like her, Sami had been hurt badly. Maybe because they had something in common, their friendship could work.

"My boyfriend did it," Li Jin said, then took a deep breath. She'd done it. It was the first time the words had come from her mouth but it actually felt good. Suddenly her body felt lighter. "He beat me and raped me so bad I thought I would die. And it wasn't the first time." She was glad Sami was behind her and she didn't have to look her in the eyes. Saying the words was hard enough, but the eyes were the windows to the soul and Li Jin wasn't ready to let anyone know just how deep Erik had hurt her.

Behind her Sami's fingers stopped their braiding. Li Jin waited for her to say something, or to continue working at her hair, but the girl didn't. Li Jin turned around and saw Sami was sitting there with her eyes closed, silent tears running down her beautiful cheeks and an expression of total torment spreading across her face. Li Jin's heart broke for the girl, and she leaned over and gathered her against her with her good arm. In the embrace Sami finally let go and the sobs erupted from her small body. The room around them went dead silent and Li Jin raised her eyes to see the other women staring solemnly at them.

One by one, they turned away and padded quietly to their beds. The few children followed their mothers and climbed in beside them, knowing a milestone had been reached in the room. Until Li Jin came, no one had been able to break through the tough exterior of the girl. Now even Li Jin's own tears began to flow as she rocked Sami back and forth, sharing in the anguish the girl finally released.

Chapter Twenty-Nine

The next morning Li Jin woke to find Sami fully dressed and waiting on the bed beside her. The girl sat cross-legged, staring serenely at Li Jin when she opened her eyes. It was a bit eerie, she had to admit. Then Sami spoke softly.

"'Waiting forever, searching for your face so fair. Just one small touch, reaching for you, and I know I'm almost there.'"

Li Jin sat up and rubbed her eyes. "That was nice, Sami. Did you write that?"

"No, it's by a poet who died trying to catch the reflection of the moon goddess in the waters."

Li Jin didn't know how to respond. She wasn't surprised that Sami could recite poetry and she felt sorry for the girl that she was robbed of her chance to further her schooling. It was unfair to be so intelligent but held back because of poverty.

"The others are downstairs having breakfast," Sami said, her voice low and even but not as unfriendly as it usually was. "I waited for you."

Why was Sami waiting for her to wake up? Li Jin wasn't going to ask. She looked at her watch and saw that she had only half an hour before Shuwen's driver expected her. She climbed out and went to the trunk at the end of her bed. She opened it and pulled out her clothes and bag, then turned to Sami.

"I probably won't have time for breakfast. I have to be ready to go back to the police headquarters and then the train station to look for Jojo." With that she walked past her and down the stairs to the bathroom to wash up and get dressed. She was finally at the point where it didn't hurt so much to take off her sling, so she guessed she was healing. As quickly as she could manage, she tugged on her jeans and shirt, brushed her hair and teeth, and washed her face. She looked in the mirror and grimaced at her face. She reached up and touched a line around her eyes. She looked at least a hundred.

"This could be the day." She said a prayer under her breath and opened the door.

She was startled to find Sami leaning against the wall outside the bathroom, a small paper bag in her hand.

"Auntie Wan put us something together to eat on the way." She gave Li Jin her usual sullen look, then headed down the hall. "The driver is waiting for us. Hurry up."

Li Jin sighed. What would a day with Sami be like? She didn't know if she was glad for the company or nervous about what lay ahead. But she followed, quickly passing by the kitchen door and the hushed morning chatter from the others. Auntie Wan was cooking something spicy and the aroma almost tempted Li Jin to stop, but thoughts of Jojo kept her moving behind Sami.

The police were even less helpful than they'd been each day before, and Li Jin and Sami were soon on their way to the train station.

"So do you have a picture of your little boy?" Sami asked, munching on one of Wan's steamed buns. The girl had already harassed Li Jin until she'd eaten half of one.

Li Jin picked up her backpack and dug around until she found her wallet. She flipped it open and pulled out the most recent photo of Jojo. It was from the year before and he had a gap where his front tooth had fallen out. Li Jin stared at it a moment, smiling as she remembered the day they took it. It was an unusually balmy winter day and they'd spent it at the local park.

She handed it over to Sami. "Here he is. He was hamming it up for the camera. And he doesn't have that gap anymore. Both his front teeth have grown in."

Sami studied it. "He doesn't look like you."

"I know." She didn't say aloud that he also looked nothing like his father, and she hoped Sami wouldn't bring up the subject. Speaking about Erik and what he'd done to her was hard enough, and nothing could make her tell the story about her foster mother's son.

Sami handed her back the photo. "So what do you really think happened to him?"

Li Jin looked out the window. She wasn't going to cry. She'd done enough of that and her heart felt emptied.

"I think someone took him to be their son. But I know Jojo and he is smart enough to find his way back to the train station. As soon as he gets a chance to get away, he will come."

Sami nodded. "So that's why you go every day. The other girls are saying you're just trying to get out of working."

Li Jin jerked around and looked at Sami. "Don't they know about my son?"

Sami shook her head. "No, Shuwen doesn't tell us anything about the new girls. She lets us give our stories in our own time. I only knew because I overheard her talking to Auntie Wan the night you came in." She narrowed her eyes at Li Jin. "And you haven't been exactly social, you know?"

Li Jin laughed and pointed her finger at her chest. "Me? Who are you to talk?"

Sami gave her a small smile. "That's just me. I'm naturally quiet. But usually when new girls come in, they want to talk about their experiences. Everyone has expected you to join them, but so far you've stayed to yourself."

"Like you, you mean?" Li Jin asked softly.

"Yes. Like me." Sami stared out the window.

The silence settled around them as the driver weaved in and out of traffic. It was the same driver that she'd met the first day. He knew the story about Jojo, and Li Jin was astonished that even he had kept it to himself. She thought about her conversation with Shuwen the night before. She really hoped today would be the day Jojo made it back to her, but if it wasn't, she planned to dig in and do whatever job Shuwen gave her to show the others she could work just as hard as them.

Chapter Thirty

Calli breathed a sigh of relief when Jet pulled his car into the parking lot of the government building and turned off the ignition. Her left hand clenched the door handle so hard she wondered if she'd be able to open her fingers to let loose. Benfu reached over and patted her leg.

"You can breathe now, m'love. We made it."

"Well, it's a miracle," she muttered back at him. "Jet drives like a maniac." She was glad she'd talked Linnea into staying with the store, as she didn't want her girls anywhere near the treacherous highway between cities. Widow Zu had stepped in to take charge of the house and younger girls, leaving Calli the freedom to go without worrying so much.

Jet jumped out and opened her car door. "Sorry about that, Lao Calli, but in this kind of traffic you either have to play with the big boys or get run off the road. In town I won't have to be so aggressive. It's only on the highways that we have to go so fast."

Calli climbed out and Benfu followed. Jet led them through the parking lot to the entrance. They climbed the stairs, moving past the security guard and into the building.

"Let me do the talking." Jet turned and whispered to them. "They're expecting me. My father called ahead."

Calli looked at Benfu and saw the scowl cross his face. He hadn't wanted to ask anyone for help once he found out that Dahlia was alive. She and Linnea had spent hours convincing him that Jet's connections were the only way to track the girl further. They only knew her last official foster home was outside of Suzhou, so if luck would have it, she would have moved into the city. But Suzhou was growing and there were millions of residents, Chinese and foreigners. Finding her without any help was like locating a needle in a haystack.

Jet obviously knew his way around the building as he led them up a flight of stairs and down another hall. He finally stopped in front of a door marked with a sign that read WANG QIANG.

He turned to them. "This is it. Now please, Lao Benfu, let me do this. I've grown up around these offices here and in Wuxi and I know how to handle this." Benfu nodded. Calli hoped he'd keep his silent agreement. Jet turned the knob and opened the door. Inside was a small inner office. A young secretary sat at a desk, typing at her keyboard. She turned to them.

"Yes? Can I help you?"

Jet gestured for Calli and Benfu to sit on the polished teakwood settee as he approached the girl.

"We have an appointment with Wang Qiang." Calli watched as the girl's cheeks turned rosy under Jet's attention.

"Of course. I'll let him know you are here." She got up and went to the other side of the room and tapped on the door. She entered and shut it behind her.

Jet turned to them. "Let's hope he's in a good mood. He probably won't remember me but I attended a fancy dinner party at his house a year ago."

Calli nodded and she waited for Benfu to say something, but he didn't. This was so far out of their comfort zone. Both of them disliked official environments after what they'd experienced at the hands of the government so many years ago.

The girl reappeared in the door and waved at them to come in. Jet waited for Calli to enter first; then he and Benfu followed. The girl rushed in with an extra chair and the three of them sat down in front of the huge desk.

Across from them sat a portly older man. His buttons on his white dress shirt looked as if they were barely holding on as the man leaned back in his chair and took a deep drag from his cigarette. His secretary moved over to the buffet cabinet and began to set up a tea tray.

"Sur Jet. You have grown into a handsome young man, I'll say." He smiled at Jet, showing his yellowed teeth. "You look just like your father when he was your age."

Jet nodded. "I'll take that as a compliment, Lao Wang."

"And to what do I owe the honor of your visit?" he asked, looking over Jet at Calli and Benfu.

Calli pasted a smile on her face. He was going to make them go through the entire story, even though Jet's father had obviously told it to him already. She watched the girl nervously bring the tray to the desk and pour four tiny cups of what smelled like jasmine tea; then the girl scurried out of the room. The official gestured toward the cups for them to take one.

Jet picked one up and took a sip, then set it back on the desk. "Lao Wang, I'm sure my father told you what is going on. I'd go into it more but it's truly a family matter of extreme confidentiality. The bottom line is that Lao Zheng here, and his wife, Calli, are searching for their daughter. My father said you were going to have your people run a search to see if she had applied for anything in the government system that would show us she's been here."

The old man nodded and picked up his own tea. He slurped it loudly.

"Yes, and I have an address here for an apartment she leased, if it is the same girl. It's been over a year ago and who knows, if she is such a wanderer, she may be gone by now."

Calli could see the nervous tic start up in Benfu's jaw, the one that only came when he was trying to keep his patience. The man was walking a fine line and Calli hoped for his sake he didn't step over it.

Jet smiled brightly at the man. "That's wonderful. It will be a start, Lao Wang. We are so grateful for your help." He looked to Benfu for agreement.

"Yes, thank you for your assistance. Can we have the address now?" Benfu added in a low voice.

The man ignored Benfu and turned back to Jet. "I believe we have one more matter to settle first." He pointed at the door. "If you'd be so kind to ask your friends to step out for a moment."

Jet stood and went to the door, then held it open. Calli gathered her bag and followed him with Benfu behind her. She had a feeling what the final matter was but she wasn't going to say a word. She just prayed she could get Benfu out before he exploded. The door closed behind them and Jet disappeared again.

They were once again standing in the secretary's office and the nervous girl beckoned for them to sit. Calli breathed a sigh of relief when Benfu did so. They stared at each other wordlessly while they waited.

Jet soon emerged with a triumphant look and a scrap of paper in his hands. Calli wondered how much he had paid for it and knew Benfu would find out later and insist on giving him the money.

"I have an address." He led them out of the office and out of the stuffy building. "It's across town in the older part of Suzhou, but we'll get there in less than an hour if traffic isn't too bad."

Calli felt weak with relief as she and Benfu followed Jet back to the car and to the lane she hoped would lead to their daughter.

Calli looked around as Jet drove slowly up the street. They'd crossed through town and she was shocked at how much Suzhou had changed since she'd last been there years before for a New Year's festival with the girls. Jet explained that Suzhou was now one of the top cities for foreign businesses, and all around the landmarks had been changed or removed to make way for new buildings and industrial parks—even a few new hotels that Calli didn't recognize. Jet had told her that the city boasted at least a dozen top-of-the-line gated neighborhoods that catered strictly to foreigners. She was glad to arrive in the older part of the city where it looked more like real China with familiar houses and brown faces. The difference between the newly updated modern parts of town and old Suzhou were a world apart, just like in Wuxi, she supposed.

Jet slowed in front of an old bridge and pointed opposite it to a line of two-story houses.

"That's it. The houses have been remodeled to have second-story apartments. I'm guessing 2A is at the top of that one."

They stared at the modest concrete building. It wasn't much but it could turn out to be the most magical place in China. Calli felt her palms sweating and she reached over to grab Benfu's hand. His touch always brought her a sense of calmness she couldn't achieve without him.

"Dahlia could be in there, Benfu. We may see our daughter today," she whispered, fighting against the lump in her throat. She was so overwhelmed. And nervous! What if her daughter didn't like her or was angry? She scolded herself. *Of course she'd be angry. She thinks she was abandoned. She probably thinks we're evil and heartless parents!*

Benfu patted her hand. "I know your imagination is running amok and don't get your hopes up, my Calla Lily. She may not live here any longer."

Jet pulled the car to the curb and shut it off. They all climbed out and stood on the sidewalk. It was overgrown with weeds and looked crooked and unkempt, but the small yard still beckoned to her. Calli followed the walkway to the stairway that ran up the side of the building. Jet let her take the lead. Calli noticed an elderly lady peering out her window on the first floor and the woman gave her a friendly wave as she passed by.

The three of them climbed the staircase and found themselves in front of a door marked 2A. This was it. Calli looked at Benfu and he nodded his encouragement, then put his arm around her shoulder protectively.

With her hand shaking, she knocked lightly on the door, then held her breath with anticipation.

Calli still couldn't get over the fact that the tall, white man who'd opened the door was her daughter's boyfriend, as he'd claimed when she asked him what he was doing in an apartment rented in her daughter's name. She was sure her look of shock was as obvious to him as his was to her when she'd declared herself Li Jin's mother.

"Li Jin told me she didn't have any family," he'd said, looking at them suspiciously. Even more shocking than his pale foreign looks was his ability to speak Chinese. Though hard to understand, he had enough of a grasp of the language that they were making do.

"She said she's been alone all her life, until she met me," he added, sneering at them through his golden good looks.

Those words had put a knife through her heart and, thank goodness, Benfu had stepped up and taken over. Calli couldn't imagine what her daughter had gone through and what had made her choose such an unsavory fellow to have a relationship with. She'd almost slipped and corrected the foreigner, told him her daughter was named Dahlia. But fortunately she'd held her tongue. Something unsettling in her gut told her not to share her daughter's secrets with him.

"She didn't know she had family. It's all been a tragic mistake, but something we need to discuss privately with our daughter. Can you tell us where she is?"

The man, his name was Erik he'd said, shook his head. Now here they were a half hour later and they still hadn't gotten much information from him other than that she'd left suddenly and had been gone a few weeks. He'd made it obvious from his tone that she had left without his approval.

"Does she have a cell phone number we can try?" Jet asked.

"Nope, she left that behind. But she'll be back. She owes me something and I've got something very valuable of hers, too." The smirk spread across his face until Calli felt like slapping it loose.

"Oh, what's that?" Benfu asked. Calli could see him looking around to see what could be valuable in the home. Other than a few African-style paintings, she didn't see much to brag about but the apartment was okay. Messy—but it could be nice if cleaned up a bit.

Behind him Calli saw the door to what must be the bedroom crack open just an inch or so. A face appeared and she locked eyes with a little boy. He looked scared. And he definitely didn't belong to the foreigner—he was as Chinese as she was. As she took in the contours of his face, she realized something about him looked familiar. She felt a tingle start in her fingers and travel up her arms and to the back of her neck.

The man continued his evasive act. "Oh, just something." He lit a cigarette and leaned his head back against the chair, blowing smoke rings from his foreign cigarette into the air.

"So, do you have children?" Calli asked, trying to keep her eyes from wandering back to the boy. She knew immediately by the way he looked that he wasn't supposed to be snooping.

"Nah, never had any. Well, if you'd like to leave a contact number, I can give you a call when Li Jin comes back, man." He stood up to lead them to the door. He was obviously in a hurry to get them out of there.

Calli cringed to hear the foreigner call Benfu *man*. She knew her husband and he'd find it offensive that he wasn't being addressed with the proper *Lao* title earned by being his age. Surprisingly, he ignored it and pulled his mobile phone from his pocket. "And when do you expect her, would you guess?"

The bedroom door opened a little more and the boy poked his head out farther. "Ma's coming back, Erik? When?"

The man turned around, his face a mask of anger. "Dammit, I told you not to come out of that room, Jojo! Get back in there."

Calli knew then what looked so familiar—the child looked like Benfu. He had the same contoured face and nose she'd looked at for decades. This was their grandson! Before she could move, he stepped back and slammed the door, obviously frightened.

"Who is this boy you call Jojo?" Ignoring the angry glare of the foreigner, Calli quickly crossed the room and pushed the door open all the way. The boy had moved to the bed and was sitting on the edge, tears running down his face as he clutched a red-striped pillow.

"Excuse me—you can't go in there!" the man said, standing up and turning to follow Calli.

From the corner of her eye Calli saw Benfu also stand and put his hand up. "Stay right there. Don't go even one step closer to my wife."

"Old man, you'd better move out of my way," the guy said, starting to move around Benfu. His choppy Mandarin was getting worse the more excited he got but Calli could still understand him.

Calli sat down on the bed next to the little boy and put her arms around him. "Hi, Jojo. Are you okay?"

The little boy began to let out ragged sobs until Calli pulled him tighter to her. "What is it? Please, tell me what's wrong." Through the doorway she looked up to see the man ignore Benfu's command, then Benfu whip the man's arm around his back and throw him up against the wall. The poor foreigner likely didn't know what hit him—as her husband was as strong as an old oak tree when his ire was up.

Benfu held him there until Jet stepped in. Calli turned the little boy to the side so the scene wasn't within his view. She had a feeling the poor boy had seen enough.

"Let me go!" the man yelled, adding a long line of curse words.

"Be still and I will," Jet calmly answered, pushing the man's arm even higher until he yelped.

"I'm calling the police and they can sort this out," Benfu answered, looking around the floor to see where his phone had dropped in the scuffle.

"Wait! *Hao le, hao le.* I'm good. No police, please." The man suddenly calmed and gave up his struggle. Jet still held him against the wall, burying the man's face against the concrete.

Benfu stayed only a foot or so behind him. "I'm going to tell Jet to let you go, but if you make one move toward my wife or that child, you'll be right back there and this time with that foreign beak of yours broken."

Calli had never heard him sound so formidable and she believed he would truly hurt the foreigner if the man was dumb enough to come at her again. She prayed he wasn't. They didn't need the trouble getting mixed up with a foreigner could cause.

"Okay. I swear. Just don't involve anyone official." With that Jet let him go and Calli saw Benfu point to the chair the man had bolted from.

"Sit. Now."

The man obeyed and Calli turned her focus back to the boy. Not just any boy! Her own daughter's child! "So tell me, why are you so scared? Do you know where your mother is?"

Jojo nodded. "We took a bus to another town and when I got off the bus, Erik's friend snatched me and brought me here. My ma doesn't know where I am. Can you call her?"

Calli gasped. She could only imagine how frantic Dahlia was in the disappearance of her son. And why would the foreigner do such a thing? Why didn't he just try to talk it out with Dahlia and get whatever it was he thought she owed him? She struggled to keep a calm face to console the child.

"I heard that man call you Jojo." She used the end of her sweater to wipe the tears from his cheeks. "Is that your name?"

Jojo nodded, sniffling. Calli shook her head. The poor kid looked like he hadn't bathed in at least a week and his clothes smelled horrible. He obviously needed his mother.

"Well, Jojo, we have a lot to talk about. How would you like to come with me for a little outing?" Now that she'd seen the fear in his eyes from the foreigner, there was no way she was leaving him.

The boy looked up at her. "But who are you? Do you know my ma?"

Calli swallowed against the sudden lump in her throat. "I don't anymore, Jojo, but I really want to. I knew her a long time ago and I've missed her so much. Maybe you can help me out with that."

She looked out the doorway at the tense scene in the living room. She wanted to take Jojo out of there but didn't think it was safe yet. Both Benfu and Jet stood beside the foreigner's chair, waiting for him to try to move. She met Benfu's eyes and he looked from her to Jojo and then back to her. In his face, under the glint of anger, she saw astonishment and hope. They'd found a piece of their daughter, and with the discovery of the boy, they'd been given an unexpected gift. A grandson.

Benfu broke the gaze and sat down across from the man. When he began to speak, Calli felt the hairs on the back of her neck rise up at the low, lethal tone of his voice.

"This is the way it's going to go. You are going to tell me where to find my daughter and I'm going to take her boy to her. Obviously that's what you meant by having something valuable of hers, you blithering idiot." He glared at the guy. "And then if you know what's good for your future, you are going to disappear from their life."

Erik held his hands up helplessly. "I'd love to know where she is, but I don't. I only know that when she figures out Jojo is here, she'll come back. She'll do anything for her kid, man."

Even from a distance, Calli saw Benfu's face turn red and knew he'd had enough of the insulting slang title.

"Don't call me—" Benfu's reprimand was interrupted when they heard the doorknob turn and the front door open. Calli peered around the men and saw a small old woman standing there with her hands on her hips and a half-knit scarf hanging from her hands.

"I know where Li Jin is but I didn't know he'd gotten ahold of Jojo," the woman said, giving Erik a defiant look. "But I'm not telling you where Li Jin is in front of him." She pointed at Erik. "She had to run from this foreign devil. He hurt her terribly."

Chapter Thirty-One

Li Jin picked up the bucket of cleaning supplies and closed the door behind her. She crossed the hall to the room opposite hers and entered, finding Sami struggling to snap the sheet into the air just right to come down evenly on top of the bed. She was so petite that all the chores were a bit harder for her, though she'd never admit it.

"Here, let me help you." Li Jin took one edge of the sheet and together they made the bed and folded the ruby-red duvet neatly on the end. They plumped the pillows and Li Jin stood up and arched her back. Using her one good arm, she reached behind her and rubbed at the knot of tension.

"I can finish the room," Sami said, and pointed at the glass door leading to a small patio. "You go out there and take a break."

Li Jin looked toward the hallway. She'd only been helping clean the patron rooms for a week and didn't want any of the other girls, or especially Shuwen, to find her doing nothing.

"Just go! Five minutes. No one is around," Sami insisted. "Anyway, you're too clumsy with just one arm to do me much good."

Li Jin knew Sami was teasing, despite her ferocious expression. She'd become very protective of her since their friendship had bloomed. Li Jin opened the door and slipped out. She didn't dare take the chance to sit in one of the bamboo chairs; instead she leaned over the gate and stared at the small pond. The tiny courtyard was exquisite; fair enough, considering the inn only had eight rooms for rent and this was their most expensive one. Sami had told her they'd just gotten a week's rental confirmed for a German photographer who'd come through the village sightseeing and wanted to stay awhile.

So far she'd been at the inn for almost two weeks and even though she still went to the police headquarters every morning, they'd found no evidence of Jojo. The day she'd gone to the train station with Sami, they'd sent the driver to go get copies of his photo made into posters. When he brought them and they'd finished hanging them around the station, she'd broken down and wept in frustration. Sami had comforted her and since then they'd been inseparable. Shuwen had even paired them up for their daily tasks and though Li Jin would rather be in the kitchen cooking, cleaning the rooms kept her physically exhausted. Only after a full day starting at the police headquarters, searching the train station, and then finishing her workload was she able to stop worrying about where Jojo was and trick her brain into shutting down for some much-needed sleep each night.

As for the other girls, they had finally accepted her, and though she hadn't so far formed any real bonds with anyone but Sami, she felt comfortable and no longer an outsider. Sami had filled her in on a lot of their stories, and for once in her life Li Jin saw that there were others who'd suffered as much as or even more than she. She wasn't alone. Being an orphan, she'd especially felt a surge of appreciation for one young girl who bunked next to her. Sami explained to her the girl had to run with her infant so that she could keep her because the child's father had wanted his wife to abandon her.

The others had finally warmed toward Li Jin when she began doing her share of work. When it was time to settle down and enjoy the evening, they all flocked to the attic but Li Jin tried to find other things around the inn that needed doing. She watered flowers, swept the walkways, and even got on her knees and pulled stray weeds in the various gardens outside the rooms if they weren't occupied. More often than not, Sami tagged along and helped her in whatever needed to be done. Sami had even snipped the last threads of her stitches and pulled them out! They didn't talk much; instead they worked silently and comfortably together, each lost in her own thoughts.

Today had been a tolerable day. She listened to Sami vacuuming the room behind her as she watched the part of the street she could see from the courtyard. For such a small village, it was busy. She saw bicycles and scooters going by, and the sidewalks were dotted with pedestrians, but only a few cars.

Across the way she could clearly see many of the ancient rooftops that still stood after decades of modernization in surrounding cities had failed to reach Hongcun. Unlike the heavy concrete most houses were built with in Suzhou, these were all either stone or brick—some with pale pink walls and black roof tiles. Li Jin was surprised they weren't demolished during the upheaval of the Cultural Revolution when everything old was being destroyed. There was so much beauty in this village that she found it enchanting, almost as if she'd stepped back in time.

On a few of their evening strolls, she'd seen the many university students who were bussed in and left to hike to the small pond to practice their brush stroke or photography skills. The small town and surrounding scenery were the perfect backdrop for their work. It was a lovely place and though it couldn't feel like home without Jojo being there, Li Jin was sure it was one of the most peaceful places she had ever stayed.

"I'm done." Sami poked her head out the door. "That was our last room. Want to go for a walk to Moon Pond before dinner?"

Li Jin nodded and followed Sami back into the room and down the hall. They passed the kitchen and saw a few of the girls peeling what looked like turnips, with Auntie Wan behind them stirring her pots at the stove, a platter of fish and diced red peppers sitting on the counter beside her. They slipped by and out the door.

"Auntie Wan is making turnips and minced fish tonight, isn't she?" Li Jin said to make conversation. She didn't see what other recipe would accompany it, as they'd moved by too quickly.

"Looks that way," Sami answered, and led the way down the cobbled path toward the pond.

Li Jin could say one thing for sure; they were well fed by Auntie Wan. The old woman made sure to prepare enough to feed her girls as well as all the customers. Li Jin was just itching to find out how she made her concoctions so delicious. Some of her recipes were spicy ones passed down from her Sichuan heritage, and the girls who waited on the foreigners got a good chuckle from the red faces and teary eyes as they moved in and out of the dining room. Li Jin had at first wondered how they communicated with the guests who didn't speak Chinese, but she soon saw them handing out picture menus with the meal-of-the-day options printed on them. The customers only had to point to the one they wanted, making it a simple exchange. And Auntie Wan gave only two choices, after all, so not much got lost in translation and she didn't have to create multiple dishes all day.

A step behind Sami, Li Jin noticed that she turned heads everywhere she went. Her small stature and graceful walk stood out, but the girl was oblivious to the commotion she caused as she walked down the pathway. Li Jin felt tall next to her, even though she'd always thought of herself as average height. It was just that Sami looked like a tiny doll compared to most women—a perfect one at that.

"Let's sit," Li Jin suggested, and pointed at the bench she'd sat at with Shuwen. They crossed the path but an elderly man beat them to the bench. Without words they both plopped down on the grass a few feet away. Li Jin was glad they did, as the coolness under her fingers was a comfort and a distraction.

Sami stared at the ripples in the water in front of her, ignoring the people around them who passed between her and the pond.

Li Jin saw a pack of tourists pointing to the pond. It was part of the draw of the crowds, she guessed, that the movie *Crouching Tiger, Hidden Dragon* had filmed a few scenes over the pond. She started to say as much to Sami but the girl broke the silence between them first.

"I've been thinking," she said in a voice barely above a whisper.

Li Jin didn't push her. Sami didn't ever say much and she'd learned quickly to give her time to get it out in her own time.

"I might make a quick trip home."

That got Li Jin's attention real fast. "Home? What about your father and your uncle? Won't they send you back?"

Sami sighed. "They'll try. But I won't go back to that life. Ever. I'd kill someone if they tried to force me."

"Then why do you want to go home?" Li Jin didn't want Sami to ever be around her father or uncle again. The girl was lucky to still be alive, considering the beating she'd taken.

Sami reached up and unbuttoned her shirt, then pulled the collar down to expose her neck and shoulder. "Because I have a little sister, and I'm afraid they'll do this and make her take my place." Sami pulled her shirt closed and stared at her feet.

Li Jin didn't get a long look but from what she saw, Sami had been tattooed. It looked like an elaborate scene of scrolls and butterflies. Quite beautiful, but in China it was unusual for anyone to be tattooed unless they were connected to some sort of gang. No wonder Sami always wore her clothing buttoned high.

"How old is she?" Li Jin asked gently. She'd never had any siblings that she knew of but she could only imagine how terrifying it would be to think your sister would be forced into the life Sami fought to flee.

"She's twelve and her name is Xue," Sami said softly, buttoning up her shirt. "I was thirteen when my father sent me to my uncle. Before that, it wasn't so bad. My mother loved us and always protected us, until she couldn't anymore. I'm thinking of going right now, Li Jin. That's why I wanted to talk to you."

Right now? Li Jin struggled. "Listen, Sami. If you can only wait until I find Jojo, I'll go with you. And I promise you that no one will touch you if I'm there." Li Jin felt a surge of protection for Sami, almost as strong as what she felt for Jojo. Sami reminded her of herself at that age, vulnerable and taken advantage of.

Sami looked at her. "You'd do that for me? Even though it's a long way from here and might be dangerous?"

Li Jin nodded. "I will. But I can't leave here yet. Something tells me that this is where I am supposed to stay until Jojo comes back for me. Can you understand that?" She knew she was asking a lot. Her mother's instinct or maybe just wishful thinking told her Jojo would come find her if she just kept returning to the spot where she last saw him.

"I understand. And I'll talk to Shuwen to see if I can bring my sister here. If she says yes, we'll make a plan. If she says no, I'll take her somewhere else. But either way, I have to get Xue out of there before they decide she will take my place. And while we're there, maybe we can find a way to make them pay for what they did to me."

Li Jin didn't answer. Going after her sister was one thing, but she hoped with time, Sami would drop the need for retribution.

It could only get her hurt and Li Jin didn't want anything else to happen to the girl. It was time for Sami to move on and build a new life, and Li Jin hoped that maybe the two of them could work together to accomplish that.

Chapter Thirty-Two

Calli tucked the blanket over Jojo's lap and looked at Benfu. Their grandson sat nestled between them in the backseat, sleeping like a little angel. Jing, along for the ride and an impromptu visit to her sister, bravely took the seat up front with Jet and now lay against the window, snoring gently. Calli whispered a word of gratitude to the gods for the old woman and then looked back down at Jojo. Her heart felt it would burst with love.

"He's something, isn't he?" she said softly. She couldn't stop looking at him. Their life had taken a drastic turn and though she didn't know what awaited her when they met Dahlia, she wouldn't trade the last day with their grandson for anything in the world.

Benfu nodded and a proud smile worked its way across his face. He tilted his head to the side just enough that his lips touched the top of Jojo's head in a light kiss. He hadn't tried to be affectionate while the boy was awake and prattling on with stories about his life, but Calli could see he couldn't resist now. She saw him close his eyes and inhale and knew he was experiencing that same little-boy smell she'd already discovered after she'd persuaded Jojo to take a soapy bath at the hotel. So far he'd not made the connection that they were his grandparents, as they'd decided that title would only be given to them if his own mother wanted it that way.

Benfu finally looked up. "Do you think his stories are true?"

Calli sighed. "He doesn't strike me as the kind to make up things. I'm sad to say it, but I think yes, they are probably true."

In his matter-of-fact way of talking, Jojo had told them about their time before Erik when they lived on the streets and occasionally slept in a hostel or even in department stores when cold weather hit. He described it as an adventure of hiding until the employees left for the night, but to Calli it sounded like a desperate situation. But no more so than the story he told about Dahlia being taken from her first foster family, the ones who had given her a nice home. With his vivid descriptions he'd made the couple sound almost like characters from a fairy tale, but the unhappy ending of her being returned to the orphanage still rang in her ears. The thought that her little girl was bounced around and left to think she was unwanted was like a dagger in her heart.

She had watched Benfu as the little boy talked and could tell he was suffering as much as she. She could honestly say, however, that it sounded like her daughter was a resourceful and protective mother to her son. He obviously adored her.

Jet had listened from the front seat and respectfully not intervened, just like Jing. Even though he was almost family now, he knew they were overwhelmed with processing all of the newest information in their hands and didn't need the opinion of anyone else.

Calli was just glad that Jet had offered to drive them to Hongcun. Calli also knew it was his way of helping her get Benfu away from the foreigner before he totally lost it and put his big hands around his neck and squeezed. When Jing had explained she lived downstairs and told them what had been going on right above her, Calli thought Benfu would surely kill the stunned man. The foreigner had accused Jing of lying but there was no doubt the old woman had no reason to lie. They'd believed her and followed her down to her apartment to listen to the entire story. Jing had offered to lead them to Dahlia and they'd accepted. Her presence obviously made Jojo comfortable, so they were glad to have her.

Jojo jumped up and down, almost unable to contain himself, when they'd told him they would take him to his mother. Now they'd been on the road for over five hours and Jojo was spent.

"Did you talk to all the girls?" she asked Benfu, wondering if their daughters were okay.

"Yes, I talked to them all."

"Even Jasmine?" That one she was worried about, as she was the most attached to her Ye Ye and would take their extended absence the hardest.

"Yep—I told her I loved her to the moon and back, just like always."

"Did she say anything in return?" Calli asked, holding her breath.

She heard him sigh. "Now Calli, you know the answer to that. And you need to try to sleep, m'love," Benfu said, breaking her away from her thoughts. "We still have a few hours to go."

Calli smiled at him. "How can I sleep when I know at the end of this trip I'll see my daughter?"

She didn't even want to stop but so far they'd made a few detours. They'd had dinner at a tiny roadside restaurant and they'd been astonished to watch such a small boy put away so many noodles and even top it off with red bean ice cream. And they'd forgotten what tiny bladders children have. Jojo had asked to stop more than a few times to relieve himself. He'd stuck to Benfu each time like glue, afraid to be whisked away again by a stranger. He'd described the gangster-looking boy to them, and even though he wasn't treated roughly, Calli wondered how long it would take him to forget what he'd been through.

They passed a billboard of a beautiful girl modeling a line of clothing and Calli thought of Linnea. She hated that everything had happened at the same time as her success, and hoped it didn't take away from her joy too much.

"Jet? What did Lin say when you told her we'd be gone another night? Is everything okay at the store?" With all the commotion, he'd offered to call Linnea while they talked with Jing and decided the travel details.

"She was excited for you that we're so close to finding Dahlia," he answered, looking in the rearview mirror at Calli. "And she said business is still going well and people are still asking for her autograph. She's already ordered another double shipment of her shirts."

Benfu chuckled. "Our girl is quite the entrepreneur. She also asked Jet to take photos of anything he sees that would make a good design for her shirts. She's always thinking ahead, that one."

Calli nodded. She felt like Jet and Linnea were keeping something from them. She didn't know what but mother's instinct told her something was up. She knew one thing for sure; Linnea was definitely going to be an even bigger success than she could imagine. Of that she had no doubt. They wouldn't have to worry about her future. She just hoped she and Benfu could help Dahlia straighten out her life and get off to a new start. She closed her eyes. More than anything she wanted their daughter to allow them into her life. If Dahlia would just give them a chance to explain everything, Calli would work to make it right for her.

A few hours later Calli listened as Jing directed Jet through the small streets. From what they could see it was more of a village than a town. Jing had called her sister and there was room at the inn she owned. Though Jet had driven as fast as the law would allow, it was after midnight, and Jing had suggested waiting until morning to meet their daughter and turn over her son. Jing's sister said she had paying customers and didn't want to wake the entire house. Calli had balked, but Benfu had calmed her down, reminding her that Jojo had been through so much and would be better seeing his mother in the morning after a few hours' rest.

"Turn here," Jing instructed, "then pull into that alley and go to the end."

Calli's skin was covered in goose bumps as Jet followed the narrow lane and then parked the car behind a building the old woman pointed out.

"This is it," Jing said from the front seat. "The girls live in quarters above the inn, and my sister rents out rooms on the first floor."

They piled out and Calli fretted as Benfu easily lifted Jojo into his arms. Jet offered to take him but, not surprisingly, Benfu refused. Calli could see a fresh look of amazement briefly cross Benfu's face when he cradled his grandson next to his chest. The boy looked small in the big arms wrapped around him, but he didn't move—he was too exhausted from the trip and the excitement of it all.

Jet opened the trunk and got their bags; then he and Benfu followed Jing up the path as she led them to the back door, with Calli trailing behind. She couldn't believe that she was only feet from her daughter! How was she ever going to go to sleep knowing that somewhere over her head the child who was taken from her lay sleeping?

The door opened, and a woman who looked eerily like Jing stepped out and waved them in. It had to be Shuwen. "Come on in. Hurry up before the mosquitos follow you."

Calli reached out and put her hands around Jojo's head to protect him from the door frame as Benfu turned sideways to bring him through, the boy's long legs dangling almost to the floor.

"This way, I'll show you to the room and you can lay him on the bed," Shuwen said, and led her and Benfu through the hall. They went past a big kitchen and a few other doors to the last one on the end. The woman opened it and switched on the lamp. Calli rushed to turn down the covers and Benfu laid Jojo gently down. She covered him up, then turned to Benfu and Shuwen. She saw Jet standing patiently in the hall.

"Lao Shuwen, I'd appreciate it if you'd show Jet to a room—he's exhausted from the drive. Benfu, you can sleep beside Jojo. I'll take the chair." She pointed to the chaise near the window. "I don't feel like sleeping, anyway."

Shuwen waved her hand in the air. "Nonsense. My housekeeper is bringing a cot. Both of you can sleep. But first, come to the kitchen for a cup of tea and then I'm off to bed. What a long day I've had."

Calli didn't feel much like talking. Her mind was spinning out of control with what-ifs. She looked at Benfu and could see he was thinking the same. "Do you mind if we take a rain check? Thank you so much for your kindness, but you go ahead and visit with your sister and we'll take a walk before we settle in."

Shuwen nodded. "Just leave this door cracked a bit and I'll check on him in a few minutes. You two go walk around Moon Pond. Try to let your *qi* resolve itself so you can get some rest."

She pointed down the hall the opposite way they'd come in. "Use the front door and the cobblestone path will lead you right to the pond. I'll have your cot set up when you return, and you can wash up and go to bed. First thing in the morning, you'll find Li Jin having breakfast with the others."

"Thank you so much for everything, Lao Shuwen." Benfu bowed to the woman.

"No thanks are needed. In only a limited time, I've found your daughter to be an exceptional and devoted woman. I cannot wait to see her reunited with her son. Oh—I'll be sure to pull her out so the reunion won't be in front of the others. I'll come get you when I have her ready. Jet, you follow me. We'll fill your belly with some buns and tea, then get you off to bed."

"That will be perfect," Benfu said.

Calli followed him out the door, then took one last look at Jojo. He was still sleeping soundly.

Shuwen waved her hands again. "Go. He's fine."

Something told Calli she could trust the old woman, so as Shuwen led Jet toward the kitchen, Calli let Benfu take her hand. They left for one more walk in which they'd both wonder what sort of woman their daughter had turned out to be. It would be a long night for them both, this she knew. She marveled that in only a few hours, they'd finally get their answer with their own eyes.

Chapter Thirty-Three

Li Jin tossed and turned in the bed, feeling hot all over. She and Sami had worked just as hard as usual earlier in the day, but still she couldn't go to sleep. She was too restless and didn't know why. She sat up and looked over at Sami in the bed next to her. She *looked* like she was sleeping . . . but maybe she was still awake and wanted to talk. Lately they'd had many long conversations about the hardships both of them had overcome and the parallels in their lives. Talking with someone about it after years of keeping it all inside was proving to be therapeutic. Tonight she wanted to talk about Jojo. She could not stop thinking of him.

"Sami," she whispered.

The mound of blankets didn't move.

Li Jin looked at the other beds. From the complete stillness she could see everyone except her was sleeping. She quietly went to her trunk and unlocked it, took out her clothes and shoes, and got dressed. She'd take a walk to clear her head and, she hoped, tire herself out more. Six in the morning was right around the corner and it was going to be a rough day if she couldn't get any sleep. She carefully reattached her padlock and tugged on it to make sure it was secure; she didn't want to come back and realize she'd been robbed—even if it wasn't really her money, it was her and Jojo's only way to build a new life.

She reached up to smooth her hair and tiptoed out of the attic and down the stairs. She heard voices in the kitchen and wondered who was awake so late, but didn't want to talk to anyone but Sami, so she slipped out the front door. The night was cool and she shivered, then crossed her arms over her chest. She probably should have felt more nervous being out so late alone but she didn't. She'd traveled around much scarier places in her life.

The village was also asleep, and the quiet sounds of the cicadas and the water were soothing to her restless spirit. Li Jin wished Sami had come with her, as the area surrounding the pond during the day was usually packed with people and tonight it was serene. She'd just sit on the bench for a while, then go back and try again to get some sleep.

As she got closer to the bench, she could make out the form of a couple sitting there. From the back it appeared to be a man and woman, his arm around her shoulders as they stared at the pond. Li Jin didn't want to intrude, and she also didn't want company herself. She began to cross behind them to get to the other side. She walked as quietly as possible in the grass, trying not to make any noise.

Now that she was closer, she could see from the moonlight that it was an older couple. She thought they were out fairly late for their age, but she smiled at the obvious closeness they shared. The woman's head lay on his shoulder and the protective way he held her made Li Jin's heart ache. She could only hope to feel that kind of love one day.

She stepped on a twig and the man turned to see what was behind them.

"It's just me," she said. She didn't want to scare the elderly people into a heart attack. "Sorry. I was only taking a walk."

The old woman turned at the sound of her voice and Li Jin found herself under close scrutiny from them both. She supposed a stroll wasn't in the cards and turned to go.

"Wait," the woman said. She looked tired but even with the obvious fatigue on her face and in her voice, Li Jin thought she was lovely. The woman looked at her so intensely it made her uncomfortable. Then she called out to her again. "Wait. Please."

"Excuse me?" Li Jin stopped. Maybe they wanted directions or something. She waited as the woman leaned her head in and whispered to the man. With her words, the man abruptly stood, his wife rising, too. He also looked at her for a few seconds, as if he wanted to ask her something important. Finally he spoke.

"Is your name Li Jin?" the man asked, his voice sort of gravelly and shaky. He was a big man—not in a huge way but in a way that made Li Jin think when he walked into a room he owned it, even if it wasn't his intention.

Li Jin was confused. Who were these people and how did they know her name?

The woman stepped around the bench and came toward her. "Li Jin, I know it's you. This is going to come as a shock but we came here to meet you. We're staying at the Moon Harbor Inn. Lao Shuwen told us we could talk to you in the morning."

Li Jin squinted in the dark and stepped closer. "Oh. Hello. But who are you?" She moved even closer and was shocked to see tears glistening on both of their faces. What was going on? Had someone found Jojo?

The woman started to answer but seemed to choke on her words. The old man put his arm around her and comforted her for a second, then looked up.

"Li Jin, we are your parents and we've been searching for you for a very long time."

Li Jin felt like the world was swirling around her as she tried to take in the words the old man spoke. She felt someone at her side and then an arm slipped around her back, giving her support. She opened her eyes to find Sami beside her.

"Li Jin? Who are these people? I woke up and you were gone. I came to look for you."

"They claim they are my parents," Li Jin said in barely more than a whisper.

The old man stepped up and took control. "Here. Come sit over on this bench. We've had a few days to process this and you've only had a few seconds. I know it must feel like you've been hit over the head with a sledgehammer."

He moved to Li Jin's other side and gently guided her to the bench. She sat down and the old woman lowered herself onto the seat beside her. Li Jin looked at them both and saw nothing but sincerity. Whoever they were, they truly believed they were her parents. Sami crouched beside the bench, watching them and giving Li Jin a feeling of security.

"Please, say that again." She finally pushed the request out of her mouth. Even if it couldn't be true, she'd waited her entire life to hear those words.

The woman sat down beside her and took her hand, holding it in her lap and patting it comfortingly. It took her a few tries between her sobs but she finally choked out the words again. "I know this is going to sound impossible, but I am your mother." She nodded at her husband. "And that handsome fellow over there is your father. But best of all, we have some very good news for you. We've found Jojo."

Li Jin could barely believe her ears. Everything else the woman said faded away and only one word remained. Jojo? They'd found him? She stood quickly, feeling the blood rush to her head too fast, and staggered. Sami was right beside her, holding her steady.

"Where? Where's my son?" She looked around frantically. She could deal with the other stuff later. She wanted her son. Now.

"He's in bed asleep back at the inn. I promise you this," the old man answered. "We tracked you from Beijing to Suzhou. From there we found your apartment and Jojo was there with the *waiguoren*. Your neighbor, Lao Jing, heard the commotion and came upstairs. When she found out he had Jojo and who we were, she led us here."

Li Jin felt dizzy with the range of emotions that ran through her, but the sudden rage she felt at Erik topped them all. He'd pay for taking her son.

The old woman nodded. "And we *are* your parents. It's true, Li Jin. It took us thirty years, but we've found you. I have orphanage photos of you back in the room, I can show you."

Li Jin shook her head. "Thirty years plus some, you mean." She didn't want to sound so angry but she couldn't help it. She'd fantasized about this day for her entire life but it wasn't going as she'd planned. Instead of embraces and declarations of love, the bitterness threatened to envelop her if she didn't spit it out. "What took you so damn long? Wasn't I important enough to look for earlier?"

She could barely see through the tears that sprang from her eyes, but from the look on the woman's face, her words had cut like a knife. Even the old man looked astonished at her anger. What did they expect? She'd lived on the streets, begged for money, been beaten and coerced, and almost killed. Was she supposed to be grateful they'd decided to finally claim her?

"Li Jin," Sami whispered. "I wouldn't trust them, but if you want to decide for yourself, you're going to have to let them tell their side of the story."

The couple stood together, watching her and waiting for her next words. They were hurt, Li Jin could see that, but it was unavoidable and anyway—so was she.

"And how do I even know I'm their long-lost daughter?" She looked from Sami to them and back to Sami for encouragement. The whole idea of her parents' finding her after three decades sounded far-fetched. And just coincidentally they showed up with her missing son?

Sami held her hands up and shrugged. Li Jin didn't know what to say. She didn't even know what to think! "I'm sorry but I can't think of anything right now but seeing my son." She turned and ran down the path, leaving Sami behind with them. As she sprinted, she heard the old woman call out behind her in a strangled voice.

"Li Jin, wait—your real name is Dahlia. And you've got the flower tattooed on your heel!"

The woman's words rang in her ears as she burst through the door of the inn. Shuwen met her in the hallway, her face a fright. The noise had scared her out of bed and she struggled to tie the sash around her gaping robe.

"What are you doing out there, Li Jin? I thought you were upstairs asleep!"

"Where is my Jojo, Shuwen? What room did you put those people in?" Li Jin stomped down the hall, ready to fling every door open to find her son. She'd even tear them off the hinges if she had to.

"The Orchid Room, Li Jin. Hush! You're going to wake all the customers!" Shuwen led her to the Orchid Room and pushed open the door. "Didn't *those people* tell you who they were?"

Li Jin ignored her and moved around her into the room. She looked but with the dimness saw only a lump under the covers. She bent down and switched on the lamp, then froze.

There he was. He lay curled up on his side with his hands balled into fists the way he always slept. She dropped to her knees beside the bed, unable to stand any longer. The tears ran down her face as she leaned over and stroked his hair and inhaled his familiar smell. She had her son back. He was alive and well. Her crying turned ragged and his eyelashes fluttered.

"Ma?" He opened his eyes.

Li Jin climbed onto the bed. "It's me, Jojo." She sobbed and held her arms out. Jojo bolted up and fell into them and all felt right with the world once again. Li Jin held him tight and he squeezed her back just as hard.

"It was that gang boy, Ma. He got me from the bus and took me to Erik."

Behind her she heard Shuwen close the door softly. She hugged Jojo tighter and thought he felt a bit skinnier.

"Oh, Jojo. I'm so sorry. It was my fault. I never should have taken my eyes from you. Did they hurt you?" She prayed they hadn't laid a hand on his little head and if they had, God help them.

"No, but Erik only cooked that weird foreign stuff. I was starving."

Li Jin laughed through her tears, then guided him to lie down beside her. She pulled him closer and spooned his body against hers. "I'll fix you up, Son. First let's get some sleep. Tomorrow I'm going to cook you all of your favorite things. Anything you want, and Auntie Wan is going to have to just move over and let me have her kitchen."

"Who is Auntie Wan?" Jojo murmured, already falling back asleep. Li Jin stroked his hair, her eyes wide open in the dark room. Now that her son was back in her arms, she couldn't stop thinking about the couple. *My parents? A real mother and a real father?* She could hardly believe it was true. But if it was—*aiya*—parents? She stared at the window and watched the clouds moving in front of the moon, wishing morning would come early. She had a lot of questions.

Chapter Thirty-Four

Feeling a bit sluggish but relieved, Li Jin stood at the kitchen stove with one of Auntie Wan's colorful patchwork aprons tied to her waist. As she waited for the batter to bubble in her pan, the old woman bustled around her. With the help of one of the other girls, Auntie Wan worked on the other dishes for their celebratory breakfast while Li Jin made Jojo's favorite *jian bing* crepes for everyone. Every few minutes she glanced behind her to see if Jojo was still okay. She knew she shouldn't worry; all the girls had taken to him immediately and he was putting on all his charm to keep them won over. As a matter of fact, the young man who'd driven him there, Jet, sat on one side of him and Sami on the other. The girls giggled and stammered in the fellow's company while it was apparent Sami had already charmed Jojo by the way he kept looking shyly at her. Of course her son would choose the prettiest girl in the room to sit beside.

"Here're the green onions." Auntie Wan passed a small bowl to Li Jin. She pointed to a cupboard over the stove. "Chili sauce is in there. Don't drown the crepes with it or we'll have to put out some belly fires."

"*Xie xie,* Auntie Wan." Li Jin didn't tell her she'd been making the special crepes since Jojo was about three and didn't need any guidance. She quietly poured her beaten egg over the batter and added the green onions. She poured a dab of chili sauce, flipped the crepe over into a quarter size, and then added it to the platter. She immediately poured more batter for the next one.

This morning no one would allow Shuwen to do a thing except sit at the table with her sister, Jing. The girls were all captivated by how alike the two were, even though one was older and they wouldn't say who. It was amusing to watch them interacting, catching up on the family gossip and telling tales of when they were younger.

The room suddenly silenced around her and Li Jin turned to see what was happening. The couple she'd met the night before—who'd brought her Jojo back to her—had entered the kitchen. Shuwen jumped up from the table and beckoned to Li Jin. "Li Jin, Auntie Wan has set up a private space for you and the Zhengs. You can all talk over breakfast. Jojo can stay with us or go with you, whichever you prefer."

Zhengs? So that was supposed to be her name? She'd always wondered every time she'd had to write down the name *Dang* the institute had given her. It might not be true but she had to admit that *Zheng Li Jin* sounded much better than *Dang Li Jin*. She put the spatula down and untied the apron. The couple waited in the doorway for Li Jin to answer. They looked so earnest and Li Jin did owe them everything for bringing Jojo to her. She looked over at Sami and despite her expression of doubt, she still nodded her approval to Li Jin.

"Okay. Which room?" She picked up a towel and wiped her hands. "Jojo, you stay here with Sami."

Shuwen sat back down as if she'd won a battle. "The Weeping Willow Room. You can eat outside in the courtyard. Auntie Wan will get one of the girls to bring your food on a tray."

Li Jin sighed and moved past the couple and down the hall. She opened the door to the Weeping Willow Room and thought it fitting as she held it for them to enter. If she had to guess, she'd say neither of them had slept at all through the night.

The woman—Lao Zheng—looked anxious as she clutched a small red silk bag to her chest. Her husband kept a steady hand on her as if to comfort her. They walked through the sleeping area of the room and right to the patio, opened the door, and went outside. Li Jin followed.

In contrast to the rolling waves her nerves were causing in her stomach, Li Jin thought the courtyard looked serene and beautiful. Though only a small area, a huge weeping willow brought a magical feeling to the surroundings. She hid a smile when she saw that Auntie Wan had set the table prettily with a cloth and some of her finest dishes and chopsticks. In the center she had placed a vase with one simple white flower in it. Wan obviously wanted the talk to go well and Li Jin felt a rush of affection for her efforts to minimize the awkward situation.

"So, what would you like me to call you?" she asked, looking at the woman.

She'd caught her off guard and the woman looked at her husband for help. He cleared his throat.

"You can call us whatever you'd like. I'm Zheng Benfu and your *muqin* is Zheng Calli."

Muqin. Mother. There was that word again. It sounded so foreign to Li Jin. How could it be true? If she were to admit it, she'd have to say the couple looked like a storybook picture of what she would have imagined her parents to look like. But that still didn't make it true.

"Okay, Lao Calli and Lao Benfu. So you think I am your daughter. Can you give me more details as to why?" She felt foolish. She'd never thought she'd find herself asking someone to prove she was their daughter. It felt like an interview. It was just way too strange.

"Did you hear what I said last night about your name? And the tattoo?" the old woman asked, then began digging around in the bag she'd brought.

Li Jin nodded. "I heard you."

"Perhaps you were never told your real name, but do you have the flower on your heel?" the man asked. "Can you let us see?"

Li Jin ignored their question as Auntie Wan came through the door carrying a tray of tea and a few crepes. She also brought a dish of sliced watermelon. No one spoke as she laid it out on the table, then went back into the room, sliding the door shut as she left.

Li Jin watched the man pick up the teapot and turn over the three cups. He poured and set one in front of Li Jin, then another for him and his wife. Beside him the woman finally found what she was looking for and pulled out something wrapped in tissue paper and set it on the table.

"What is this?" Li Jin asked.

"Open it, please," the woman kindly requested as she sipped her cup of tea.

Li Jin reached over and pulled the package closer, then unfolded the sheet of tissue paper. It was an infant's outfit. She picked up the tiny red shirt and matching pants, then looked at the flowers intricately embroidered across the chest. The tiny frog ties were pink and still looked new.

"Who is this for?" she asked, looking at the couple.

The woman dabbed at her eyes with her napkin. Her husband reached over and put his arm around her. She took a deep breath before answering. "It was yours, Dahlia. It was to be the outfit you wore at your one-month party. But I never saw you in it because you were stolen as I slept. Someone snatched you out of your cradle and we searched and searched, but we couldn't find you. I can still see your tiny face in my mind. You were such a beautiful child."

Li Jin reached up and touched the scar on her face as she listened to the old woman's voice break. The man pulled a leather pouch from his inside pocket and opened it. There were photos inside, and he picked them out and set them on the table, fanning them out for her to see. They were old snapshots; she could see that by the tattered edges.

"We just got these recently and were told you were still alive. As soon as we had a strong lead, we came to find you. We speak the truth."

As a mother, Li Jin couldn't imagine what the woman had gone through. Her son had only been gone a few short weeks and she'd almost lost her mind over it. She felt the first stirrings of pity—or maybe forgiveness? The pain in the woman's eyes was so raw, she had to look away. She reached over and picked up the photos.

She sorted through them, remembering each and every day that they were taken. How could she forget the photographer telling her to smile so that someone would pick her to be their daughter? At first she had believed him and been hopeful. But later she knew no one would ever truly want her. In the last photo she remembered the indifferent expression she had perfected to hide the loneliness she held in her heart.

From the empty room beside the Weeping Willow Room, Sami quietly slid the window open and leaned in to listen. With her eyes trained on the patio, she could feel her heart racing as she watched the scene unfold before her. She was a bit stung that Li Jin hadn't asked her to be with her for this important meeting, so she decided to listen from the shadows. Only a second ago Li Jin looked strong and stubborn, but now something had changed in her demeanor. Sami could feel it even from so far away. *Was she so easily going to forgive them for the years of neglect?*

"So tell me how you got your first clue to how to find me." She heard Li Jin say this as she laid down a stack of photos, then calmly took a sip of tea.

"Way to go—stay strong, Li Jin, don't fall for their story of undying love", Sami whispered under her breath. She couldn't believe how composed Li Jin was after how upset she'd looked only the night before. Unable to go back to sleep, Sami had crept down the stairs a few hours after Li Jin had lain down with Jojo. She'd opened their door only a crack to see them sleeping wrapped in each other's arms. It was sweet but Sami couldn't help feeling a pang of jealousy. She was glad Li Jin had found her son—she really was—but it put a wrench in the new relationship they were building.

Now Sami would have to share Li Jin and she admittedly didn't like it. And what about the trip they were planning? Would Li Jin really go with her now that she had a *family*? Only yesterday they were just alike because they had no one else in the world, but now everything had changed.

She listened as the sad old woman told Li Jin more about how she'd always suspected her mother-in-law of stealing her baby, but finally got proof only a week or so ago. *Was Li Jin really going to believe that story?* Sami wanted to shake the common sense back into her.

Sami could see the anguish mixed with relief on the man's face as he waited for Li Jin to open up and accept their explanation. Beside him, the old woman dabbed at her cheeks with a piece of wadded handkerchief.

Enough with the tears already, Sami wanted to say. But under the bitterness at the happy scene before her, Sami found herself wishing she'd had a father who loved her like this one must love Li Jin. She reached up and plucked first one hair, then a few more as she watched and waited to see if Li Jin would allow the people into her life. *Whatever happens,* she silently promised herself, *I will be glad for Li Jin, and I will not resent her newfound happiness.*

But Sami would make sure their paths remained linked together as she knew fate intended.

As the woman spoke softly yet confidently, Li Jin peeked at the man who claimed to be her father and saw something she'd not noticed before. In his old but kind face she could see familiar eyes and the same stubborn tilting jaw she knew so well. Even the nose was a larger version of one she'd come to adore. The similarity between him and Jojo was almost uncanny. She looked at the old woman holding her cup of tea. Even though her fragile hands shook nervously, Li Jin could see what her own hands would look like in the years to come. She looked back at the old man and their eyes met. He had seen her examining their features and Li Jin felt like he knew what she was thinking. A small smile started on his face and gradually spread bigger. She was astonished at what she saw there. It was pride—coming from looking at her!

As they waited for her to speak she realized something. Their features, the flood of emotion, and the smile he wore told her something that no words could—they told her that maybe this *was* her father and the woman he hovered over protectively could really be her mother. She suddenly wanted to know more.

Li Jin reached down and pulled off her shoe, then showed her foot to the couple. Lao Calli, as she'd said she was called, looked at the dainty flower etched on her heel and began to cry again.

Jojo saved the moment from becoming too much by bursting through the door.

"Ma! Come with me and Auntie Wan to Moon Pond! She said there's fish there!"

Li Jin smiled at him, then patted the empty chair beside her. She studied his dear little face, then looked at the man across from him. Yes, it was clear. She'd never before seen another person who carried her son's facial features. Never before until now. She felt something shift inside her and wondered if it was the burden of resentment finally lifting, after years of feeling abandoned. Whatever it was, she was going to embrace it. Her heart felt lighter and a smile worked its way across her face, probably the most genuine and heartfelt smile she'd ever worn. She squeezed Jojo close to her and whispered in his ear, but loud enough for everyone to hear. "Okay, I will. But first sit down and let's get to know your grandparents. I'm sure your Ye Ye would like to take you fishing."

"*My* Ye Ye? He's my Ye Ye?" Jojo asked, looking from his mother to the old man, his eyes open wide. "For real? Ma, are you telling the truth?"

Li Jin laughed softly, then nodded. "I sure am, Jojo. And that woman right there"—she pointed at the old woman—"the one who brought you such a long way back to me, she is your *real* Nai Nai. Jojo, I know this is going to sound like another fairy tale, but I've finally found my mother and father."

With those words, the old woman's body began to shake with sobs, and the man pulled his handkerchief from his pocket and passed it to her. Li Jin's own tears started and before she could react, Lao Calli stood and made her way over to her.

Li Jin stood and she stared into her mother's eyes, searching for truth in them. Jojo clung to her, somehow knowing she needed his support. Only a second passed but she felt a lifetime of questions suddenly answered between them. With that she let herself be pulled against her mother's chest, something she never thought she'd experience. Then Lao Benfu—*her father*—was up and enveloping all of them, his arms wrapping around them like the protective branches of an old oak tree as in that moment, they became what she'd always longed for—a family.

Bitter Winds

Enjoy a Sneak Peek of Book III
of the Tales of the Scavenger's Daughters.
Coming soon from Lake Union Publishing.

Lily shivered as she pulled her Ye Ye's jacket tighter around the stiff clothes they'd made her put on. The sterile smell of the room mixed with what reeked of old urine was nauseating, and she filtered her breath through her mouth as she waited. She listened intently, hoping the sound of footsteps wouldn't come. She'd been crouching on the icy cold floor in the corner for hours, ever since that nasty excuse for a man had slammed the door on her. The turning of the lock and his threats to return later that night still rang in her ears. She felt a wave of revulsion remembering how he'd taunted her, coming close enough that she could smell his rancid breath as he hissed what he'd like to do to her.

But she wouldn't let him touch her—he'd have to kill her first. If he thought because she was blind she wouldn't be able to defend herself, he was in for a surprise because she'd fight until there was no breath left in her. She'd pull from that place deep within her, the reserve that so far had kept her from becoming hysterical. Ivy would be proud of her for being so strong. When she'd wished for independence she hadn't meant this—being jerked away from her sister and sentenced for something she hadn't even done. She only wished she could go back and live the morning again, just start completely over.

Her face burned with shame. It was her own fault. Given another chance, she'd do it differently and stay within the protection of her family—she'd forget her *independence* nonsense.

Her ears perked as she heard the faint slapping of plastic slippers coming closer. She reached out and pulled the mattress from the bed, then crouched under it. If it was him, maybe he'd think she'd been moved to another room. As she waited, a high-pitched shriek filled the hall and then her room. A chill went through her at the sound, a scream that could only be triggered from complete torture or hysteria. *What were they doing to that poor woman?* She tried to still the new onset of trembling.

She would not let them break her.

She would not let them break her.

She would *not* let them break her.

Sign up for Kay Bratt's newsletter on her website to be notified when new books in the Tales of the Scavenger's Daughters are released.

Glossary

R ed Guards, [*AsianHistory.about.com*]..............During the Cultural Revolution (1966–1976), Mao Zedong mobilized groups of young people to enforce communist dogma and rid the nation of the so-called "Four Olds"—old customs, old culture, old habits, and old ideas. Millions of youths formed groups known as "Red Guards." The first Red Guards groups were made up of students, ranging from elementary school to university students. As the Cultural Revolution gained momentum, mostly young workers and peasants joined the movement as well.

The Red Guards destroyed antiques, ancient texts, and Buddhist temples, and publicly humiliated teachers, monks, former landowners, or anyone else suspected of being "counter-revolutionary." Thousands of people were killed outright, and many more committed suicide as a result of their ordeal.

Aiya (pronounced I-yah)	Expresses surprise or other sudden emotion
Anjing (Ann jing)	A command to be quiet
Ayi (I-yee)	Auntie or a woman performing household duties
Bai jiu (bye joe)	Chinese wine
Bai Yao (bye-yow)	Sleeping tonic made from herbs
Bu Yao (Boo yow)	No or don't want
Chengguan (Chung gwan)	Local police
Dagga (Dah guh)	South African slang for marijuana

Dui le (Dway luh)	Right/correct
Dui bu qi (dway boo chee)	Sorry
Duo shao qian (Dwoh sh-oww chee An)	How much?
Gambei (gom bay)	Bottoms up! (a toast)
Fuyang Jiating (Foo yong jah ting)	Foster family
Hao de? (How duh)	Okay?
Hukou (Who koh)	Residential permit all Chinese must carry
Hutong (Who tong)	Lane or residential area
Jianbing (Jee on bing)	Chinese pancake/crepe
Kuai yi dian (kwy ee dee an)	Go a little faster
Laoren (L-oww run)	Respectful way to address the elderly
Laowai (L-oww why)	Foreigner
Li Jin (Lee-Jean)	Girl's name meaning beautiful, gold
Mao tai (Moww tie)	Chinese liquor
Mahjong (Ma jong)	A Chinese game
Meiguo (May gwoh)	America
Muqin (moo cheen)	Mother
Nai Nai (Nie Nie)	Grandmother or other elderly female
Ni hao (Knee how)	Hello
Nuer (New are)	Daughter
Pai dui (Pie dway)	Queue up or get in line
Qi gai (Chee guy)	Beggar
Qingwen (Ching one)	Excuse me
Waiguoren (why-gwoh-rin)	Foreigner
Xiangqi (She-an-chee)	A form of Chinese chess popular in Asia and around the world
Xiao Jie (Sh-oww jee ah)	Miss

Xie Xie (She she)	Thank you
Ye Ye (Yay Yay)	Grandfather or other elderly male
Yi bei cha (ee bay cha)	One cup of tea
Zao (Zow)	A short morning greeting

Author's Note

Tangled Vines, book two in the Tales of the Scavenger's Daughters series, was a story that begged to be written. Research for this story taught me a lot about the plight of abused women in China. Some, like Li Jin, fall into the trap of being drug mules as a way to improve their quality of life. Anyone involved in drugs should be punished accordingly, but, sadly, many Asian women have faced execution because of choices made out of desperation. My heart goes out to their families.

I also wanted to bring attention to domestic abuse. As a survivor myself, I've found that burying those shameful memories is a woman's first instinct, but I also know to stop the madness we must acknowledge it happens in every circle. On a brighter note, in Linnea's story of success I wanted to emphasize for readers the amazing sense of entrepreneurship the Chinese people have. I spent more than four years living in China, and I still marvel at the multiple small businesses many Chinese locals juggle in their quest to raise their family's status in life. They are an astonishingly resilient people, and my time in Asia changed my own perspective on life and encouraged me to reach for my own dreams. In real life, the concept for Linnea's T-shirts was inspired by Dominic Johnson-Hill, the creative director of Plastered, who in 2005 started creating T-shirts that incorporated iconic imagery from China's streets in a celebration of everything beautiful about China. Plastered T-shirts are available in Beijing and online at www.plastered.com.

If you enjoyed this book, a short review posted on Amazon or GoodReads would be much appreciated. Also, please visit kaybratt.com to sign up for my newsletter, which will notify you of new releases, including *Bitter Winds,* the next book in this series.

Acknowledgments

Writing can be a lonely process, but because of a group of people who have accepted me for my meager contributions to their community, I am never alone in these endeavors. So a huge *xie xie* goes out to the international adoption community for always being my sounding board when I hit a wall. Using the platform of social networking, you've helped me name characters and towns, and you even gave me ideas of where to take the plot of *Tangled Vines*. But more than that, you've shared your own stories with me and allowed me to be a small part of your lives, and for that I am grateful.

To Gina Barlean, Karen McQuestion, and Kate Danley, I'm so glad to have found other successful (and superfun) authors to be my critique partners. This book is so much stronger because of your input, and in gratitude I hope you sell a million of your own amazing stories! To Charlotte Herscher, my developmental editor—as we continue to work together I've come to depend on you to help me grow as a writer, and you never let me down. Thank you to Terry and others on my Amazon team who continue to support my efforts and take my titles to a bigger audience. To my husband, Ben, thank you for filling my life with laughter. Lou Hsu, thank you again for your insight into the Chinese culture and for being my official fact checker. Most important, to my readers: If you didn't read my books, I would still write, but it wouldn't be nearly as much fun. Thank you, thank you, thank you.

About the Author

ECLIPSE PHOTOGRAPHY STUDIO (GAINESVILLE, GA)

KAY BRATT is a child advocate and author. She lived in China for more than four years, and because of her experiences working with orphans, she strives to be the voice for children who cannot speak for themselves. If you would like to read more about what started her career as an author, and also meet the children she knew and loved in China, read her poignant memoir, *Silent Tears: A Journey of Hope in a Chinese Orphanage*. Her works of fiction include *A Thread Unbroken* as well as *The Scavenger's Daughters* the first book in the Tales of the Scavenger's Daughters series. Kay resides with her husband, daughter, dog, and cat in a cozy cottage overlooking Lake Hartwell in South Carolina.